BREAKER'S REEF

BOOKS BY TERRI BLACKSTOCK

THE MOONLIGHTERS SERIES
1 *Truth Stained Lies*
2 *Distortion*
3 *Twisted Innocence* (Available February 2015)

THE RESTORATION SERIES
1 *Last Light*
2 *Night Light*
3 *True Light*
4 *Dawn's Light*

THE INTERVENTION SERIES
1 *Intervention*
2 *Vicious Cycle*
3 *Downfall*

THE CAPE REFUGE SERIES
1 *Cape Refuge*
2 *Southern Storm*
3 *River's Edge*
4 *Breaker's Reef*

NEWPOINTE 911
1 *Private Justice*
2 *Shadow of Doubt*
3 *Word of Honor*
4 *Trial by Fire*
5 *Line of Duty*

THE SUN COAST CHRONICLES
1 *Evidence of Mercy*
2 *Justifiable Means*
3 *Ulterior Motives*
4 *Presumption of Guilt*

SECOND CHANCES
1 *Never Again Good-bye*
2 *When Dreams Cross*
3 *Blind Trust*
4 *Broken Wings*

WITH BEVERLY LAHAYE
1 *Seasons Under Heaven*
2 *Showers in Season*
3 *Times and Seasons*
4 *Season of Blessing*

NOVELLA
Seaside

OTHER BOOKS
Shadow in Serenity
Predator
Double Minds
Soul Restoration
Emerald Windows
Miracles (The Listener/The Gifted)
The Heart Reader of Franklin High
The Gifted Sophomores
Covenant Child
Sweet Delights

CAPE REFUGE SERIES

BREAKER'S REEF

BOOK FOUR

Terri Blackstock

New York Times Bestselling Author

ZONDERVAN®

ZONDERVAN

Breaker's Reef
Copyright © 2005 by Terri Blackstock

This title is also available in a Zondervan audio edition.
Visit www.zondervan.fm.

Requests for information should be addressed to:

Zondervan, *Grand Rapids, Michigan 49546*

ISBN 978-0-310-34278-6

Library of Congress Cataloging-in-Publication Data

Blackstock, Terri, 1957 –
    Breaker's reef / Terri Blackstock.
        p. cm. — (Cape Refuge series; bk. 4)
        ISBN 978-0-310-23595-8
        1. Bed and breakfast accommodations — Fiction. 2. Detective and mystery sto-
ries — Authorship — Fiction. 3. Teenage girls — Crimes against — Fiction.
4. Novelists — Fiction. 5. Georgia — Fiction. I. Title.
PS3552.L34285B74 2005
813'.54 — dc22

                                                                    2004025174

Scripture taken from the *New American Standard Bible.* Copyright © 1960, 1962, 1963, 1968, 1971, 1972, 1973, 1975, 1977, 1995 by The Lockman Foundation. Used by permission.

Published in association with the literary agency of Alive Communications, Inc., 7680 Goddard Street, Suite 200, Colorado Springs, CO 80920. www.alivecommunications.com

Interior design by Beth Shagene

Printed in the United States of America

14 15 16 17 18 19 /QG/ 24 23 22 21 20 19 18 17 16 15 14 13 12 11 10 9 8 7 6 5 4 3 2 1

*This book is lovingly
dedicated to the Nazarene.*

ACKNOWLEDGMENTS

I'd like to offer special thanks to my friends at the Hinds County Detention Center for all you've taught me about Christ's love, forgiveness, grace, and redemption. Your valiant struggles and victories have shown me God's enormous power and strength. Some of you have shared your hard-earned wisdom with me, others of you have broken my heart, and still others have thrilled me beyond words as I see you embracing God's deliverance, and letting Him change your lives . . . even when you're released into freedom, where the choices are hard.

Thank you for giving me the soul of this series—characters with pasts, whose lives have not always been neat and clean, who have known the depths of hell on earth and have been bound to it like slaves. Characters for whom the Father scans the horizon each day, searching for His prodigal children to come home. Characters like you.

"But while he was still a long way off, his father saw him and was filled with compassion for him; he ran to his son, threw his arms around him and kissed him" (Luke 15:20).

Oh, my sisters, how He loves you! Never, never forget it!

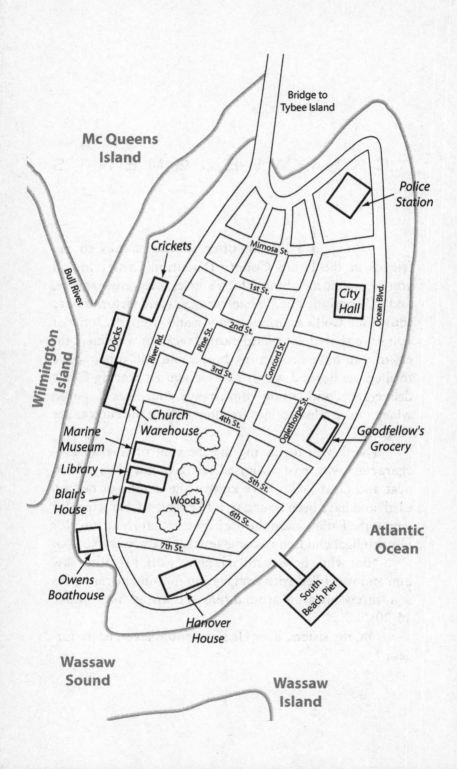

Mc Queens
Island

Bridge to
Tybee Island

Police
Station

Crickets

Mimosa St.

1st St.

City
Hall

Ocean Blvd.

Docks

River Rd.

Pine St.

2nd St.

Concord St.

3rd St.

Bull River

Wilmington
Island

Church
Warehouse

4th St.

Oglethorpe St.

Goodfellow's
Grocery

Marine
Museum

Library

5th St.

Blair's
House

Woods

6th St.

Atlantic
Ocean

Owens
Boathouse

7th St.

South
Beach Pier

Hanover
House

Wassaw
Sound

Wassaw
Island

BREAKER'S REEF

CHAPTER
1

Chief Matthew Cade rarely considered another line of work, but the 4:30 a.m. phone call about the dead teenage girl made him long for a job as an accountant or electrician—some benign vocation that didn't require him to look into the eyes of grieving parents. He sat on the side of his bed, rubbing his eyes as he clutched the phone to his ear.

"She's from Cape Refuge, Chief." Myrtle, his night shift dispatcher, sounded shaken. "That new guy, Scott Crown, just found her floating in a boat on the Tybee side of the river. Looks like a homicide."

Cade braced himself. "Who is it, Myrtle?"

"Didn't give me a name yet. If they know it, they're keeping it off the radio for now. But Chief Grant from Tybee is hot about how Crown handled things, and he wanted you to come to the scene as soon as you can."

"All right, give me the address." Oswald, Cade's cat, jumped onto his lap, purring for attention as Cade fumbled for a pen and jotted the address down. The cat stepped onto the bed table and plopped down on the notepad. "So what is it Crown did?"

"I'm not clear on that, Chief. But he's young. Go easy on him."

He clicked the phone off and thought about the nineteen-year-old rookie. Crown had joined the force straight out of the academy; he hadn't even been in Cade's department a week. His zeal to be the best cop in the department had led to a few mishaps already, but nothing serious. Cade knew he just needed to give the kid some time to grow into his position. But what had he done to aggravate the neighboring chief?

He got up, wincing at the arthritic ache he always felt in his leg first thing in the morning. It had healed from the multiple fractures he'd sustained in an injury a year ago—and he'd overcome his limp for the most part—but the mornings always reminded him how far he'd come.

He got dressed and hurried out to his truck. It was cool for May, but he knew it would warm up to the upper eighties by the end of the day. Life would go on as it always did—murder or not. As he drove across the bridge that connected Cape Refuge to Tybee Island, his mind raced with the faces of teenage girls who'd grown up here. Whoever this girl was, the murder would have a rippling effect, shattering her family and shaking her friends. There would be a life-size hole in the heart of the small town.

He found the site and pulled up to the squad cars parked there. One of the Tybee officers met him as he got out. "Oh, it's you, Chief Cade. I didn't recognize you in your truck."

"Where's Chief Grant?" he asked.

The man pointed to the riverbank, and Cade saw him with the medical examiner looking over the body.

As he approached, Cade saw the girl lying on the grass. She was small, maybe a hundred pounds, and looked as if someone had carefully laid her down there, her arms out from her body, her knees together and bent to the side. In the flickering blue light, he couldn't yet see her face, and her hair was wet, long . . . He walked closer, and Keith Parker, the medical examiner, looked up at him. "Hey, Cade. You recognize her?"

Chief Grant handed him a flashlight, and Cade stooped down and illuminated her face. His heart plunged. She was Alan Lawrence's girl, Emily. She couldn't be more than sixteen. Cade didn't think she'd even gotten her license yet.

Anger stung his eyes, and he rubbed his jaw. His throat was tight as he swallowed. Who could have done this? Who would have wanted to end the life of an innocent, sweet girl whose parents loved her?

He cleared his throat. "Yeah, her name's Emily Lawrence. Her parents are Alan and Marie." He paused, trying to steady his voice. "You know the cause of death?"

"Gunshot," Grant said. "Looks like she was shot in another location, then apparently brought here and put into that boat. Your man found her."

Cade stood and looked in the direction Grant nodded. Scott Crown stood with the other cops, answering questions. His uniform was wet, and he looked shaken and nervous. Cade felt sorry for the kid. Odds were he hadn't expected to find a dead girl his first week on the job.

"Unfortunately," the Tybee chief went on, "your man compromised the evidence. Moved the body out of the boat before he called us. Got her wet trying to get her onto the shore. Who knows what evidence might have been washed off? I would think you'd train your people better than that."

Cade's anger shifted from the faceless killer to the rookie. "What was he even doing over here? He was supposed to be patrolling Cape Refuge."

"He saw the boat floating in the river between the two islands, saw that someone was in it. Right then he should have called my department instead of coming onto my turf and handling the matter himself."

Cade sighed and looked toward the kid again. He'd had reservations about hiring someone so young right out of the academy, but Crown was Joe McCormick's nephew. When his detective vouched for the kid, Cade decided to give him the benefit of the doubt. But he'd recognized Crown's hero complex his first day on the job. He was something of a loose cannon, and Cade had wondered if he could trust him to follow the rules.

Apparently, he couldn't.

He crossed the grass toward Crown. The kid turned, saw him, and burst into his explanation. "Chief, I know I did wrong. It was stupid. I don't even know what I was thinking. But there were vultures, and I thought there must be a dead animal in the boat . . . I crossed the bridge and came over here—"

"Your first mistake," Cade said.

"But if I hadn't, they might not have found her!"

"Crown, if you had called Tybee to tell them what you saw, they would have been there in minutes. Not only did you step outside of our jurisdiction, but you botched up the evidence."

The kid looked at the cops around him, as if humiliated that he'd been reamed in front of them. "I didn't botch it up."

"Yes, you did! I *know* they taught you in the academy never to move a body. And then you go and wash off the evidence!"

In the light of the police cars' headlights, he could see the kid's face turning red. "Okay, I'm sorry! I got out to the boat and recognized Emily. I wasn't sure she was dead. I was trying to *save* her!"

"You should have checked before you got her out of the boat!"

"Right." Crown's voice rose as he shot back. "So let me get this straight. Next time I see a girl dying in a boat, I'm supposed to sit on my hands until the right people get there? I thought we were emergency personnel. I thought it was our job to *save* lives!"

Crown was livid, stepping over his bounds. Clearly, Cade wasn't going to teach him anything right here in front of his peers. Besides, there was a dead girl lying there—and a killer to be identified. He didn't have time to deal with the rookie.

"Go back to the station, Crown. Wait for me there."

"I don't *want* to go back. *I* found her!"

Cade stepped nose-to-nose with the kid, speaking through his teeth. "Now, Crown. If I hear one more word, you're fired."

Crown backed down then and, without another word, stormed off to his car. Cade watched him until he drove away, then breathed a frustrated sigh and turned back to the body.

Emily. He remembered watching her at the Hanover House Easter egg hunt when she was three. She'd practically tripped over the "hidden" eggs and celebrated when she found her first one, while those around her snatched up all the rest. Who would want her dead?

He went back to his car and radioed in. "Chief Cade here. Get all available units to secure the bank of the Bull River across from where the body was found. I don't want anyone traipsing through there until I have a chance to get over there. We don't know which side the boat was put in on."

The radio crackled, and Myrtle's voice rasped across the airwaves. "Will do, Chief." As she began radioing the other cars on duty, he went back to the body and stooped down next to the medical examiner. "Where's the gunshot wound, Keith?"

The ME pointed to the hole in her stomach. "No exit wound, so it probably didn't happen at close range. The bullet's still in there. But she was shot hours ago. Bled out before she was put into the boat."

Cade stood, a sick feeling twisting in his gut as he anticipated having to go to her home and break the news to her parents. They might not even know she was missing yet. If they'd gone to bed before her curfew, they wouldn't know until morning. But if they were more diligent, as he knew Alan was, they might be up even now, waiting to confront her when she came in.

In a million years, they would never expect news like this.

He wished he was in charge of the investigation, but the murder hadn't happened on his turf. Still, he looked over the body as the medical examiner knelt beside her.

"That a bruise on her jaw?" Cade asked.

"Yep. Several more on her arms and legs. There was definitely a struggle. And look at this." He pointed to the chafed skin around her mouth. "Looks like duct tape was pulled off of her mouth and wrists."

It had clearly been an abduction. Cade looked across the dark water. Was there a murderer still lurking on his island, looking for young girls?

"We need to notify the family, Cade."

He turned to Grant. "I'll do it. They're friends of mine."

"I'm waiting for the GBI to get here. I'll need their help on this."

Cade knew the GBI, Georgia's Bureau of Investigation, had the resources to solve this case. He was glad they'd been notified so early.

"One of our detectives is going to need to go through her room, see what we can find," Grant said. "If you can just break the news to the parents, then my detective or the state's men can take it from there."

Right. Let me do the dirty work, then be on my way. "That's fine. I'll seal off her room, make sure nobody goes in there."

He strode back to his truck, trying to get his head together. How was he going to break it to them? The muscles in the back of his neck were rock hard, and his jaw hurt as he ground his teeth together. What would he say? How would he phrase it?

Lord, give me the words.

As he drove his pickup back to Cape Refuge, Cade rehearsed the hated speech in his mind. *Alan and Marie, I'm afraid I have some bad news . . .*

CHAPTER

2

The ringing phone snapped Blair out of sleep, and she sat straight up and grabbed it. "Hello?"

"Blair, it's me." Her sister Morgan's voice sounded strained, rushed.

"Oh no. You're in labor."

Her sister was eight months pregnant, far past the danger of the miscarriage she had experienced a year ago, but it was still too soon for the baby to be born.

"No, I'm fine."

Blair shoved her hair out of her eyes and blew out a sigh of relief. "Oh, good. You had that bad news tone."

"I do have some bad news, Blair. Jonathan had to go in to City Hall early this morning, and he just called to tell me there was a murder last night. Emily Lawrence, Alan and Marie's daughter."

Blair caught her breath. "She was *murdered*? How?"

"I don't have any details, but I knew you'd want to cover it for the paper."

Blair stood, thinking of the girl who'd frequented the library when Blair still ran it. She had tried to guide Emily to literary maturity, but the girl had rarely deviated from the Baby-Sitters Club and Nancy Drew Mysteries. She'd often given Blair lists of books she wanted her to order.

A sick feeling twisted her stomach. How could she be dead? "I'll call Cade right now."

"No, don't," Morgan said. "He's at their house with the family. Jonathan did know that much."

Blair tried to think as she grabbed some clothes. She'd need to take her camera. Where was it? "Morgan, I think Sadie took the camera home last night. Is she up yet?"

"No, but I can go wake her. Do you want her to come to work early?"

School had ended last week, and Sadie was working for her full-time during the summer. She wouldn't want to be left out for the sake of sleep. "Yeah, tell her I'll come pick her up in fifteen minutes."

"She'll be ready."

CHAPTER

3

Sadie was crying as she ran down the Hanover House steps and opened the car door.

"What happened to Emily?" she asked as she got in. "I just saw her a few days ago at school."

"I don't know yet, honey. Was she a good friend of yours?"

Sadie's face twisted as she struggled to hold back her tears. "Not a good friend. But I like her. She's one of the good ones."

Blair knew Sadie didn't relate well to most of her classmates. She had come to Cape Refuge as a sixteen-year-old ninth grade dropout, and when she went back to school, she was two years older than those in her class. As an eighteen-year-old junior, her background made her the subject of ridicule, but Blair knew that the cruelty of some of the girls at school was due to jealousy. Sadie's fine blonde hair and big blue eyes were the stuff of beauty pageant queens. But such things didn't interest the girl. She spent her free time working for Blair as a reporter and photographer. Despite her age, she was already a gifted journalist.

Over the last year, since Blair had hired Sadie to work for her, the girl had turned into a more self-assured young woman, one who wasn't that concerned about her classmates' approval. Strangely, as she put less emotional emphasis on her acceptance at school, she began to make more friends.

Sadie wiped her eyes. "What did Cade say about it?"

"I haven't talked to him yet. He's at the Lawrence house. That's where we're going now."

"The Lawrence house." Sadie repeated the words with great thought. "Are you sure we should? I mean, it seems like a violation, the press showing up when they've just found out."

"We won't intrude, Sadie, I promise. We won't be the only press there, guaranteed. I just want to get the facts down. Be there for any statement the police give. We're a vehicle for helping find the killer, and we're responsible to get the news out to our readers."

Sadie drew in a long, deep breath. "You're right. I was just thinking of her parents . . . What they're going through . . ." Her voice squeaked, and the words fell off.

"I'm thinking of them, too, honey. Trust me, okay?"

Just as Blair predicted, a television news van sat parked in front of the Lawrence house. Several people stood clustered in the yard, members of the Savannah media, waiting to get a statement. Blair saw Cade's truck in the driveway, next to a Tybee Island squad car.

Sadie had stopped crying, but her face was tight. She peered up at the front door as if imagining what was going on inside.

Thank heaven Cade was the one talking to the family. He'd notified Blair when her parents were killed. He had a gentle touch, and if any comfort could be given, she knew he was the one to give it.

Her heart swelled with love for him, and she whispered a silent prayer that God would grace him with all the strength he needed. She wished she could go in and hold his hand as he did this, comfort him when being strong began to take its toll. They'd grown so close over the last year that she felt his burdens as keenly as her own, and she wanted to help shoulder them.

As if her very thoughts summoned him, the front door opened, and Cade stepped out. The press members descended on him with microphones and shouted questions, but Blair hung back. She would get the story soon enough.

"Chief Cade, did the family have any ideas who might have killed their daughter?"

"How did her parents take it?"

"Were they aware that she was missing?"

He came down from the porch and stepped across the yard before speaking. "The Tybee Police are working with the state on this case," he said as he walked. "They're inside now. They'll make a statement soon." Cade met Blair's eyes and jerked his head toward his truck.

Blair handed Sadie her keys. "I'm going to ride with him and get the story. Can you stay in case the police make a statement, then drive my car back to the office?"

"Sure."

Blair hesitated. "Sadie, are you sure you're all right?"

"Yeah, I'm fine. Go ahead. This is important."

Cade was getting into his truck, and Blair slipped in on the passenger's side. "They're going to claim favoritism," she said.

"Let them." He looked out the rear window and began to back out of the drive. His face was tight, and the corners of his mouth trembled.

"Cade, are you all right?"

He ignored the question. "Marie fell apart, started screaming that it wasn't true, that it couldn't be her daughter. Alan couldn't help her. He was crying like a baby." Tears glistened at the rims of his eyes. "I remember when Emily was three. At the Easter egg hunt at your house. Your dad hired Jonathan and me to help hide the eggs, and I was trying to help her find some. She was such a cute little kid."

"Oh, Cade." She took his hand, and he squeezed hers, but didn't look at her as he drove.

"I think Marie's going to have to be sedated. I called Doc Spencer, asked him to come over. He's their family doctor, so he should be able to help."

"I'm sure Morgan and her comfort brigade will be over soon. Cade, what happened? How was she found?"

He took a turn that put them at the newspaper office and pulled into the parking lot. Shutting off the engine, he sat there for a moment and told her what he could. He gave the facts in fits and starts, struggling to control the emotion in his voice and on his face.

She reached across the seat and pulled him into a hug. "I can't imagine being a father and getting news like that."

"Neither can I."

He held her for several moments, clinging to her as if she kept him from sinking into the depths of despair, drowning in the sheer tragedy of it all. When he let her go, he drew in a deep breath. "I'd better get to the station. I have to brief the department."

"You'll be all right?"

"Yeah, I'm fine."

She gazed up at him, wishing he would let go and cry instead of struggling so hard to hold it back. She knew his heart was breaking.

He touched her face and kissed her gently. "Thanks for being here. You want me to take you back to the Lawrences'?"

"No, that's okay. I'll wait here for Sadie." She got out of the truck, walked around to his open window.

He was staring vacantly through the windshield. "They're good people, the Lawrences. Strong Christians, active in their church. And they love their children. I'll never get used to horrible things like this happening to people who don't deserve it."

"Neither will I." She leaned in through his window. "But I remember what you said to me after my parents were killed, when I thought of God as some divine terrorist who used homicidal maniacs to carry out His will. You said God is a loving father, with purposes we can't understand. You said we may never see the purpose in their deaths, but that we can be sure God has one."

Cade looked into her eyes and brushed her hair back. "I still believe that, but I needed to be reminded." He kissed her again. "You're good for me, you know that?"

"Of course I know. I've been trying to tell you that for the last year." She stroked his unshaven jaw, and he took her hand and kissed her knuckles.

"I knew it long before that."

Smiling softly, she stepped back, and he put his truck in gear. "I'll call you later."

Her smile lingered as she watched him drive away.

Sadie stood among the reporters in the Lawrences' yard, waiting for one of the state's detectives to come out and make a statement. Neighbors came out to see what they could see, and a few of them approached the door and knocked, probably hoping to offer their help, but the family never answered.

A carload of teenagers pulled up behind one of the TV vans, and as they piled out, Sadie turned away. They were all her classmates—two cheerleaders and a quarterback-in-training.

"Sadie!"

She turned back to them, surprised they even knew her name, when they had always ignored her before. They cut across the lawn toward her.

"Sadie, is it true about Emily?" April Manning addressed her as if they talked every day.

"I only know what's being reported."

"But you work for the paper, right?" Courtney Gray flipped her three-tone hair back. "You would know."

"I'm waiting for a statement. The police are still inside."

"The radio said she was found in a boat. Was she, like, shot or something?"

Sadie fought the irritation rising inside her. Couldn't these people hear? "I told you, I really don't know."

Steve spoke up. "She seemed straitlaced, but there are rumors that she may have had a drug problem."

A drug problem? Sadie knew that wasn't true. "Emily was a Christian. She didn't do drugs."

"You never know," April said. "People aren't always the way they seem at school."

Steve nudged her. "You ought to know."

The girl grunted.

Sadie didn't have the energy to deal with their rumors and speculation. "I have to . . . change my film." She left them standing there, working out the inane details of Emily's life and death, and got into Blair's car. She could sit here until the police came out to make a statement. It was better than standing in the yard like one of the grief groupies.

She leaned her head back on the seat and wished she had more charitable thoughts toward them, but the snubbings she'd gotten from these very people since she'd started attending Cape Refuge High still stung. The snubs had subsided over the last several months—either that, or she had stopped noticing them—and she didn't feel self-conscious when she walked down the halls anymore. She had more important things to worry about—like her mother and her job.

Her life was full now, much fuller than before, when her mother was in jail and Sadie spent her days trying to protect herself and her baby brother from his rabid father. She had come here physically and emotionally broken, and found refuge at Hanover House. Morgan and Jonathan Cleary had taken her into the home that housed other of life's refugees and had become foster parents to her and her little brother, Caleb, until her mother was released from prison a year ago and joined them here.

With all the adjustments, Sadie didn't have time to mope over her status in school anymore. And since she'd stopped caring, she'd found herself with friends and she'd become less of a curiosity to those she avoided.

The front door opened, and Sadie sat up. Police were coming out of the house. She jumped out of the car and snapped pictures while the officers were still elevated on the porch. She joined the cluster of reporters at the foot of the porch steps and pulled her small tape recorder out of her pocket. She held it among the microphones and other tape recorders.

An officer stepped forward. "I'd like to make a brief statement on behalf of the Tybee Island Police Department and the Georgia Bureau of Investigation. At approximately 4:00 a.m. this morning, May thirtieth, a body was discovered in a boat floating between Tybee Island and Cape Refuge. The body was pulled out on the Tybee Island side of the river, and has been identified as sixteen-year-old Emily Lawrence. Cause of death was a gunshot wound. At this time, we are treating it as a homicide and we have no suspects. The autopsy is scheduled for tomorrow. We'd ask people in the community to call the police if you have any information that might relate to this crime. The family will not be making a statement at this time. They ask that you please respect their need for privacy today and clear off of their lawn. That's all."

He and the other officer pushed through the crowd and moved to their cars as reporters shouted questions.

Letting her camera drop around her neck, Sadie pulled the notepad out of her back jeans pocket and began jotting some notes. Her three new "friends" headed toward her again.

Amy had tears in her eyes. "It's terrible, just terrible. Who'd ever think one of our own class could be murdered?"

Sadie swallowed her emotion back and looked up from her notepad. "Do you guys know who Emily hung out with mostly? When she wasn't at school, I mean?"

"Sure, yeah," Steve said. "She, like, spent a lot of time with Danny Brewer and Lourdes Grant, and that bunch."

Sadie made a note.

"Are you going to interview them?"

"Maybe."

"You could interview us." Courtney smiled hopefully at her.

Sadie shrugged. "Okay, do you have anything you'd like to say about Emily?"

"Yeah," Courtney said. "Put that she was a nice girl. That people liked her and stuff."

Original, Sadie thought. *The stuff of awards.*

"And spell my name with an *e* instead of an *a*. G-R-E-Y."

"I'll do one," Amy piped in. "Say that it's a creepy feeling to know that somebody's out there murdering your friends. Makes you scared to go out at night."

That was one she could use. She jotted it down. "Anything else?"

Steve was ready for his fifteen minutes. "Yeah, I talked to her last week, and she seemed fine. She let me use her cell phone. She didn't seem depressed or weird or anything."

"And what's your last name?" She knew his last name as well as she knew her own. Who didn't? But she didn't want him to think she'd ever noticed him.

"Singer," he said. "S-I-N-G—"

"I got it." She flipped her notebook shut. "Well, thanks, guys. I have to go now. I have a story to write."

She left them standing there and headed back to Blair's car.

Matt Frazier had pulled up behind the car in his father's florist van and called out to her.

Sadie smiled at him. "Hey, Matt."

He'd been her very first friend on Cape Refuge. The day she'd been dropped off at the door of Hanover House, and no one had been home, he had come up to bring a floral wreath for the door. They had gotten to know each other better over the last year and a half.

"Sadie, have Emily's parents come out to make a statement?"

She shook her head. "No. Just the police."

He looked up at the door. Some of the press still milled around in the yard, unwilling to leave. "My dad wanted me to bring them a wreath. I'm just numb. How could this happen?"

Sadie shook her head. "Poor Emily."

They both stood there, quiet, and Sadie saw the look of helpless anger in his eyes. Finally, he looked down at her. "You okay?"

She smiled up at him through unshed tears. "Yeah, thanks."

"I know she was in your class. She was a cool kid. I used to see her at the ballpark, working the concession stand. She was always so happy and bubbly. She never hurt anybody."

Sadie was afraid she might cry, so she reached for the car door. "I have to go."

He took the door, opened it for her, and watched as she got in. "Call me if you need to talk, okay? I have classes later this morning, but I'll have my cell phone with me."

"I might do that."

He closed her door, and she drove off. A tear rolled down her face, and she wiped it away. Leave it to Matt to treat her as the wounded one, when he'd probably known Emily longer than she. But that was the way he was.

Blair had suggested several times that the college sophomore had a crush on Sadie, but she couldn't say for sure. He'd never asked her out, not on a real date, anyway, but he'd recently started coming to her church and always sought her out to sit with her. She enjoyed being around him, but she wasn't sure it would ever be more than friendship.

Still, it was nice to have a guy care about her feelings. It was like sunlight breaking through a thick canopy of gray.

She wondered what her mother would say.

CHAPTER
5

So, Miss Sheila Caruso, tell me why you're right for this job." The famous Marcus Gibson stood like an accuser in front of Sheila, his hands splayed on the two clean spots on his desktop.

She hardly knew what to say. The truth was, she probably *wasn't* right for the job of assistant to the author, and if he knew she had a felony drug conviction and had spent a year in prison, he'd send her on her way. But Sadie, her daughter, had encouraged her to try, and she couldn't let her down. "Well, your ad called for someone who could type, and I'm a fast typist. I just finished a secretarial course at the community college. I also know how to use a computer."

She glanced at the laptop on his desk and hoped she knew how to use that one. It didn't look anything like the computer she'd learned on in school.

"I also need help with filing." He rose to a less accusatory position and waved a hand over his desk. It was cluttered with ragged stacks of papers and magazines and books. "But I don't want someone coming in here and throwing things around helter-skelter. I have a system, so whoever comes has to be teachable. Do you have any experience with this kind of thing?"

As he waited for her answer, he picked up a Panama hat off of one of the stacks, lightly punched his fist into it, and seemed to consider the result.

"Uh . . ." She hesitated. Should she wait until he'd finished with the hat? "Well, not really. I've never worked for a writer before."

"Good." He flung the hat across the room, and it landed on an old wooden file cabinet. "That's what I'm looking for. Someone with no experience."

She thought he was being sarcastic, and her hopes deflated. She waited for his dismissal, but instead he started digging through one of his stacks. He found the book he was looking for under a pile of handwritten pages and started to furiously flip through it.

"What do you know about forensics?"

She searched her mind for an answer. "Uh . . . well, just what I've seen on TV."

He looked at her as if she were stupid. "Do you seriously believe the tripe you see on a one-hour yawn written by Hollywood hacks?"

She swallowed. "I didn't say I believed it all—just that it's all I know about it."

"So you learned nothing about crime investigations during your incarceration?"

Then he knew. She closed her throat. "How did you know I was—?"

"I Googled you."

She stared up at him, wondering if she'd heard him right. "I'm sorry?"

"I Googled you. Checked you out on the Internet. I know all about your prison sentence."

"I see." So this had been a foolish pipe dream. Of course he'd checked her out. What had she expected?

"I've changed a lot in the last year." She leaned forward, bent on helping him understand. "See, my kids, they were staying with some people here in Cape Refuge while I was doing time. I came here when I got out—to a place called Hanover House, to keep from uprooting them."

His eyes strayed to his computer screen, and he began to type. She didn't know whether he was taking notes or checking his email. She swallowed and kept talking.

"Hanover House—you may know it, it's over there by the Sound, the big yellow house across the street from the beach on Ocean Boulevard?" He didn't indicate whether he knew it or not. "Anyway, it's kind of a halfway house, with a real strict Bible program, and it's made me a better person." She was rambling, she realized, and her voice trailed off. "I've come a real long way in my personal life, and my kids are doing real good, and I know I can do this if you just give me a chance."

There was a long moment of silence, broken only by the clicking of his fingers on the keyboard. Had the man forgotten she was here?

"I may wish to interview you about prison life," he said finally. "I find that fascinating. I usually try to put myself in the shoes of my characters—living what they live—but I haven't managed to get thrown in jail just yet."

She frowned, not certain she'd heard him right. "Well, yes. Of course. Anything you want to know."

He kept typing. "It pays four hundred dollars a week. Forty hours, give or take. I'll need to know within twenty-four hours."

She froze and gaped up at him. Did that mean he was offering her the job? Did her prison sentence not matter?

As if he'd forgotten his last statement, he turned back to the credenza behind his desk. It looked like something he'd dragged out of a garbage dump. One of the legs was broken, and a cement block replaced it. He paged through another book. She wondered if he was still interested in forensics, or if he'd moved on to some other subject.

He came to whatever page he was looking for and ran his finger down the paragraphs. "I can't work with you in the room. I usually won't be here when you are. I like to write out in the world. Experience real life. I'm not like those wannabes who sit in four walls all day hammering out their drivel. And I know what you're thinking, but having research books does not make me weaker as a writer."

She caught her breath. "Oh, no, I wasn't thinking anything."

"I simply have to confirm things now and then, find words, details, history, explanations . . . Do you know what they call the clicker on a lamp? The little black thing that goes in and out, turning the blasted thing on and off?"

"Switch?"

Anger flashed across his face. "Do you honestly doubt that I could come up with *switch* on my own?"

"No . . . I—"

"Never mind." His face twisted as if he'd just tasted arsenic. "If there's one thing I hate it's stuttering inanity. It would have been the perfect metaphor, if I could find the cursed word." He looked around, as if he hoped to find the answer lying on one of the other cluttered surfaces. "If you take the job, you can start tomorrow. I have papers somewhere."

She caught her breath and wondered if she'd heard him right. "I do want the job," she said quickly. "I can be here tomorrow."

"Fine. I'll have a roll of red tape here for you to fill out tomorrow. We don't want to give the government another reason to harass me. I have enough to do."

"All right."

He left his book open and went to one of the stacks, began digging through. "Your job at first will consist mostly of typing several of my earlier books into the computer. I composed those on typewriter, but I'm having them reprinted by my current publisher, and I'll need them entered onto a computer disk."

"I can do that."

"I want them exact. No comma out of place. No quotation mark left off. Just as I've written them."

"No problem."

"Then I'll see you tomorrow."

She blew out her relief as she left his cottage but knew she would have to get used to the eccentricities if she was going to work for him. She could do it, she told herself. She'd dealt with difficult types among the guards and her cell mates in jail. Even since getting out, she'd had to adjust to the different personalities at Hanover House.

Besides, it might be interesting. Certainly not your ordinary nine-to-five.

She couldn't wait to tell Sadie that she was gainfully employed.

CHAPTER
6

The former Laundromat that served as the police station was full to the brim with cadets from the local Girl Scout Troop, who'd come for a Saturday morning tour. Cade had completely forgotten his promise to Joyce, their leader, to get someone to show them the workings of the police station. It looked like Alex Johnson had stepped in for him.

In addition to the chattering girls, five computer guys from the GBI were setting up the upgraded equipment the mayor's office had approved for them and running cables to get them online with the Georgia Criminal Justice Information System Network. Myrtle, the dispatcher, sat at her station with her headphones on, trying to hear the radio exchanges over the confusion around her.

Cade stepped over some of the cables and touched the Girl Scout leader's shoulder. "Sorry about the mess, Joyce. I forgot you were coming today. You didn't confirm."

"Didn't think I had to, Cade. I talked to you three weeks ago, and you said it was fine."

He nodded to Alex. "Take them back and show them the jail cells, and then you can lead them out and show them the bells and whistles in Crown's squad car."

Alex winked, understanding that Cade needed them out of the building.

"Tell Chief Cade thank you, ladies," Joyce said. "He's a very busy man with a lot of work to do."

"Thank you, Chief Cade," the girls said in chorus.

Cade forced a smile, but he felt sick at the thought that they would all soon learn of the murder of one of the town's teens—a girl who could very well have been their babysitter.

When the girls left the squad room, Cade looked around at the mess. The computer guys from the state police had opened up the cases of several of the computers, and cards and peripherals lay open on the desks. Two guys stretched belly-down across the floor, running cable along the walls. It was the worst possible day for them to do this, but he'd been so vehement in requesting the upgrades that he could hardly run them out now.

The moment Jonathan Cleary—Cade's best friend and Blair's brother-in-law—had been installed as mayor last year, he'd begun raising funds for a bigger, better police station. So far, it was still a dream. But even if he managed to secure the blessings of the City Council and get the budget to build a new station, it would be at least a year before the CRPD could take possession. Until then, Cade hoped the computer equipment would get them up to par with departments in other cities, so they could get more done from the tiny quarters they had now.

Scott Crown sat at his desk in the corner of the room, and from the look on his face, he was still brooding over what had happened that morning. Cade hadn't had time to deal with him before going to talk to the Lawrence family. Instead, he'd ordered Crown to do his report on the discovery of the body, and let him stew in his juices for a while.

But defiance still shone in his eyes as he looked up at Cade. "My shift is over. If I'm not going to be used for anything worthwhile, I might as well go home."

"You know we called in all available officers to help search the riverbank."

"Then let me go search it."

His tone made Cade want to send him home. For good. "Come into my office, Crown. Let's talk."

"Fine."

Cade led the kid into his office and closed the door behind him. "Sit down."

Crown sat, crossing his arms like a child being reprimanded.

Cade took his chair behind his desk. "I don't have time for attitude, Crown. I'm not a babysitter or a grade school teacher. If you can't show some respect and admit when you're wrong, then you don't belong on my force."

"But I—"

"I don't want to hear your excuses, Crown. You messed up big-time this morning. This is not just some minor infraction. You may have jeopardized a homicide investigation. And until you admit that and learn from your mistakes, you're of no use to me or my department."

"You didn't have to chew me out in front of those other guys." Crown slumped back in his chair. "You know I was trying to do the right thing. How do you think that made me look?"

"I'm not in the image business, Crown. You made your*self* look bad. You were trying to be the hero, and it backfired."

"I knew her, okay? She's my buddy's sister. What did you expect me to do?"

"I *expect* you to follow protocol. You didn't even know who she was until you splashed out to the boat."

His lips curled, and Cade waited for him to say something that would get him fired.

But then Crown's face softened. His mouth trembled. "I'm sorry, Chief. I really am. Don't fire me, man. I want to be a cop. I've wanted to be one since I was a little kid. It was a dream come true."

"Didn't sound like it, the way you talked to me earlier."

"I know." He folded his hands between his knees and swallowed. "I shouldn't have talked to you that way. But give me another chance, Chief. I'll learn from this. I swear."

Cade leaned back in his chair and tapped his chin with his finger. "All right, Crown. But I expect better of you. You go by the book, you hear me? You follow policy. You don't go off half-cocked doing whatever feels right."

"Okay." His expression held a trace of residual anger, but he sounded contrite. "Do you want me to go back to work?"

"Not today. Just go home, get some sleep. I'll see you when you come in tonight."

Crown groaned, but didn't argue. He got up, went to the door, then turned back. "Thanks, Chief. I won't let you down."

Cade met his eyes. "Make sure you don't."

He watched as Crown left his doorway, and hoped he'd done the right thing, keeping him on. He got up and went back into the squad room. Through the front glass he saw that the Girl Scouts were in the parking lot, taking turns sitting in the squad car and turning the lights on and off. He stepped over to Sarah, who had replaced Myrtle for the day shift. "Have you managed to reach all of the off-duty officers?"

"Most of them. Some had already come in, so I sent them over to the river."

"Get them in here. I need to brief them and give out assignments."

He went back into his office. One of the computer guys had taken over his desk now and sat in his chair, working at his computer. "How much longer you think you'll be?"

The man looked up. "Not long, but these things take time."

Cade leaned back against the door. "I'm not trying to rush you. I just have work to do."

"Well, you'll get it done a lot faster and more efficiently when I get this set up. You do want this, don't you?"

"Yeah, I want it."

"Okay, then." Clearly the technician, who looked like Bill Gates before his billions, had a superiority complex. "So I heard on the radio about the girl who was murdered. She your case?"

"No. She was from Cape Refuge, but she wasn't found here. Not my jurisdiction." He didn't bother to tell him he'd just broken the news to her parents.

"These things often cross city lines." The technician patted the computer. "This baby will help you get all the information you need. Want to know who the repeat offenders are in your area? Child molesters? Rapists? One touch of a button. Want to tap into FBI files? State files? Want to get forensics reports, autopsy results? Check in with the crime lab, or do an ACIS search?"

"I could pretty much do all that before."

"But not this fast. One touch, my friend, and the world is yours."

"I'll look forward to that."

The man looked as excited as a NASA engineer on launch day. "Don't worry. I'll show you how to use everything. We plan to give a training class for all of those who'll be using it. Can you get everyone here for tomorrow?"

"It's done. We set it up a week ago."

Cade slipped out while he had the chance and went into the small interview room. McCormick was just entering the building, followed by two of the uniforms just coming on shift. "In here, guys," he said.

He went in and waited for the rest of his force to show up.

When they were all finally there, he closed the door and briefed them on the murder. Chief Grant had asked Cade's department to help with the investigation since the girl was from Cape Refuge. Grant thought they might make more headway doing informal interviews with her family and friends than outsiders might.

Cade had hoped to motivate them all into pushing harder tonight, but as they spilled back out into the squad room, the computers were just beginning to work. They all gathered around the monitors to see what the new system could do. Like kids with new PlayStation games, they were distracted from what truly mattered: the murdered girl and her grieving family.

But it wasn't so easy for Cade. No matter what mundane chores required his attention, he couldn't get his mind off the terrible truth that one of Cape Refuge's children had been violently murdered.

And her killer was walking free.

CHAPTER

7

I saw this crib at the antique auction last weekend, Morgan, and I thought it was perfect for you." Clara Montgomery climbed up in the back of her pickup truck and struck a pose beside the crib. "I'll give it to you at cost. Only five thousand dollars. It's made out of real mahogany, solid all the way through, probably a hundred years old."

Morgan stood on the steps of her porch, her hand moving over her belly. The baby was active today, kicking like a soccer player. "It's beautiful, Clara. But I can't afford that. Besides, I already have a crib. Caleb's started sleeping in a bed already, so we're ready for the baby."

"Oh, honey, it's an investment! You don't want your baby sleeping in that cheap thing you've got. It's practically made of particle board." She ran her hand along the antique crib's wood. "Come on, honey, let's get it in the house, and then you'll see."

Morgan didn't *want* it in the house. She knew how Clara worked. She was a good saleswoman. When business

39

was slow, she was known to show up at people's houses with individual pieces of furniture, insisting they were meant for them. Usually, her tactics worked.

Thank goodness Morgan didn't have five thousand dollars lying around.

"I don't think I need to be lifting furniture, Clara, and there's no way I could pay you for that."

"I could give you credit, darlin'. If anybody's good for it, it would be our preacher-slash-mayor."

"You don't understand. I don't want to go into debt for a piece of furniture I don't need. Have you thought of Marissa Brown? Her baby's due any day now."

Clara's face twisted. "*Her*? She wouldn't know a valuable antique if it bit her on the toe." As she spoke, she tried to move the crib off the truck.

Thankfully, the old car they let their residents drive pulled into the driveway, momentarily distracting Clara. Sheila was behind the wheel, and as she got out, Clara called to her. "Sheila, come here, honey. Help me carry this in the house."

Morgan groaned and came down the steps, putting herself between the truck and Sheila. "That won't be necessary. It's not coming in."

Clara grunted. "Morgan, don't be that way."

She breathed a laugh. "I'm not buying your crib, Clara. You're wasting your time."

The woman finally gave up, came off the bed of the truck, and slammed the tailgate. "You're a stubborn woman, Morgan Cleary."

Morgan laughed and turned back to Sheila. "So how did the job interview go?"

Sheila squealed and threw her hands up. "Tell me, ladies, do I look like the assistant to a famous novelist?"

Morgan just looked at her. "You got the job?"

"What job?" Clara looked from Sheila to Morgan. "What famous novelist?"

Sheila clearly loved Clara's surprise. She paused for effect. "Marcus Gibson, the *New York Times* bestselling mystery writer."

Clara gasped. "Marcus Gibson is in Cape Refuge?"

"Yes. He bought Gabe Stone's beach cottage a few weeks ago. But from the looks of the place, you'd think he'd lived there for forty years. He must have just moved his stacks of papers in boxes and piled them all around his room, exactly like they were in Atlanta."

"And he hired you?" Clara looked the woman over. "Does he know your background?"

Sheila's smile faded. "Yes, he does. He Googled me."

"He what, dear?"

"Googled. He did a computer search." Morgan turned back to Sheila, trying to look excited despite her reservations. "So he knows everything?"

"Yes, and he doesn't care. He wants me to start tomorrow."

Morgan hadn't expected the writer to offer the job to Sheila, so she hadn't expressed her concerns before. But she and Sheila would have to sit down and talk when Clara left.

"I love his books," Clara went on. "For heaven's sake, I read one last week, and it kept me up all night. Scared me slap to death, if you want to know the truth. I kept feeling like there was someone staring in the window at me, standing in the shadows with an ax in one hand and a machine gun in the other. See, it was about this woman who married this guy . . ."

Morgan had a bad feeling she was about to hear the play-by-play of the entire plot, so she looked at her watch. "Goodness, I need to get back inside. Caleb might wake up."

Clara was still studying Sheila. "Guess that pretty blonde hair didn't hurt any in that interview, huh? Almost can't blame a red-blooded male for wanting to hire somebody like you, even if you are an ex-con."

Clara had a talent for compliments that cut. Morgan saw the joy fade from Sheila's face, and her patience with the woman reached an end. "Thanks for coming by, Clara."

Clara opened her truck door and slipped inside. "You call me now, if you change your mind about the crib."

Morgan could hardly make herself answer as the woman drove away. She sighed and smiled at Sheila. "Ignore her."

"Don't tell me she means well."

"I won't because she doesn't."

Sheila broke into a smile again. "Can you believe it? He actually hired me!"

Morgan tried to mirror Sheila's excitement as she led her into the house. "So tell me about this interview. What was Marcus Gibson like?"

"Weird. Eccentric. A little scary. Remember the crazy scientist guy in *Back to the Future*? He reminds me of him." Caleb, who'd been sleeping on the little cot inside the office off the kitchen, was just waking up as they went in. Sheila went to pick him up and kissed his rosy cheek. "Hey, bud. You have a good nap?"

He nodded and laid his sleepy head against her shoulder. She sat down at the table and cuddled him close. Morgan got his sippy cup of milk out of the fridge and gave it to him.

"You can hardly hold a conversation with the guy," Sheila said, her voice softening. "He goes from one random thought to another, like he's trying to think of twenty things at once but can't quite finish a thought. Talk about a poster child for ADHD. I can't imagine how he writes novels."

"What will you do for him?"

"Typing, mostly." Caleb slipped out of Sheila's lap and went to play with his toys in the corner of the room. His mother followed him and sat on the floor behind him as he played. Stroking his curls, she said, "The great thing is that I won't be working nine to five every day. He said it would be forty hours a week, give or take, but that he doesn't really want me there when he's there."

That was good news. "Then you won't see him that much?"

"He said I wouldn't. He likes to write in other places on his laptop." Sheila looked up at her. "It's not true, what Clara said, Morgan. He didn't hire me for my looks. He's not interested in me at all. He probably couldn't tell you what color my hair is.

He hardly looked at me the whole time, and when he did, he had this blank look, like he was seeing something else. He was more interested in the word for the switch on a lamp. I'm telling you, he's weird. But the job pays really well. And if you haven't noticed, it's the first offer I've had. It's not like people are beating my door down to give me a job." She leaned over and kissed Caleb's forehead. "Are you sure you won't mind keeping Caleb while I work?"

"Of course not. You know I love Caleb." How could she not? She'd been a mother to the child for almost a year. As she'd watched Sheila resume that role herself, Morgan had had to force herself to step back. But she longed to have time alone with him again. "Sheila, are you sure this is the right thing for you? There's no hurry for you to find a job. You've only been out of school a few weeks. Maybe you should just take your time and look for something else, something a little more predictable."

"He's paying four hundred dollars a week, Morgan. Everything else I've looked at has been minimum wage. And the temptations aren't going to be as great working there, alone most of the time, as they would be if I worked in a restaurant or around people who may do drugs. I could actually use my brain. I used to be smart, Morgan, until I went off the deep end and started doing drugs. If I hadn't gone that way, I might have gone to college. I can *do* this. I'm trained on the computer, I can do word processing, and I'm a fast typist. I'm excited about it."

Morgan chose her next words with care. "If the writer were a woman, I wouldn't be concerned. But I don't want you to be vulnerable."

"I can take care of myself. I have street smarts, don't forget. If he comes on to me, I'll quit."

"Unless your heart gets involved." Morgan sighed. "Marcus Gibson must be making a fortune. Being around a man like that, with money and fame and power, might be a little dangerous for you."

Sheila covered her face as if the thought disgusted her. "He's not my type, okay? He's not even attractive to me, and he's way too old. And if you could meet him just once, you wouldn't think of power, or even money or fame. He's just . . . flaky. I'm going to try it, okay? Just give it a week or so to see if it's something I can do. I promise, if it's too weird or things get crazy, I'll quit."

Morgan just watched as Sheila stacked some blocks for Caleb to knock over. Maybe she was overreacting. Maybe it was a good thing, after all. Sheila was going to take the job with or without her blessings.

She only hoped her fears would be proven wrong.

CHAPTER

8

Marcus Gibson wasn't answering the door. Sheila looked down at her watch. She was ten minutes early for her first day of work. She had left extra early since she had to walk and she wanted to make a good impression. Marcus Gibson's car was there, so he had to be home. Maybe he was so quirky he wouldn't answer before the prescribed time. She decided to wait until nine o'clock sharp, then knock again.

The day was already growing warm and muggy, and the walk hadn't helped. Still, it was a beautiful day. Over the last year, she'd grown to love the ocean and even found the muggy heat worth it.

She heard the sound of a child's laughter and walked to the side of the porch. From that vantage point she could see the beach behind the writer's house. A young family— probably from one of the neighboring cottages—played there, the mother and father holding a toddler between them, dipping his feet into the foam as the waves rolled across the sand.

A scene from long ago came back to her—her own mother, wobbling in the lapping waves as the breeze lifted her hair. Her mother was drunk, as she so frequently was, and her lecherous companion was three sheets to the wind as well. Still, Sheila, probably six or seven years old, had sat with her red bucket, shoveling sand into it and pretending she was part of one of the happy families playing in the surf.

Did that little family at the water's edge have any idea how rare and special they were?

She reeled her thoughts back in, determined not to feel bad today—and went back to the front door. It was straight-up nine now. She knocked and rang the bell, waited . . .

Still no answer.

Had he forgotten he'd asked her to report this morning? Had he thought better of hiring her? Had the information he'd gathered on Google finally registered in his mind?

What should she do? Maybe he'd gone out. If she just waited, maybe he would come home soon.

She sat down in the white rocker on his porch and tried to think. If he didn't show up, should she assume that the job was just a figment of her imagination? Would she have to tell Morgan she'd misunderstood? Would Sadie be disappointed in her all over again?

Minutes ticked into half an hour, and the sun grew hotter. The clothes she'd dug out of Morgan's donation closet felt sticky, and her hair clung to her neck. If he did finally come home and let her in, she wouldn't look like someone ready for a full day's work. She'd look like someone who needed a good bath.

After forty-five minutes, she decided that waiting was use-less. He'd forgotten about her or simply changed his mind. Or he was in the house flipping through books in some mad search for a piece of trivial information.

She got up and started down the porch steps, when she saw a man trudging up the road toward her. Was that him?

It was. She watched as he grew closer. He wore a pair of camouflage pants, a big wrinkled T-shirt plastered to his body with sweat, army boots, and a vest that hung open, its pockets full of stiff-looking items. On his back, he carried a huge knapsack.

He made his way up the driveway and looked up at her, sweat dripping down his face. "Oh, yes. You're here."

It wasn't the greeting she'd imagined, but she swallowed hard. "Hello, Mr. Gibson. You told me to report for work at nine this morning, remember?"

"Is that what I said?" He shrugged off the pack and left it lying on the porch, then slapped his pockets, probably searching for his keys. "Yes, I suppose I did."

"Is it a bad time? I could come back when it's more convenient."

Finally, he pulled out some keys and opened the door. "It's never convenient. But there's work to be done. It has to be done."

He led her into the dark house, flipping on lights as he went, revealing unopened boxes in the front room, furniture that looked as if it had been carried in and set down anywhere. It was as if he hadn't noticed that the couch was in the center of the floor, the coffee table against a wall, the grand piano rolled in and left just inside the door.

He led her into the kitchen and went straight to the cabinet. He pulled out a box of Fruity Pebbles cereal and poured it into a bowl.

He'd forgotten her again. "Would you like me to go on into the study? I could start filing, or . . ."

He looked up at her, as though annoyed that she was still there. He patted his pockets again. This time she had no idea what he was searching for.

He hesitated, unzipped a pocket, pulled out four microcassette tapes and a handheld tape recorder, and thrust them at her. "Type these. I numbered them. Should be five hours' worth of dictation." He counted the tapes in his hand. "Only four. Grief. I must have dropped the fifth one in the woods."

The woods? She took the tapes and the recorder. Glancing down, she said, "There's one still in the recorder."

"Ah, yes. Five. I didn't drop it."

"Were you . . . camping last night?" She knew she shouldn't have asked, but curiosity was killing her.

"Yes. Slept in the woods, no food, no water, just like Ryan Casings."

"Ryan Casings?"

"My character. I had to feel what he felt . . . However, I know what you're thinking. You're thinking no character named Ryan would be roughing it in the woods, prowling around like a soldier in enemy territory, eating only what he could kill . . ."

"I didn't—"

"And of course you'd be right, which is why I'm going to change his name today. So after you type it all up, do a find-and-replace and change his name to—"

He froze, agony twisting his features as he racked his brain for the perfect name. She wanted to help. *Rocky, Rambo* . . .

"Reed," he bit out finally. "Name him Reed."

Reed? That was it? "Okay. Reed, it is."

"Yes, Reed." He stood over the sink and dug the spoon into his cereal.

She went into the study and cleared off the chair in front of his computer. Taking out the fifth tape, she loaded number one.

His voice, deep and rumbling—and a little creepy—narrated the opening pages of his book. Sheila smiled as she typed. She felt part of something important, something big, as if her work contributed to a piece of art that would take shape until it was something huge, immortal—something millions would share in.

After a while, she heard him leaving again and looked out the window. Still wearing his camouflage, he trudged through the sand toward the water, walking like a man on a mission. He walked straight into the waves, still fully dressed, until the water was over his shoulders. Waves beat against him as they slammed toward the beach. He swam into those waves, stroking, stroking, until she lost sight of him in the sun's glare on the water.

Weird. Did he even realize he was fully dressed? Would it occur to him when his boots began weighing him down?

She went back to work, typing as fast as her fingers would move, hoping to get it all done before he came dripping back.

CHAPTER

9

The funeral visitation had been somber, as hundreds of kids came and went, paying their respects to their dead classmate. Sadie heard the others talking about meeting at the ballpark that night to commiserate. Though she hadn't been invited, she knew it was a good place to get more for her article, so she armed herself with her camera and walked over as night fell.

Cars lined the parking lot, and one baseball game was already going. A crowd of her classmates had gathered on the bleachers at one of the empty fields.

The concession stand—where Emily had worked—was closed in honor of her memory, and several bouquets of flowers had been laid around the little building.

Sadie looked toward the kids clustered in the stands. Crystal Aimes and Kelly Jackson, two of her nemeses who often ridiculed her in front of others for being a former dropout and the daughter of a convict, were there. Some of the football players and cheerleaders mingled with the class nerds and the group so proudly dubbed the "freaks."

They all hugged and cried together. Death had a way of bringing unlikely people together.

Carrying her legal pad and pen, Sadie started toward them, her heart pounding in her chest.

"Sadie."

She looked toward the voice. Courtney and April, whom she'd last seen in Emily's yard, gestured for her to join them. She started toward them.

"I'll bet she knows," someone said. "Sadie, do you know where Emily was shot?"

Everyone turned to look at her.

"Sadie, set all the rumors to rest and tell us what you know."

She felt like a celebrity of sorts, the gatherer of facts . . .

As the kids gathered around her, Sadie pulled her notepad out of her back pocket. "The police haven't released details of how she was killed yet. They had an autopsy scheduled for today. Did any of you see Emily Wednesday night?"

"I did." Cameron Ward looked as if he might burst into tears. "I had a soccer game that night, and Emily worked concession."

Sadie jotted that down. "Did you see her talking to anyone unusual?"

"No, not that I can think of. I've racked my brain, but nothing. There were so many people here. It could be anybody."

"How did she leave?"

"She was still here when I left. She usually was one of the last to leave the park."

The police probably already knew that. Chances were someone approached her after the crowd cleared out. "Emily seemed pretty straight. She was, wasn't she?"

"She was." Emily's best friend from school looked like she'd been crying all afternoon. "She mostly worked and went to church and hung around with her friends."

"Sadie, who found her?"

That she could answer. "Remember Scott Crown, who graduated last year? He's a cop now, and he found her."

"Scott Crown, a cop? No way!"

Sadie nodded. "That's right. He was on patrol and saw the boat in the water. The boat wound up belonging to the Craven family who lives upriver, on the Tybee side. They said it was stolen from their dock last night."

Even the girls who'd made themselves her enemies had lost their looks of disdain and hung on her words as if she were an authority.

"Sadie, did anybody tell you about the memorial service tomorrow night after the funeral?" Courtney asked her. "Emily's youth group at the Methodist Church is putting it on."

Were they telling her as a reporter or inviting her to participate? "No, I didn't know."

"They want people to stand up and tell stories about Emily. They're taping it so they can give a copy to her family."

Sadie swallowed. She didn't have any stories that would comfort Emily's brokenhearted parents. What would she say? *Emily was nice. She treated me like I mattered.*

No, she couldn't say that, but she wanted to be there anyway.

She took down the information, then sat there with the kids as they talked about Emily in low voices—each person accounting for the last time they'd seen her, what she'd said, what she'd sold them at the concession stand.

Finally, when Sadie couldn't hold her emotions back any longer, she left the group and headed home. She didn't choose to walk on the sand along the beach as she normally did. Even though it was still light, she walked along the road, afraid to be alone.

Not wanting to go home just yet, Sadie walked to the scene of the crime and sat on the Cape Refuge side of the river, staring across to where Emily's body was found. The police were still there. The Craven property—where the boat had been stolen— was taped off as officers searched for clues.

The place where the boat was found was also blocked off, but several people were there with binoculars, watching the police activity across the water.

A couple of boats drifted downstream, as other oglers strained to get a look.

Sadie sat in the grass, leaning against a tree, her arms around her knees, praying for Emily's parents, her closest friends, her siblings. What a terrible time they must be having.

"You here for business or just killing time?"

Sadie looked up to see Scott Crown. She'd known of him in school, since he'd been a senior just last year. He wasn't in uniform, so he looked like he had in the hallways of CRH. "Hey. I didn't see you coming."

"You were a little preoccupied." He sat down on the grass next to her, leaning back on his hands. "Weird, huh? All this excitement over a girl we actually know. Whoever would have thought?"

"Must really be weird for you, since you found her."

"Yeah, it was awful. Never expected to find a homicide victim my first week out of the gate. Especially not someone I knew."

"It must have really freaked you out."

"You have no idea. I was just patrolling around here and I saw that boat floating in the middle of the water. A turkey vulture was circling, which was strange. Vultures are normally afraid to strike at night since they can't see to protect themselves. I knew whatever that bird saw in that boat had to be dead, and he wanted it bad enough to take a risk."

She must have winced, because he stopped himself. "I'm sorry. I forget that others don't want to hear the gory details."

"No, I do. I work for the paper, you know. I need to know."

He grinned then. "You can quote anything I say, if you want."

She pulled her pad and pen out of her back jeans pocket and crossed her legs Indian style. "So you went to Tybee to pull the boat in?"

"Yeah. I headed across the bridge to Tybee. The boat was just a few feet out from the Jacksons' pier. I started trying to catch the rope with a pole and pull it in, but then I saw what was in the boat. I about died."

"Good police work." She jotted it down. "I'll bet you got a lot of pats on the back."

He was quiet for a moment. "Not really, since everybody was kind of in a tailspin about the death. But I'm sure it was noticed. I was just doing my job, though."

"So what part is Cape Refuge playing in the investigation?"

"Well, since she was from here, Chief Cade has us doing a lot of legwork talking to friends and trying to retrace her steps the few days before her death."

"Do you have any leads?"

"Dozens. People have been calling tips in all day. Cade's had to turn most of them over to the GBI, but we're following up on a few. Hey, I'll be happy to talk to you anytime. Keep you updated."

Sadie managed to smile. "We pretty much stay on top of things, since Blair's dating Cade. He tells her what he can. And what he can't tell her, she usually hunts down on her own. Sometimes I think she would make a great cop. She has an instinct for crime-solving."

He breathed a laugh. "It's not as easy as it looks, you know. People have all these ideas about cops from watching TV. It's actually a whole different thing."

"So does it take a lot of training?"

"Ten weeks at the academy."

"I thought it was longer. No wonder you can be one so young."

"Chief Cade hired me even before I went for training, so I had the job when I got out. But it's not just the training that makes you a good cop. It takes a gut instinct, and a certain amount of courage."

"I guess so." She could see he was proud of his job. It was probably warranted. "That gut instinct helps in reporting too. I don't know if I have it or not. I guess that's why I mostly get stuck with the mundane reports of local happenings. Boring stuff. But Blair said I could do some on the murder, since I knew Emily. I've been talking to people all afternoon."

"Guess you have an advantage, since you knew her."

She wouldn't have called it that, but she supposed it was true. "I guess. People might tell me things that they wouldn't say to Blair. Not that most people want to confide in me, either."

"Yeah, I noticed you were pretty much a loner at school."

She shrugged. "I'm a little older than the kids in my class, since I dropped out for a couple of years. I'm eighteen."

"Then you're only a year younger than me. I *thought* there was something different about you."

She smiled, surprised he'd given her any thought at all. "There's a lot different about me."

"Well, that's what makes you special." He looked down at the grass blades he sat on, tore some up. "You know, I always wanted to talk to you in school. But you looked so self-contained. Like you didn't need anybody else. I was afraid I'd get shot down."

"Shot down?" She stared at him. "Me, shoot you down? I would never do that."

"You wouldn't? Then we ought to go out sometime."

Sadie caught her breath. Had she heard him right? Could he really be interested in her? "That'd be nice," she managed to say.

"How about a movie or something? Say, tomorrow night?"

He was serious! "Sure. Do you know where I live?"

"Hanover House, right?"

"That's right." How much did he know about her? Everyone at Hanover House had a sad, tangled past. Did he realize she was no exception?

"How about six thirty? We can probably find a seven o'clock flick."

Sadie shook her head. "I can't go that early. I need to go to the prayer service for Emily after her funeral. But I can go after that."

"All right. I'll pick you up from there."

"Aren't you going to the service?"

"No, I don't think so. Sounds a little morbid."

She sat there for a moment, awkward and uncertain. She couldn't wait to tell her mom, pick out something to wear, practice how to wear her hair. She got up and dusted her jeans off. "I have to get home now. My mom started a new job today, and I know she'll want to tell me all about it. She's working for Marcus Gibson, the author."

"No kidding? He's my favorite. Have you read his latest?"

"No, I haven't read any of them."

"You should. They'll blow your mind."

Sadie wasn't sure she wanted her mind blown.

Scott offered her a ride, but she declined and walked back home, up Ocean Boulevard, along the busy street. She felt a little guilty for getting a date out of a terrible tragedy like Emily's. But it wouldn't hurt to go out with him.

Her step was lighter as she hurried home, anxious to share her news.

CHAPTER
10

Sheila had just come in when Sadie got home, and she chattered in the kitchen with Morgan and Blair. Sadie hurried in to share her news, but her mother was mid-story.

"Hey, baby. Come here and listen to this. Mr. Gibson shows up an hour late from camping out, and then he walks into the ocean fully dressed in camouflage gear, boots and all, and swims until I can't see him anymore. Comes back in an hour later, dripping wet, and heads off again. I didn't see him the rest of the day. Meanwhile, I'm typing this dictation he did in the woods last night, an extremely creepy narration of this killer who's stalking someone he's planning to kill. And I keep feeling like he's going to sneak up on me."

Sadie shivered. "Are you sure you're comfortable being there all alone?"

"So far. He hasn't really bothered me. Practically ignores me. I think it surprises him every time he realizes other people actually live in his world."

Sheila put Caleb into his high chair and got him a cookie from the pantry. She smiled up at Sadie. "So how was your day, baby?"

"Terrible. I went to Emily's visitation." She glanced at Blair. "I talked to a lot of people, got a lot of quotes."

Blair turned back to her. "Anything we can use?"

"No hard facts. Just comments from friends and mourners."

Her mother looked at her. "Sadie, until this killer is found, you don't need to be out walking around at night."

"She's right," Morgan said. "You could have used the car."

Sadie lowered into a chair and contemplated her mother's newfound sense of authority over her. She'd never given her parameters before—not until she'd come to Hanover House, and watched how Morgan and Jonathan drew limitations.

Sadie got a cookie and took a bite. "What would you think if I'm with a cop when I go out?"

Morgan and Blair turned to look at her, and Sheila frowned. "What cop? Cade?"

Sadie grinned. "No, Scott Crown. He kind of asked me out."

Blair grinned, but Morgan was clearly troubled. "The new cop? How old is he, Sadie?"

"One year older than me. He's nineteen. And Cade thinks he's trustworthy enough to be upholding the law."

She could see Morgan was searching for a reason to keep her from going. She never liked for her to date, since Sadie had shown poor judgment in her choices before. It was as if she was sure of Sadie being led down the proverbial "wrong path" again. Blair looked triumphant, though, and Sheila seemed to gauge both of their reactions, before reacting herself.

"He's the one who found Emily's body yesterday," Blair said. "Seems like a nice guy. Cade wouldn't have hired him if he weren't."

"Still," Morgan said. "Sadie's in high school. He's already out, probably has his own apartment."

"I won't go there," she said. "I know better than that. We just want to go to the movies."

She saw the struggle on Morgan's face, but finally, her mother saved the day. "When are you going, baby?"

"Tomorrow night."

"Then we need to go through your closet and figure out what you're gonna wear. No hand-me-downs for a first date. Has to be something nice if you're going out with somebody important like that."

Sadie looked at Morgan, and saw that she was biting back her reservations. She'd deferred to Sheila, and Sheila was letting her go.

She hoped it didn't cause problems between them.

The front doorbell rang, and Sadie heard the door opening. "Anybody home?"

Blair came out of her seat. "In here, Cade!"

He appeared in the doorway. "How's it going?"

Everyone greeted him, and Blair went to reach up and kiss him. The sight of that did Sadie good. Blair and Cade—two of her favorite people on the island—deserved each other.

"Just the man we needed to see," Sheila said.

Sadie noted a flicker of something as Blair turned to look at her mother. Blair clearly thought Sheila had a crush on Cade. The truth was, Sadie thought so, too.

"Oh, yeah?" Cade smiled.

"Yeah. Sadie has a date with Scott Crown tomorrow night. Should we let her go?"

"Mom!" Sadie felt sick. What if Cade went back and ribbed Scott about it, or worse, chewed him out for dating a school-aged kid? She wanted to crawl under the table.

Cade looked from Sheila to Sadie, as if he didn't quite like the idea. But then he shrugged. "He's a good man. I wouldn't worry too much."

Sadie breathed a sigh of relief.

He turned back to Blair. "Can I talk to you out back for a minute?"

"Yeah, sure."

As Cade took Blair's hand and led her out to the backyard, Sadie turned back to her mother. Sheila was watching them with a trace of longing in her eyes.

If she was interested in Cade, maybe it was a good thing. Maybe it meant that her tastes had changed. And since Cade wasn't exactly available, maybe it would keep her from making any mistakes with other men.

There were worse things than setting her sights too high.

So what did you want to tell me?" Blair asked as they stepped into the backyard.

Cade pulled her to the side of the house, and leaned down to give her a crushing hug. "That I missed you. I saw your car here and wanted to see you for a minute before I go back to the station."

It was too good to be true, having Cade care about her this way. She felt small, protected, in his arms. "I miss you, too. Are you going to be working all night?"

"Until late. We had the computer training session today, which slowed me down, so I still have all our local leads on Emily's murder to process. I'll drive by when I start home, and if your light's on, I'll stop. That okay?"

"The light'll be on."

She smiled up at him, wishing they were more than just an item. If they were married, she wouldn't have to fall asleep with her light on, hoping he'd come by. He would come home to her, and crawl into bed next to her. And he'd be there when she woke up.

But Cade hadn't spoken much of marriage just yet, and neither had she. The very idea of his being in love with her in the first place was a blessing she'd never expected. Wouldn't he wake up any day now and realize how repulsive she was, with the burn scars that marred the side of her face? Wouldn't he realize there was a reason no one had snapped her up before now?

But he didn't seem repulsed. He seemed enchanted.

Headlights lit up the drive next to them, and they saw Jonathan pulling his pickup into the driveway. Cade let her go, and she stepped back.

Jonathan got out of the truck, wearing a pair of dress slacks and a button-down shirt. His fisherman's wardrobe had been relegated to the back of his closet once he was sworn in as mayor, but Blair knew he would never get used to "office-wear." He looked tired, but he was grinning as he came toward them. "Hey, don't let me interrupt anything," he said on a chuckle.

"You weren't," Blair said. "I was just going in."

Cade grinned. "I'll see you later tonight."

She smiled and nodded, then headed back inside. Later tonight couldn't come soon enough.

Jonathan didn't follow Blair inside. Instead he closed his door and leaned back against the truck, crossing his arms. "So, Cade. Just what are your intentions with my sister-in-law?"

Cade returned his best friend's grin. Jonathan had asked him that dozens of times in the last year, and Cade always evaded. But Jonathan knew his intentions. If he didn't, he was blind. "I have to go."

Jonathan caught his arm. "One day you're gonna answer that question."

Cade couldn't hide anything from him. They'd been closest friends for over fifteen years. Jonathan had seen Cade with every date he'd ever had. He'd critiqued his relationships in college, advised him through romances in his twenties.

"Never mind," Cade said. "When something happens, you'll be the first to know."

"I want to know before," Jonathan teased. "Come on, Cade. You've got it bad. The question is, what do you plan to do about it?"

"I'd tell you, but then I'd have to kill you."

Jonathan laughed. "So you do have plans?"

"I have plans. But you're not exactly confidant material, since you're married to her sister."

"Hey, my lips are sealed, man."

They heard the back screen door slam, heard Sadie's voice talking to Caleb on the porch.

"Go ahead, she can't hear you."

Cade just stared at Jonathan for a moment. Finally, he caved. "All right. But if word gets out, I know where you live."

Jonathan moved closer to hear Cade's secret.

CHAPTER
11

Marcus Gibson wasn't home to greet Sheila when she reported for work the next morning, but he hadn't forgotten her. He'd left a note taped to the door, addressed to *Sharon*.

Since it gave her instructions on what to type today, she assumed the note was for her. She hoped he'd get her name right when he wrote out her paycheck.

The note directed her to the key hidden under the mat. Why hadn't he just left the door unlocked? Did he think there was more security in a note and a doormat?

Amused, she went in, found the latest tapes among the clutter on his desk. As she began to type, his dictation threatened to put her to sleep. He spoke in a rumbling monotone, with less inflection than Ben Stein in *The Wonder Years*. How he'd managed to teach college students was beyond her. They must have had to pop caffeine pills just to keep their eyes open.

Background noise of chirping crickets and squawking birds broke up the monotony, along with the occasional sound of a car engine or the ocean. Finally—thankfully—she got to the end of the tapes and decided she would go ahead and start typing the old, out-of-print book he'd given her to enter into the computer.

Thank heaven she could type it from printed copy rather than the drone of his voice. As she did so, she found herself getting involved in the story. The protagonist was a teenage girl who had a stalker following her, watching her through windows, recording her every step. His obsession grew more threatening on every page, building to the climax, when he captured her. After a significant struggle that lasted three chapters, he shot her, then dumped her body in a boat, and set it free to float downriver—

She stopped typing and picked up the book, read that scene again.

I arranged her carefully in the bottom of the boat, her knees bent, her feet crossed. Her fingers lay curled against her face, as if she'd lain down there for a nap, and bled out while she dreamed.

I launched the boat downriver, knowing that someone would find her soon. It was important that they knew. Part of the thrill.

It was just the way Emily Lawrence's killer had disposed of her, right there in the pages of Gibson's book!

"You're still here, are you?"

The writer's voice from the doorway startled her, and she yelped and swung around. He stood there, dripping with sweat again, but this time instead of camouflage, he wore a gray pair of sweatpants and a white threadbare tank top, with a towel around his neck.

"I didn't hear you come in."

"Did you finish the dictation?"

"Yes. It's all done." She touched her chest, trying to calm her breathing. Her heart was racing. "I was starting on the out-of-print books."

"Start on them tomorrow. I need to work and I want to be alone."

Relief flooded her. "All right. Just let me save what I've been doing."

She made a mental note of the incriminating book, then said a nervous good-bye.

He gave a vague nod. "I may not be here when you arrive tomorrow. I haven't been sleeping at home. I'll leave the key under the mat again."

She didn't want to ask where he *had* been sleeping. "All right," she managed to choke out.

She got out of there as fast as she could and practically ran until she was off of his street and back on the main thoroughfare. She hurried along Ocean Boulevard, until she came to the police station.

She wished she looked a little better as she stepped into the air-conditioned building and looked around for Cade.

He wasn't in the small squad room, but she saw his detective, Joe McCormick, sitting at his desk, glued to his computer.

"Hey, Joe."

He looked up, then got to his feet and tucked his shirt in better. "Sheila, what brings you here?"

"I wanted to talk to Cade."

He looked a little disappointed, which surprised her. Had he hoped she'd come here to see him?

"I'll get him." He headed to Cade's office, and she watched him until he was gone. He wasn't a bad-looking man. His shaved head had put her off at first, but now that she knew him, she thought it looked kind of suave. She wondered if he did it to hide baldness, or if he simply liked the Bruce Willis look.

Joe came back out, Cade following. As attractive as Joe was, Cade was more so. He looked like a calendar model of a hero in uniform. It was a shame that he belonged to Blair.

"Sheila, what are you doing here?"

"Can I talk to you, Cade? Actually, maybe I should tell Joe too."

Joe's eyebrows came up. "Sure, let's go in here."

He led her into the interview room, Cade following behind them. Once again, she wished she'd gone home to fix herself up before coming here. A little perfume wouldn't have hurt, or even a little deodorant after walking here in the heat. She finger-combed her hair.

Cade sat on the table. "What is it, Sheila?"

"I think I might know who killed that girl." There. She had their full attention.

Joe pulled out a chair, dropped into it. "Go on."

"I don't know if Blair told you or not, Cade, but Marcus Gibson—the writer—hired me to do some typing for him."

"No, she didn't mention it."

"Well, he did. I've been typing his dictation and also entering some of his older books into his computer. And as I was typing today, I found a description of a murder that is really similar to Emily Lawrence's murder."

Cade and Joe exchanged looks. "Similar in what way?"

"A girl was shot, and her body was put into a boat to float down the river so someone would find her."

Joe shot Cade another look, and Sheila knew she'd brought them important information. "We need the name of that book, Sheila."

"It was *Crescent Hill*. I probably should have brought it with me, but he was there, and he's so creepy. Sleeping out all night in the woods, swimming fully dressed, sneaking up on me when I least expect it . . ."

"Sleeping in the woods?" Joe stood back up. "He told you that?"

"Yes. He's trying to get into the head of his character. But his main characters seem to always be the killers, so that in itself is creepy. I'll tell you, I don't know if I can go back there tomorrow. I'm starting to be afraid of him. But I know where his key is, and I can go if you need me to help you with the investigation . . ." She smiled, trying to work a smile out of Cade, as well. "If you promised me some personal protection, I might be willing to go back and try to see what I could find."

Joe shook his head. "Not a good idea. Maybe you'd better stay away until we have time to look into this. We don't want you to be in danger."

Warmth flushed through her. "Well, thank you, Joe. I appreciate that."

"He's right," Cade said. "We need to look into this before you go back. We'll take it from here, Sheila. Thanks for coming by."

Cade opened the door for her—the perfect gentleman—and she stepped out into the squad room. Blair stood just inside the front door.

The smile Sheila had been trying to get out of Cade blossomed on his face, and her own heart took a nosedive.

Sheila recognized the look on Blair's face too. Her expression held a combination of jealousy, anger, insecurity, and fear—at least that was how Sheila saw it. Blair's usual self-confidence seemed to slip a couple notches whenever Sheila was around Cade. She should tell Blair she had just come on police business, but she kind of liked the idea of having someone think of her as a threat.

"Hey, babe."

At Cade's warm greeting, Blair lost that threatened look and smiled up at him. He was a good head taller than she. Like it or not, they looked really cute together. "Bad time?" Blair asked.

"No, actually. It's a good time. I need you to go somewhere with me."

Sheila's chest tightened. Cade had forgotten she was there.

"Where?" Blair asked.

"The library. I have a book I need to check out, and you'll know right where it is."

"That's me—" Blair grinned—"Marion, the former Librarian. I'll help if the Ladies' Auxiliary hasn't recataloged everything. They're liable to have revamped the whole system."

Sheila followed them out. "I'll see you later. Cade, call if you need to ask me anything."

"I will," he said. "Thanks, Sheila."

She stood there and watched as they got into Cade's truck.

"Are you walking?"

She looked back at Joe, standing in the doorway. He was tall too, even a little taller than Cade. Sheila had always had a weakness for tall men. "Yeah, trying to get my exercise."

"You don't need it." He smiled almost awkwardly.

She grinned. "Joe, are you flirting with me?" She'd known the comment would hook him—she had lots of experience, after all.

"Maybe," he admitted on a chuckle. "Come on, I'll give you a ride."

She tossed her hair back. "You're my hero. I'd love a ride."

He walked her out to his unmarked car and opened the door for her. She slipped in, feeling like Cinderella stepping into her pumpkin chariot.

"Hanover House?" he asked.

"That's right."

As they drove, Sheila told him about Marcus Gibson's quirks. He hung on every word, laughing at her descriptions, occasionally looking at her with a smile in his silver eyes. It had been a long time since a man had looked at her that way.

Maybe her crush on Cade had been misplaced. Maybe she should give Joe a little more consideration.

CHAPTER

12

Blair understood Cade's reason for not wanting to check out Gibson's book himself. His very presence in the library during a murder investigation would attract undue attention and invite a million questions he didn't have time to answer. It might also give someone the idea that Gibson was a person of interest before Cade had time to talk to him.

She stepped into the small library, and a flood of nostalgia washed over her. She'd spent so much of her life here before her competence had been called into question by some of the City Council members. She had thrown the job back in their faces and boxed up her belongings. The Ladies Auxiliary, who was behind the complaints about her, had arrogantly agreed to "take over" the running of the library until a replacement could be found. But none had been found yet.

Blair went to the shelves of reference books and breathed in the dusty scent of those old volumes, gently running her fingers over some of their spines. The books were like old friends, welcoming her with their riches. She'd missed this place, but she would die before she admitted it.

Her shoes clicked on the old hardwood floor as she crossed the room to the fiction section. She stopped and perused the Gs. There, right before John Grisham's collection, she saw the dozen books Gibson had written.

Sue Ellen Jargis must have heard her footsteps, because she emerged from the back office. "May I help you, hon?"

When Blair turned around, Sue Ellen caught her breath. "Oh, it's you."

Blair gave her a saccharine smile. "I'm fine, Sue Ellen. And how are you?"

The woman bristled. "What can I help you with?"

"I don't need help." Blair insisted she'd forgiven the woman for edging her out of her job, but now as she stood face-to-face with her, she found herself hoping Sue Ellen felt oppressed by the dimly lit room and the dust floating on the air in the rays of sunlight coming through the front windows. Did they ever dust the place? When she ran the library, she'd dusted a different area each day, and managed to keep it relatively fresh, in spite of the age of some of the volumes. "I'm assuming you haven't reorganized the fiction section. You haven't done anything outrageous, like categorizing it by subject matter, or the names of the characters, have you?"

The woman's chin came up. "Of course not. They're exactly as you left them."

Blair decided not to respond to that, so she pulled the books off of the shelf until she had an armload. "I'll take all twelve of these." She dumped them into Sue Ellen's arms.

The woman stared at her, mouth agape. "Blair, you know you can't have twelve at a time. Ten is the limit."

Blair sighed. "Since when? I never had a limit."

"Well, you should have. If not, the college kids who come in here would take all kinds of advantage. They would hog all the research and reference books for themselves and keep them for who knows how long."

"If the college kids need the books for research, then what's the harm? I never had any problems. If they were late, I usually knew how to get in touch with them, and I reminded them to bring them back. Simple as that. And you know where I live. Right next door. If I'm late returning the books, you can cross the yard and come get them."

Sue Ellen huffed out her distaste at the plan, but took the books to her desk and began checking them out.

"So, do you work here every day? I thought your ladies were taking turns."

"I do Mondays and Thursdays."

"Any closer to finding a qualified librarian?" She knew the answer already. As mayor, Jonathan had made a valiant effort to find her replacement, but the Ladies Auxiliary frightened most of the candidates away.

The woman slammed one of the back covers and jerked open the next one. "We have some things in the works." She clearly didn't want to talk about it, and Blair couldn't help her amusement at the woman's plight. Sue Ellen was a socialite and a world traveler. The last thing she probably wanted was to be stuck in a library all day. But since she was the one who'd gotten the city into this mess, Blair knew she was determined to serve whether it killed her or not.

Blair sneezed. "You know, you should dust these shelves more often. I'm getting a sore throat just standing here."

"We dust plenty, thank you very much."

"Hey, don't jump on me. I'm just suggesting—"

"I don't *need* your suggestions."

Blair took the books, uttered a syrupy sweet good-bye, and made her way back out to Cade's car. He got out and relieved her of the load. "Why so many? I only wanted one."

"I thought it might be helpful to look at his other murder scenes. Plus, I took a little pleasure in aggravating Sue Ellen. That woman makes me forget the Golden Rule."

"Uh-oh. *She* was working?"

"If you want to call it that. She has a limit of ten books now." She smiled. "I got twelve."

Cade tried not to grin. She knew he didn't want to encourage her.

McCormick was pulling back into the department parking lot when they got back. They went in and looked up the scene Sheila had mentioned.

Cade read it aloud. "It is very similar."

Joe took the book and scanned the scene. "So the question is whether Marcus Gibson is involved in the murder."

"That would be pretty stupid," Cade said. "Why would he describe the murders to a tee, then perpetrate them in real life, and think he'd get away with it?"

Blair shrugged. "Maybe he's just crazy. Sheila thinks so."

"Or maybe it's a copycat crime."

"I still say we need to dig into Gibson's life, see what we can find out," McCormick said. "Put him under surveillance. Especially if he was sleeping in the woods on the same night the Lawrence girl was murdered."

Cade nodded. "You're right. We can't ignore the obvious. But meanwhile, we need to read this whole book and see if there are any other similarities. Whether he's our man or not, we might get some insight into what really happened."

C H A P T E R

13

Cade used his new computer system to gather all the information he needed on Gibson in a matter of minutes. The man had no criminal background. Before his work had hit the *New York Times* bestseller list, he'd worked as an English professor for a small college in Maine. He'd started out with a couple of short, literary novels. Critics had hated them. One review called his books "complicated to the point of being obscure." Another one wrote that the "depth of his thoughts, and the convoluted concepts therein, came off as superficial and shallow—the pompous efforts of a man who thinks more highly of his intellect than he should."

In articles about Gibson's life, old colleagues and former students commented that he had taken those reviews hard and stolen around campus with a bitter, distant look on his face. He'd been described as a man "tormented by his own misunderstood genius."

Then one day he decided to do what his colleagues disdained, and "sold out" by writing a crime novel. But not just any crime novel. This was from the point of view of the killer, a dark, macabre look at the inner workings of a murderer. He sold it to a new publisher, who heavily promoted it with a major ad campaign months before its release and booked him for a twenty-city tour. The novel debuted at number one on the *New York Times* list. He subsequently signed a multibook contract for millions and quit his job, ignoring the turned-up noses of his fellow academicians, who accused him of writing drivel for the masses.

Since that time, he'd been a virtual loner, by all accounts. He'd never married, and reports said that he did meticulous research on every book, even to the point of living as a homeless person on the streets of Atlanta's inner city for months at a time.

Cade found a death certificate for Gibson's father, who had died two months after Gibson's birth. His mother, who'd also worked as an English professor, raised him alone. He had very little contact with her now.

"Excuse me, Chief?"

Cade looked up to see Scott Crown leaning in his doorway. "Yeah, Crown. What is it?"

He came in. "Here's the paperwork you asked for. I'm knocking off now. I switched shifts with Bruce."

"Okay, see you tomorrow night."

Scott glanced down at the books all over Cade's desk. "You a Gibson fan?"

Cade shook his head. "No, not really. You?"

"Yeah, I've read almost everything he's written."

Cade turned from his computer and looked up at the young man. "Did you notice that the victim in *Crescent Hill* was killed and disposed of exactly the same way that Emily Lawrence was?"

Crown picked up that book and paged through it. "Now that you mention it . . ."

Maybe this was a chance for the kid to redeem himself. "I want you to do me a favor, Crown. Can you spare another hour or so?"

"Sure. I have a date tonight, but I have some time left."

Cade didn't tell him he knew who his date was with. "Since you've read all these, could you give me a rundown on the plots, paying careful attention to the way the murders are committed, who is killed, the motive, that sort of thing?"

"Sure. I'll just need to refresh my memory on some of them, but it shouldn't be too hard. Is this part of the homicide investigation?"

"Could be."

Crown's eyes widened. "Then you think Marcus Gibson may be our killer?"

Cade didn't want to go that far. "I didn't say that. Maybe it's a copycat. Just in case, though, we're putting him under surveillance. He has some odd habits. The night of the murder we know he spent the night in the woods."

"Can't they bring him in, before he kills anybody else?"

"Nope." Cade rubbed his eyes. "Until we gather enough evidence for probable cause, we'll just be watching him to make sure he stays out of trouble."

Scott stacked all the books from Cade's desk. "I'll get right to work on this, Chief. I'll have it to you before I leave."

Before Scott left his office, Alex Johnson leaned in. "Cade, you got a minute?"

"Sure, whatcha got?"

"The state just faxed this over. It's the initial ballistics report on Emily Lawrence."

Cade took the report and read about the bullet lodged in Emily's chest. It was from a .40 caliber Glock—the same weapon he carried.

Crown stood there, holding the books and watching Cade read. Ignoring him, Cade turned to his computer, pulled up his database on registered weaponry, and typed in Gibson's name. One entry came up.

He sat back hard in his chair. "Marcus Gibson owns a .40 caliber Glock."

Crown balanced the books under his arm. "That the probable cause you need?"

"Not yet. But if I could get that gun, then we could match it to the bullet. If there was a match, it would be a slam dunk. But to get the gun, we'll need a search warrant, and the DA won't issue it *until* we show probable cause."

"Kind of a vicious cycle, huh? Maybe you could just question him and ask for the gun."

Cade's phone rang, and he heard someone in the outer room answering, then Alex came back to the door. "For you, Chief."

Cade picked up the phone. "Chief Cade."

"Hello, Cade. I hope life is well for you today." He recognized the Pakistani accent of Zaheer, the jeweler in town.

"It is, Zaheer. How about you?"

"Very, very good," the man said. "And I wanted to tell you that the ring is ready. It is quite radiant, if I do say so myself."

Cade glanced up at Crown, wishing he'd leave. "Thank you. I wonder if you could do one further thing for me."

"For you, anything."

Crown kept standing there, straining to see the report. Cade put his hand over the receiver. "Close the door on your way out, will you?"

Crown nodded and, since his hands were full, pulled the door closed with his foot. It didn't close all the way, but it would do.

Cade lowered his voice. "Could you somehow put it in an oyster shell?"

"An oyster shell?"

Cade knew the jeweler thought he was crazy. He glanced at the doorway again. "It's part of my plan, Zaheer. I was thinking that I might take her snorkeling at Breaker's Reef Grotto. It's one of our favorite places. I wanted her to find it there, in the cavern."

A deep, low rumble of laughter rolled in the Pakistani's throat. "Ah, very romantic. Yes, I will see what I can find. I enjoy being your confidant in this matter. I will call you as soon as it is ready."

Cade hung up the phone and sat staring at it for a moment. He hoped he wasn't jumping the gun. Marriage was something he and Blair had not yet discussed. All he knew was that she was the one he wanted to wake up next to every morning for the rest of his life. And he didn't see any reason to put that off any longer.

He only hoped Zaheer could keep a secret.

CHAPTER

14

Emily's funeral service was both tragic and celebratory, a memorial to her life even as the mourners wept over the suddenness of her death. Her family stood strong from eulogy to burial, breaking Sadie's heart with their courage and faith.

As the graveside service broke up, Sadie saw her friend Matt, standing across the crowd. He'd been crying, as she had, and somehow that moved her.

"Hey, Matt," she said softly as he came toward her.

He reached down and gave her a hug, something he'd never done before. She suddenly felt close to him, bound by a common thread.

"You going to the prayer service the youth are giving?" she asked when he let her go.

He glanced in the direction most of the students were heading, into the church next to the cemetery. "Am I too old?"

"Of course not. It's for anyone who wants to come."

"Okay, I guess I will."

He walked with her into the big room where the youth held their Bible studies, and they took seats near the back. As the kids quietly filed in, talking in low voices, Matt leaned his elbows on his knees and closed his eyes, shaking his head. "This is horrible. Her death is so senseless. I can't even believe it. What could he have been thinking?"

"Who?" she asked.

"The one who did this. She was just a kid. She never hurt anybody."

She saw the tears in his eyes behind his glasses, and she touched his back. Slowly, he sat back up, took her hand, and held it in his. He looked down at it, as if contemplating it. "Sorry. I'm just having a hard time with this."

"Me too."

He drew in a deep, ragged breath and let her hand go. Taking off his glasses, he rubbed his eyes. "I'm so angry I don't know what to do."

"At who?"

He shrugged, shoved the glasses back on. "God, maybe. He should have protected her. Watched over her."

Sadie didn't know what to say to that, but his honesty and openness made her feel closer to him than ever before. She almost wished she didn't have a date after the service. Maybe she would have been able to hang out with him and talk the anger through.

The prayer service started with the Mercy Me song "I Can Only Imagine," sung by the guitar-playing youth minister. The kids around her closed their eyes in tearful worship. Sadie did the same.

After the song, the microphone was open, and one by one, Emily's friends came up to share personal stories about the girl whose personality had never shone more brightly. With each successive story, the sadness lifted, and tears turned to laughter. It was good to see teens who didn't know Christ being touched by Emily's life as well as her death. It helped, knowing God might, indeed, have a purpose for it and a plan to reap a harvest from the sleep of one of his beloved children.

As Sadie left the church after the service, the burden of Emily's death became lighter. Matt still seemed down, but his tears had dried. He followed her out into the church's foyer.

"Hey, you want to go somewhere and talk?"

She looked up at him. "I wish I could. I really do. But I'm meeting somebody."

"Oh." He nodded, looking almost embarrassed. "Well, I guess I'll see you around then."

"Maybe tomorrow? I do want to talk to you."

He softened then, and met her eyes. His were a soft brown behind those glasses. A slow smile worked itself into them. "Okay. I have class and have to work at the florist, but I'll call you if I can get some time free. Will Morgan and Jonathan let you talk to me?"

"Of course. Why wouldn't they?"

"I've just heard they're pretty strict. And me being a college guy . . . That's kind of why I haven't suggested it before now."

"I think it'll be okay."

She followed him out of the church and watched him walk to the parking lot. Scott Crown was already waiting for her in his little Toyota, idling on the street out front. She hoped this was worth it.

The radio was playing a rap song too loudly for her mood, but thankfully, he turned it down as she got in.

"Hey."

He studied her face. "You okay?"

"Yeah. The service was actually nice. I'm glad I went."

"Good. I thought we'd go get a hamburger. Hungry?"

"Yeah, I am. That'll be great."

As he drove, she realized he looked like a teenager who'd just walked out of algebra class, instead of a full-fledged police officer.

He wore that teasing grin that he'd worn in high school when he strolled down the corridor, keenly aware that he could have dated any of the dreamy-eyed girls who spoke to him. And he'd dated quite a few.

He took her to Beach Bums, a hamburger joint on the water, where the beachcombers hung out and where a lot of the high school kids usually congregated in the parking lot each night. Since most of the kids had been at the service, the place was relatively empty. Scott chose a table by the window with an ocean view, and though the sun wasn't visible as it set in the west, its hues filled the sky in a watercolor pallet, lending an air of romance to the night.

Scott smiled at her. "I'm glad you came out with me. I was afraid you might not, since I'm out of school and all. Did your mom give you any trouble?"

"No, but the age thing did come up, until I reminded them that you're only a year older."

"Hard to believe you have another whole year of school left," he said as he bit into his burger. "You ever feel like quitting? Since you have a job and all?"

"All the time." Sadie picked at her french fries. "But then I realize I need to finish. Maybe even go to college and study journalism."

"Why? So you can spend four years learning to do what you're already doing, then come back here and work the same job?"

She smiled. "How do you know I want to stay here? Maybe I want to go to New York or Washington and work for one of the major papers."

"Is that what you're gonna do?"

"I'd want the option, even if I didn't take it. Didn't you ever think of going to college?"

"Yeah, I thought about it. But my family couldn't afford it."

"What about scholarships, grants? Jonathan says no one should have to skip college because of finances, with all the financial aid available. I mean, you might not get to go to the college that's your first choice, but you could go somewhere and get your degree."

He bit again and chewed, thinking. "Well, to be perfectly honest, my grades weren't good enough in school to get academic scholarships. I wasn't a good enough athlete to get an athletic scholarship. And when it all came right down to it, and I started thinking about loans and grants and all that, I realized I'd rather get on with my life now. Now I have a steady income and a place of my own and I don't have to live in some dorm room waiting for real life to begin."

"Real life? You don't think college is real life?"

He chuckled. "No, I don't. When else can you take four years to party and hang out, live in a place all expenses paid, with no one to answer to?"

"You answer to the professors."

"Not much. If you can pass their tests, they're satisfied. But they don't care when you come in at night or how much you drink. Even the studying isn't real life. Think about it. How often in life are you going to use calculus?"

"I don't know. But don't you think it's good for your brain to learn? It makes you sharper. More disciplined."

He rolled his eyes. "Most people come out of college with their brains fried, not sharper. I have friends who've gone to college and wound up just as messed up as those who dropped out in high school. I figure, who needs it?"

"You sound like you've given this a lot of thought."

He smiled. "Yeah, I have. I decided that being a cop was the way to get what I want. People respect cops. They admire them. Bad guys fear them."

Sadie grinned. "And you like being feared?"

"There are worse things."

Sadie thought about the impressions she'd had of cops in the past. They'd arrested her mother, dragged her off in handcuffs. . . . But they'd also rescued Sadie when she was alone and broken. "I don't fear cops. I respect them. I owe my life to Cade. Ten college degrees wouldn't make you more important than one police badge, in my book."

His smile told her he appreciated that.

"And look what you did, discovering Emily's body. You're practically a hero."

"Just doing my job."

Sadie wasn't sure of his sincerity—since he had every reason to be proud—but she decided to give him the benefit of the doubt. "Have you always wanted to be a cop?"

"Since I was a kid. But I also like working with computers. Maybe I'll move into something with cybercrimes. Maybe for the FBI or something."

"Ever thought of being a detective, like your uncle?"

"Maybe. But I wouldn't settle for what he's settled for. Small town crimes that would put you to sleep—"

"Hey, Joe's helped solve some major cases. Cade says he's one of the best."

"Yeah, but I want more. I'm starting young enough to make my mark."

"And you're being trained by the best. Cade's top-notch."

"Yeah, he's great. A real role model."

Was that a note of sarcasm in his voice?

He gazed out the window, then his face changed. "Hey, if it isn't the old gang. Let's go out and see them."

Sadie followed his gaze to the group of her schoolmates that had gathered in the parking lot. They'd been at the church, and like her, they seemed to need some levity after the sadness of the last few days. She didn't want to join them, but Scott was already sliding out of the booth. Reluctantly, she followed him outside.

"Hey, it's Scott!"

At Don Sandifer's exclamation, everyone turned to look. Sadie wanted to shrink back, but Scott headed into the midst of the crowd.

"Hey, guys. What's up?"

"Are you really the one who found Emily the other night?" Annie Malone's voice gushed with adoration.

"Yeah, that was me, but I can't talk about an ongoing police investigation, guys."

"Do you have your gun with you?"

Scott shot Bret Ames a look that suggested he was an idiot. "No, Bozo, I'm not carrying a piece, and even if I were, I wouldn't let you see it. It's not a toy."

Sadie watched Scott bask in the admiration of his former classmates. He deserved it . . . but it was the last way she wanted to spend their date.

As if he sensed her feelings, Scott reached back and took her hand. "You guys know my date, Sadie, don't you?"

The gesture surprised her. The gossip would be all over the island within an hour. She wasn't sure how she felt about that.

Then, through the crowd, she saw someone watching her. Matt stood there, his hands in his pockets, looking at her holding Scott's hand.

She let his hand go and crossed her arms. Why had she done that? Was it worry for his feelings, when she didn't even know for sure how he felt? Or was it because she didn't want him to think she and Scott were an item?

She honestly didn't know.

Matt didn't come closer. Instead, he walked away and was gone before she could stop him.

She considered running after him, but what would she say? If he was interested in her, why hadn't he ever made a move?

Scott Crown had done so, and he was proud to be with her, even if she was a high school student.

And there was something to be said for that.

C H A P T E R

15

The sun melted into the horizontal clouds that seemed to hang over Hanover House, and Amelia Roarke realized it would be dark soon. The sight of that peaceful sky—like a banner that promised nothing bad could ever happen here—should have relaxed her. Instead, she couldn't breathe.

She needed a paper sack to blow into, to signal to her lungs that they didn't have to coil up like tightly balled fists. "I can't do this. Keep driving."

Her best friend Jamie clutched the steering wheel. "Come on, Amelia. We came all the way here. We've driven by that house four times. We're going to stop and knock on that door."

Amelia thought she might throw up as they rolled toward the driveway. "No, I *can't!* Please, don't turn in there. We'll do it tomorrow."

She'd never figured herself for a coward, yet here she was, shivering like her life depended on the person behind that door, the woman who had given birth to her nineteen years earlier.

The mother she'd never met.

The truth was, she was scared of how she'd feel when that door opened. What if her mother answered the door and mistook her for an encyclopedia salesman? What if she slammed the door in her face?

Or worse, what if she invited her in and listened as Amelia told her that she was the child she'd given up for adoption? She could get angry and rail about sealed records and ruined lives. She could throw her out without even a smile.

Anything could happen.

Her parents had warned her—her *real* parents, who had loved her and raised her, stayed up with her when she was sick, and wept when she went off to college. Still, no matter how much they loved her, they just didn't get it. They'd been hurt, as if her search was a personal assault on them.

But the questions ate at Amelia, and she often woke up thinking about this mystery woman who gave her up. What did her mother look like? Did she have any other kids? Who was Amelia's father? Was he alive?

She'd had to do the search behind her parents' backs, using the computer and the resources she'd learned about on a Listserv for adoptees. It took more than a year to find out her mother's name and another year to locate her.

When Amelia learned she lived in a place called Cape Refuge, she thought the name sounded like shelter, peace, a place where you were a part of things without even trying.

She didn't expect such terror at the prospect of finding what she'd searched for all this time.

"You'll have to do it sometime, Amelia." Jamie's look was pointed. "We don't have enough money to stay longer than a couple of days."

Jamie was a good friend. She'd come along for moral support—knowing that Amelia's nerves would get the best of her and she'd need a hand to hold. Amelia hated letting her down.

"I know, and I will. Tomorrow, I promise." She twisted her long blonde hair around her finger until it almost cut off the circulation; she was like a little girl at vacation Bible school, clinging to her mother's knees and begging her not to make her go in.

It wasn't supposed to be like this. She was supposed to have more courage. She'd been relentless in tracking her birth mother down, more fearless with each phone call that got her closer to her goal.

Was she going to let it slip through her fingers because of a case of nerves? If she did, she'd never forgive herself. "What if she doesn't want to see me?"

"We've been through all this." Jamie came to a stop sign and gave her a long look. "You said you were ready. You've been building up to this for a whole year."

It was true. Jamie had been with her every step of the way, rooting her on and offering ideas. The day Amelia got a copy of her original birth certificate and learned her mother's name, Jamie was there, just as excited as she.

Now Jamie sighed. "I'm gonna be totally bummed if we did this all for nothing."

Amelia knew that for all Jamie's encouragement, she was running out of patience. As they sat at the stop sign, Jamie pulled her bottle-blonde hair up from her neck to cool it off, since her air conditioner wasn't working that great.

"I'll be bummed too. I promise, I'm going to do it tomorrow. I just need to get my head straight first. Plan what I'll say. I thought we'd get here and have a little more trouble finding where she was, you know? I didn't expect that lady to tell us right off the bat. It threw my rhythm off."

Jamie shot her an amused look. "Your rhythm? Don't go dramatic on me, Amelia. You don't need a rhythm to knock on someone's door."

"Okay, so it sounds crazy. But I don't know yet what I want to do after I meet her. Like, if she does accept me, what relationship do I want to have? Will I want to be friends? Will I need to call her *Mom?* Will I spend holidays with her, visit her in the summers? When I get married someday, will she sit on the row with my parents, or will she sit somewhere else like anybody else who comes? I have to work through these things."

"Now you're acting mental. Normal people don't have to have the outcome for every possible scenario before they take the first step."

"So you're calling me crazy?"

"Yes. Certifiable." Jamie looked at her with those impatient eyes, and suddenly Amelia started to laugh. Jamie broke into a smile too and started to drive again.

"Okay, so we go back to the room, get a good night's sleep, you write about a hundred angst-ridden pages in your journal, and tomorrow—"

"Tomorrow we go and knock on her door. I'll be ready then."

"Promise?"

"Promise."

"Okay, then. We'll go back to the room." Jamie flicked her hair back over her shoulder and glanced at Amelia. "Now *that's* something to be afraid of."

CHAPTER

16

Cade gave the information about Marcus Gibson to the GBI, letting them know his department was available to help in any way they needed. They'd planned to put Gibson under twenty-four-hour surveillance, but they hadn't been able to locate him yet.

Cade took advantage of the lull to go to the jewelry store and pick up the ring he'd had made for Blair.

The Colonel from Crickets—Cade's favorite diner—was there, standing at one of the display counters, studying some necklaces. Zaheer, who had taken out several things to show the man, clapped his hands when Cade came in.

"Ah, Chief Cade. I have been expecting you today."

The Colonel turned around and grinned. "Well, well. If it ain't ol' Romeo hisself."

Cade grinned and shook the man's hand. "You didn't see me here, okay, Colonel?"

"Course not. Can't imagine what would bring you here." He winked. "You ain't shopping for a new watch, are you?"

Cade grinned. "Maybe." The Colonel was teasing him. Cade should have made an appointment after hours and come in here when he was sure not to be seen. Why on earth hadn't he thought of that? "What brings you here, Colonel?"

"The wife's birthday is today," he said. "I woke up this morning and realized it. Hadn't got her a thing. Looking for an emergency necklace I can afford."

Cade chuckled.

"You can go ahead and wait on him." The Colonel waved his hand. "I haven't made up my mind yet."

Zaheer smiled up at Cade. "I will be right back with your purchase, Chief Cade."

Cade wanted to tell him to wait until the Colonel left, but by then there might be someone else in the store. Sweat beaded on his temples. Maybe he should pretend he had a radio call and come back later. Before he could do so, Zaheer came out, brandishing the oyster. "Beautiful, is it not? I freshened the shell up a little, to make it a bit more magical."

Cade tried to block the Colonel's view, but he couldn't help grinning as he took the oyster in his hand. It was perfect. Zaheer had touched up the shell with some pearl paint, making it look more like a jewel than a sea creature. "May I look?" he asked in a low voice.

"Of course. Carefully . . ." Zaheer opened the shell, revealing the one-carat solitaire Cade had so carefully chosen.

His heartbeat stumbled into triple time. He was really going to do this.

He glanced back at the Colonel, saw him straining his neck to see. Quickly he looked away, pretending he hadn't seen. But the grin on his face told Cade he had.

"Colonel, I'm counting on you not to tell anybody this, okay? I want her to be surprised."

"My lips are sealed. You know I wouldn't spoil this for either of you. So how are you gonna do it?"

Cade relaxed and looked from Zaheer to the Colonel. "I'm taking her out to Breaker's Reef Grotto Saturday. I'm going to pretend I found the oyster on one of the cavern shelves. When she opens it, I'll direct her to the cave wall, where I'll have written 'Will You Marry Me?' "

The men laughed at the plan, and Cade knew he had a winner. He hoped Blair didn't hear about it before he had the chance to surprise her.

CHAPTER

17

The radio call from McCormick came when Cade was leaving the jewelry store. "GBI just located Gibson, Cade. He just came trudging up from the woods."

"So he's home now?"

"That's right. They don't plan to let him out of their sight from here on out. They said they're going to question him, but since he lives here, they wanted one of us to go with them."

"I'll go," Cade said. "I'll head over right now."

Two GBI agents—Yeager and Smith—were waiting near Gibson's house. Cade got out of his truck and greeted them.

"Did you get a warrant?" he asked as they headed for the door.

"Yep." Yeager patted his coat pocket. "Arrest and search warrants."

They knocked, and moments later the door opened. The author blinked out at them. "If it isn't the gestapo."

He seemed amused—and slightly fascinated—as they identified themselves.

"May we come in?" Yeager asked.

He looked confused for a moment, then stepped back, offering them entrance. "One hardly says no to the Georgia Bureau of Investigation, I'd suppose."

They went inside, and Cade looked around at the boxes in the front room and the furniture dropped down but not arranged. They followed Gibson into his study, and Cade saw what Sheila had described. Papers everywhere, cluttering his desk and his bookshelves and the floor, organized into toppling stacks that seemed to cover everything.

He cleared off a place for them to sit, then pulled up a chair of his own. "Forgive me if I wasn't my usual sharp-witted self when I answered the door, gentlemen, but I had just gone to bed. I've been camping to research my latest book and I haven't slept much in days."

"Where, exactly, have you been camping?" Cade asked.

Gibson gave him a long stare. "I'd be happy to answer your questions, Detective, but—"

"I'm not a detective. I'm chief of the Cape Refuge police department."

"I see," Gibson said. "Forgive me for not knowing that. I'm new to town. As I was saying, I'd be happy to answer your questions, but I'd like to know what they're in regard to. Have I done something wrong?"

Cade deferred to Yeager.

"We're investigating the recent murder of Emily Lawrence."

"Murder?" Gibson sprang up and raked his fingers through his Einsteinish hair. "And you think *I* had something to do with that?"

"Just answer the questions, please," Smith said. "Where were you on the night of the fourteenth?"

Gibson seemed to search his mind. "Well, I can see that I have a problem. I believe I was camping that night. I came home intermittently, but spoke to no one, except for the woman who does typing for me. Sandra, or Sharon, or . . ."

Cade didn't correct him. "Then you don't have an alibi?"

"Not one that can be verified for that night, unless you find a rabbit or snake in the woods that might have seen me."

Cade didn't find that amusing. "We understand you own a gun. Could you get it for us, please?"

The man hesitated, and Cade noticed him swallow. "I can't. You see, it was stolen."

"Stolen?" Yeager frowned. "When?"

"I'm not sure, but I think a couple of days ago. I had it in my pocket as I visited with some criminal types . . ."

Cade shot Yeager a look. Was this guy for real?

"Criminal types?"

"Yes. Drug dealers, addicts, prostitutes. It was research for my book. Some of them were a little too chummy, and eventually I found out why. They were robbing me blind. One of them stole my gun."

"Where were these people?"

"Different places. I visited some seedy motels here and on Tybee Island and several in Savannah before I noticed the weapon was gone. It could have been stolen at any of them."

Yeager got up and looked around the room. "Mr. Gibson, we have a warrant to search your house."

Gibson looked disturbed. "My house? Why?"

"Because the girl's murder mirrored the murder in your book *Crescent Hill*."

"So you have decided in those twisted brains of yours that I must somehow be responsible? Tell me, detectives, what would lead you to believe that I would be so foolish as to murder someone in such an obvious way, with all signs pointing to me? Don't you think if I wanted to commit murder that I would be creative enough to come up with something new?"

That thought had occurred to Cade, but the man didn't seem all there. Maybe he was mentally ill—as Sheila suspected—and hadn't thought it through.

"Fine, search my property, then. But keep in mind that murder is my business. When you find books on weaponry and poisons and forensics, don't get the idea that these are somehow clues that I'm a mad killer. I write about killers, and I research my subjects well."

"We'd like to take you in for questioning while we search."

Gibson looked at first annoyed, then almost intrigued. "Yes, of course you would. And I'll certainly cooperate. I've never been questioned in a murder case before. It might prove to be useful."

Cade hadn't expected that. Were all writers like this?

"And I'd like to take my laptop with me, if I may. I may want to take notes."

Now Cade was amused. "I'm afraid we'll be taking the notes, Mr. Gibson. And your laptop is evidence."

That seemed to upset him. His face reddened, and a vein in his temple began to pulsate against his skin. "I'm afraid that's not acceptable."

"Not acceptable?" Yeager's brows arched.

"No. You see, I have a first draft of my work in progress on that laptop. I don't show anyone my first drafts."

"Something to hide?"

"Yes! Bad writing. My first drafts belong in the garbage dump. I'm a rewriter. I rewrite extensively, and I can't abide anyone reading my work before I've had the chance to rewrite it! It's in my will. If I drop dead, they're to burn my first drafts. I certainly don't want a bunch of halfwit police critics poring over my words!"

Cade had been called many things, but never a "halfwit police critic." He doubted if *anyone* had ever been called that before.

"I'm afraid you won't be able to control that," Smith said.

Visibly shaken, Gibson threw his hands in the air. "Then I demand a lawyer. I insist on calling him immediately."

They allowed him to make the call to an attorney in Atlanta, and the man promised he would charter a plane to get there as soon as possible.

Cade hoped he would hurry. Marcus Gibson knew more than he was telling, and Cade was ready to pry it out of him.

18

By that evening, the news was rife with reports of Marcus Gibson's arrest, along with televised clips from his hastily arranged arraignment. Apparently the judge was a fan of the eccentric writer and handled the case with star-struck incompetence. He set bond at $100,000. Gibson's lawyer paid it without blinking, and Gibson was released by dark.

The police put him under twenty-four-hour surveillance and warned him not to leave the county.

Cade prayed there would be no more murders.

Maybe he should cancel his day with Blair tomorrow. He'd asked her to take the day off and spend it with him out at the grotto. Both the day and the place had special significance. Though he doubted she realized it, it was the one-year anniversary of their first kiss . . .

No, he wouldn't cancel. He'd waited this long to propose, and he didn't want to wait one more day.

The grotto held a special place in Blair's heart. Her father used to take her out there to fish, and they'd often explored the cavern, which was one of the most unique and beautiful spots on the east coast, as far as Cade was concerned. A couple of divers had discovered it fifteen years ago, and spelunkers from the Atlanta Grotto group had begun to explore it.

Because it was difficult and dangerous to get into, it hadn't become the tourist attraction it could have been. The sole entrance could only be reached by swimming twenty-five feet under the rock formation and coming up from the reef, to the one place where it jutted out. If one knew where the entrance was, and had strong lungs and a lean build, he could swim through it and come up inside the most beautiful natural work of art that God had ever created.

The entrance wasn't large enough for divers with air tanks to get through, which prohibited the average swimmer from ever getting into it. Years ago, the cities of Tybee Island and Cape Refuge had formed a commission to investigate how they could broaden the entrance to make the place more publicly accessible, but the logistics were too complicated. They'd never been able to agree on how it should be done.

Cade was glad. He liked keeping the grotto the special treasure of a privileged few.

Blair often talked of her most precious memories with her dad, when he'd taken her out there, and she'd followed him under that wall. It was one of Cade's favorite places as well, a reminder of God's extravagant artistry. He'd never forget the first time he and Jonathan went under, their lungs screaming for breath, then burst up into the cavern. Sunlight had poured through the slitlike openings at the top of the cavern, providing natural light for the beauty around them. Stalactites hung like diamond icicles from the ceiling, and helictites that looked like magnificent flowers sprang from the limestone ledges.

The breath he'd just gulped had been taken away at his first glimpse.

What a perfect place to ask Blair to marry him.

He wondered if his timing was bad. Was it irresponsible to take off now, when the state might need to call on his police force?

"Cade, you've been planning this for weeks." McCormick sat in the chair across from Cade's desk, bent on convincing him to go. "Tybee and the state guys are handling the investigation. Our part is peripheral at best. They don't need us. If something comes up, I can handle it."

"I know you can." Cade pulled the oyster out of his desk drawer and eased it open. He turned it around and showed it to McCormick. "So what do you think?"

McCormick whistled. "That's some investment. What's your plan?"

He grinned. "In the morning, I'm going out to the grotto and writing 'Will You Marry Me?' on the wall."

McCormick threw his head back and laughed. "You're doing *what*? Do you know what you have to do to get into that cave?"

Cade grinned. "'Course I do. That's what makes it special."

"So you'll deface that gorgeous place with graffiti?"

"Just in chalk during low tide. As soon as the tide comes up, it'll wash it all away. And under the sign, I'm leaving a bouquet of yellow roses, her favorites. Then tomorrow afternoon, I'll take her out there and lure her into the cavern."

McCormick was clearly enjoying this. "*Lure* her, huh? With little minnows? Pieces of tuna?"

"Nope." Cade leaned back and put his hands behind his head. "Just my charm, my friend."

They both laughed.

"So don't tell me. You'll have the ring stuffed into the mouth of a sea bass, and it'll jump out of the water at the exact moment that she sees the proposal on the wall . . ."

Cade leaned forward. "No, but that's a great idea. You know any trained bass?"

"No, but I hear they're intelligent critters. You can probably recruit one on the spot. They're always looking for good gigs."

"Yeah, but Sea World gets the best ones. No, I can't rely on some Flipper wannabe to do it. I'm gonna have the ring in my pocket and I'll slip it onto the ledge right under my sign. I'll make sure she finds it."

"She'll drown. You know that, don't you?"

Cade smiled and looked down at the ring. He hoped it did take her breath away. "We can get out and sit on one of the ledges while I make my case."

"Make your case? You don't think she'll say yes?"

Cade was pretty sure she would, but it was impossible to be sure. Blair was a complicated woman. "Hard to tell."

"No, it's not. She'd have tied the knot months ago. I don't know what's taken you so long. And the cave, that's great. Women love that stuff. They gotta have a story, women do. My sister has married three different guys because they gave her romantic proposals."

"Two of them also gave her black eyes, if I recall."

"Yeah, that. But she still talks about those proposals."

Scott Crown stepped into the doorway, and Cade looked up, hoping he hadn't heard.

"You talking about my mother?"

"Yeah." Joe looked back at his nephew. "You eavesdropping?"

The kid hesitated. "I didn't mean to. But for what it's worth, Mom quit falling for the romantic proposals. I don't think she'll ever get married again."

"No, now she just moves in with them."

Cade wished Joe would let up on Scott. He clearly wasn't amused.

"I just wanted to give you this report, Chief. It's the summaries of all the murders in Gibson's books, just like you asked."

Cade took it, but he kept his eyes on the young man. "Hey, Crown. Whatever you just saw or heard—besides the stuff about your mom—you didn't see or hear it. Got it?"

For a moment he thought Crown was going to deny he'd seen or heard anything, but then he grinned. "My lips are sealed, Chief."

Cade hoped that was true. Crown left the doorway, and Cade looked at McCormick.

"He's all right, Cade. I don't think you have to worry. And there's just no question about your going through with it. You have to do it, and it has to be tomorrow. No more discussion. I can hold down the fort."

Cade looked down at the ring again, unable to hold back his grin. "All right. I guess it's a go then."

CHAPTER

19

Amelia stared out the window as Jamie turned the car onto the road leading to the Flagstaff Motel. "You know, Amelia, the very worst that could happen tomorrow still isn't all that bad. If you meet her and she rejects you, you can leave and never come back. You forget you ever had a birth mother."

Amelia sighed. "It's not that simple. You don't understand. You know who you are. I don't."

"Yes, you do, Amelia. You're my best friend, a gorgeous girl who's good at everything she does, the daughter of two people who absolutely adore you. A 4.0 student with a full scholarship and a great future. Who you are has nothing to do with the woman who carried you for nine months."

"Oh, yeah? Then why have you been egging me on? You've been almost as invested in this search as I have."

"Because it was interesting. Challenging. I mean, it seems like anything could happen. There's a story about you, one that you don't know. It captured my imagination."

"Captured mine too."

"But it's not like you have anything to lose. Whatever happens, you still have great parents who love you. Not everybody has that, Amelia."

She knew Jamie didn't have that. Her father lived across the country with his new family, and when Jamie was a kid, he'd only tried to see her once a year at Christmas. Since she'd turned eighteen, he hadn't bothered at all. Her mother was on her fourth marriage and stayed so distracted by her own problems that she hardly noticed Jamie. She probably didn't even know she'd left town yet.

"I do love my parents," Amelia whispered. "It's not about them. It's about who I really am. My genes. My family. My story."

Jamie had the grace not to argue with her. She really was a first-class friend, and Amelia loved her. Jamie was always there for her. Amelia would never forget the summer they'd both planned to go to church camp. Despite their excitement, the morning of the trip Amelia woke up with a fever and couldn't go at the last minute. When Jamie found out, she got off the bus and refused to get back on. She told the chaperones she didn't want to have fun without Amelia. So she stayed home, and they talked on the phone and through her bedroom window until the fever broke.

Everybody needed a friend like that.

Jamie was quiet as they reached the Flagstaff, the only place with vacancies that they'd been able to afford. The look on Jamie's face revealed her dread at returning to this place. She looked around at the activity in the parking lot. Cars came and went; drivers slowed down and talked through the windows to the sleazy-looking men who hung around on the street. Women of all ages, very young teens on up to middle-aged, walked up and down the walkways in front of the open doors and, occasionally, went into one of the rooms with a visitor and closed the door.

"This place totally stinks," Jamie said. "I'd almost rather sleep in the car."

"We'll be okay in our room. We'll just lock the door."

"If we make it to our room without being attacked."

"Well, do you want to stay somewhere else?"

"With what? He made us pay up front. What were we thinking?"

Amelia sighed. "It didn't look this bad this morning."

"Guess they were all sleeping it off. But it sure looks bad now."

Amelia looked up at their room on the second floor. They could get to the stairs without walking through men, and then if they walked fast past the open doors, they could probably get to their room without talking to anyone. "We'll be okay. Let's just stay close together and walk fast."

They got out of the car, and Jamie locked the doors. As they started up the stairs to the second floor, Jamie whispered, "You kill me. You're afraid to knock on your mother's door, but *this* doesn't scare you."

"Ironic, huh?"

They heard someone knocking on the rail at the bottom of the stairs, and a man called out. "Hey, baby, you two looking for me?"

"Keep walking," Amelia whispered. "Don't look back at him."

Up ahead, a girl in a pair of shorts and a tube top leaned in a doorway, looking toward them. Black makeup was smeared under her eyes, and her hair looked as if it hadn't been washed in a week. She reminded Amelia of a child who'd gotten into her mother's makeup and substituted the eyeliner for the retouch.

Amelia's heart jolted. She wanted to stop and talk to the girl, find out where she was from, how she'd wound up here. Was she one of those outcasts in school who didn't fit into any group, so she'd latched onto the first group that came along and accepted her?

Amelia swallowed hard. Where was the girl's mother? How had someone so young ended up here, blending in with the rest of these wayward souls? Had she come to this town like Amelia, looking for something or someone, only to be stopped by drugs or men or some trouble she was in—to the point that she'd checked into this dirtbag motel and never managed to check back out?

Their steps slowed as they approached the girl, and Amelia felt Jamie pulling at her sleeve, warning her to keep walking. Jamie knew her too well.

Amelia decided she was right—the girl probably wouldn't welcome her intrusion. But then the girl's vacant eyes met hers, and she stepped toward Amelia . . . staggered a little . . . then collapsed onto the concrete.

Amelia gasped and rushed to her, falling to her knees. "Go get her some water!" she told Jamie. "Hurry!"

Jamie looked around, then darted into the girl's room and came back with a paper cup.

The girl opened her eyes, clearly disoriented, and tried to focus on Amelia.

"Are you okay?" Amelia asked.

"Who're you?" she asked in a raspy slur.

"Amelia." The minute she said her name, Jamie nudged her with her foot, as if warning her not to give too much information. Amelia took the cup and offered it to the girl. "You fainted. Here's some water."

The girl took the cup.

Jamie finally stooped down next to the girl. "Do you need us to call an ambulance?"

She blinked, then started to sit up. "No." She took another drink, then looked around to see who was watching. Amelia realized they'd become the subject of attention of everyone around them.

"We could give you a ride somewhere," Amelia whispered. "Get you out of here."

"No, I'm fine." She wobbled back to her feet. "I don't have anyplace else to go anyway."

Those words slammed into Amelia's gut. How would it feel to have no place to go? She was here in this godforsaken place for one night, and that was all. What if she had to stay indefinitely because there was no other choice? Tears stung her eyes.

"What's your name?"

"Tina." The girl stumbled into her room, fell onto the bed. Amelia got up and started to follow her in, but Jamie caught her arm and mouthed, *Let's go!*

But Amelia couldn't leave the girl, not until she was sure she was all right. She followed her into the room and looked around.

It smelled like vomit. A pair of shoes lay on the floor, next to a Kroger sack with some clothes spilling out. A dozen empty fast-food bags were wadded around the room. Garbage spilled out of the trash can. "Do you . . . do you live here?"

"What's it to you?"

Amelia looked at Jamie, then back at the girl. "It just doesn't look like a very nice place for a person your age. Especially someone who's sick."

"I'm not sick." Tina rolled onto her back and looked at the ceiling. A fine film of perspiration glistened on her forehead. "If it's so bad, why are *you* here?"

"We're just staying the night. Don't you have a home? Is there someone we could call for you?"

The girl started to laugh, silently at first, but then her shoulders began to convulse with her laughter. She rolled back over and buried her face in her pillow.

Amelia turned back to Jamie, who looked just as clueless as she. "I guess that would be a no," Jamie whispered. She tugged on Amelia's sleeve, and Amelia nodded. They should go. The girl wasn't going to let them help her.

They started to walk out, but suddenly the girl rose up. "That's right, you better run, or you might wind up like me. It's contagious, you know." Her words were thick with contempt.

Amelia stopped at the door and looked back. The words were an accusation, but she couldn't fault Tina for them. "If you need a ride somewhere, we'll just be down the hall. The next to the last door. We could buy you some food."

"Are you *crazy?*" Jamie hissed the question in her ear. "We don't have enough money!"

But it didn't matter, because Tina wasn't interested. She just looked at Amelia for a long moment, then finally said, "You don't belong here." There was no malice in her tone now, just a deep, urgent sincerity. "You should get back in your car and pretend you were never here. It's not a safe place for someone like you."

Jamie tugged on Amelia's sleeve, urging her to come. Finally, Amelia left the doorway and followed her friend toward their

room. Jamie's hand was shaking as she put her key into the lock.
When the door opened, Amelia looked back toward the girl's
room.

Tina was in the doorway, watching them, looking for all the
world like an abandoned child.

Shaken, Amelia stepped into the stale room and watched
Jamie lock the door behind them.

Cade couldn't have picked a better day to bring Blair to Breaker's Reef. She was glad she'd agreed to come in spite of all the work they both needed to do. She'd been so conflicted about taking the day off, but there wasn't anything she'd rather do. The scoop of the century would not have deterred her from exploring the grotto with Cade. The cavern was a special place from her childhood, one of her favorite places on the earth, the secret place she shared with the most important man in her life—her father. And now the other most important man in her life wanted to share it with her too.

They had taken her family's boat out, anchored it, and then gone into the water with their snorkeling gear, intent on getting into the cavern.

"Are you ready?"

Blair looked toward the big rock structure jutting up from the reef. She always got slightly panicked when she went down under that wall, fearing that she wouldn't make it up on the other side in time to fill her lungs with air. "I think so."

"Just move fast. You want to lead?"

She thought that might make it easier. Knowing Cade was behind her might keep the panic at bay. If she struggled to make it under, he could help her and get her to air. "Okay, you follow."

She pulled her mask down and dove under. He came beside her, moving his arms in long, graceful strokes, pulling himself down toward the saltwater depths until he came to the wall. His dark hair waved around his head as he waited for her. She followed as he went lower still, found the underside of the wall, then signaled her to pass him.

Her heart raced as that jolt of panic hit her, but she swam on, taking the lead, pulling with long strokes until she found the opening and squeezed up through it.

It was too far this time! Her lungs wouldn't hold the air. She'd have to release it, and then she wouldn't be able to inhale again in time. She needed to turn back, yet she was closer to the surface of the cavern than if she went back under the wall. Besides, she could feel Cade behind her, urging her on, waiting for her to clear the opening so that he could make his way to air.

She pulled out of the tunnel, and Cade swept up beside her. She raced him to the surface, pulling with all her might toward the light . . .

She burst up, sucking in air.

Something floated against her arm, and she jerked and moved back as Cade came up. A turtle? A fish? It was soft, limp . . .

She turned around in the water . . .

And screamed.

The body of a girl floated there.

Cade pulled Blair back and saw what had frightened her. Gasping for breath, Blair tried desperately to tread water as she stared, horrified, at the body. It was secured by a tether tied to her arm and hooked around a stalagmite jutting out of a ledge.

"It's okay." Breathless, Cade whispered in her ear. "Calm down."

"Is she dead?" Her words wavered across the cave. She was trembling, but so was he.

"I don't know." He pulled Blair toward a flat, smooth shelf and helped her out of the water. "Are you okay?"

"Yes. Hurry."

He swam back to the body, dread tightening his face.

"She's cold, and there's not a pulse. She's dead, all right."

He looked around as if trying to judge whether someone else was there with them. There was clearly no place for anyone to hide.

Blair was shivering. "Did she float in here on her own?"

"No, she's tied. Someone put her here."

Blair finally forced herself to look toward the body. She thought she might faint, but she had to stay clear-headed if she hoped to get out of there safely. It looked like a teenager, dressed in jeans and a red pullover shirt. Feather earrings floated on the surface, and one pink sandal with a yellow daisy was buckled onto her foot. Blair's eyes followed the rope that held the girl, drifting to the wall above her. She saw some words written in chalk, just above where the girl was tied.

Will you marry me?

She caught her breath. "Cade, look! The killer left a message."

She saw the chalk lying there next to a bouquet of yellow roses, as if the killer had placed them there. Cade's face was ashen as he turned back. When he spoke, his voice was raw.

"I think our killer is playing with me. This can't be a coincidence."

Blair tried to stop shivering. "W-what do you m-mean?"

He shook his head. "Someone knew we'd be here."

Blair was shaking harder now. "Did you t-tell anyone you were coming here?"

He hesitated again. "Yes, I told a couple of people."

"Cade, I'm s-scared. Let's g-get out of here."

Cade nodded. "Yeah, I'm going to have to radio this in." He came back to her, pulled himself out of the water, and rubbed her arms to warm her up. She tried to relax.

"You okay?"

She nodded. "I think so."

"Can you make it out?"

Again, she nodded.

"Put your mask on," he said. "Let's go."

"But the girl."

"We have to leave her here. I can't disturb the evidence."

Blair looked at the body again. Who was she? "Do you recognize her?"

"No. I've never seen her before." Cade pulled his mask on, hiding the emotions passing across his face. Blair tried not to think of more parents grieving over their child. She tried, instead, to concentrate on getting enough air to get out of the cavern.

She followed Cade down, down, down under the wall, and back up again. She burst into daylight, never so glad in her life to see the sky. Cade helped her into the boat and looked through his binoculars for any sign that the killer was still around. Then he radioed the state police.

Blair pulled a blanket around her body and tried to stop shivering.

21

Cade was thankful Blair had managed to shake off her fear and slip into journalism mode as the various law enforcement agencies involved came out to work the crime scene. "Blair, you've obviously got a scoop on this, but I have to ask you not to report any of the details of the crime scene. There are certain things only the killer knows. We want to keep those things away from the public."

"What about the writing on the wall? Can I report that?"

Cade wanted to scream out that the killer hadn't written that on the wall—that *he* had—but he didn't want his proposal to come that way. He'd wanted her to see the writing, then find the flowers, the oyster, and see the ring. He'd wanted it to be romantic and memorable, something they would tell their grandchildren.

It would be memorable, all right.

"No, especially not that," he said. "And please don't let it get out to the rest of the press."

Blair sighed. "Are you sure? It would make great headlines."

"I'm sure."

She looked toward the cave. "I guess it's the biggest clue you've got, huh? If you can trace the handwriting, get prints off the chalk, maybe you'll figure out who it is."

Cade didn't answer.

"Gibson's under surveillance, right? He couldn't have done this without being seen."

"Unless he hired someone to move the body. Maybe it was his way of throwing us off. Making us think he couldn't be the one. Look, I have to go back in." He brushed her wet hair out of her eyes. "You gonna be okay?"

"I'm fine. Don't worry about me."

Cade put his mask on and swam back under the wall. He came up on the other side. Already Yeager and Smith from the GBI were working the scene, documenting the evidence and photographing the girl.

"I have to tell you something." Cade's voice echoed off the cavern walls.

The detective in charge of the investigation looked back at him. "What?"

"The writing on the wall. It's mine."

Everyone turned to stare at him. "What do you mean, yours?"

"I wrote it. I was here earlier today. I wrote it on the wall, and I was bringing Blair here to propose. The killer must have known. The body wasn't here earlier—I'm sure of it—and he tied her to the ledge right under where I wrote my proposal, obviously *knowing* I would bring Blair right to that spot."

Yeager's eyes narrowed. "When were you here, exactly?"

"About ten this morning—" Even as he spoke, he knew he had become a suspect. He pulled the oyster out of his nylon pocket. "Here, look. I was going to have Blair come up and see the sign, and then I was going to set this on the ledge and direct her to find it. It has a ring inside it." He opened the oyster and showed the detectives.

Yeager looked as if he didn't know whether to congratulate or cuff him.

"Look, if you can keep this from Blair, I'd appreciate it," Cade said. "I obviously didn't get to propose. I don't want her to know the writing was mine."

"So you're telling me that the chalk will have *your* prints on it?"

Cade fought back his frustration. "Of *course* it will. I didn't try to hide my prints. I didn't know I would have to answer for any of this later. But someone knew."

"Who did you tell?"

"I told the jeweler, Zaheer, and the Colonel, who owns Crickets. And Jonathan Cleary, the mayor. And I mentioned it to the florist when I picked the flowers up. Some of my men knew. Any one of them could have told a dozen people, even though I swore them to secrecy." If only he knew which one had wagged his tongue. He would personally like to throttle them.

And now what would he do? If he didn't ask Blair to marry him today, word was bound to get back to her. But this wasn't how he wanted to propose. Blair deserved better. He watched the detectives work, noting the tension in their movements, their hushed conversations. And he knew the evidence was pointing to him, because the killer wanted it that way.

With all his heart, he vowed not to let him win.

CHAPTER

22

Hours later, Cade met with Yeager and Smith in the GBI's branch office.

"You won't believe what we've found on Gibson's computer," Yeager said. "A scene describing this second murder was in the book he was working on. He had it down to a tee."

Cade hadn't quite expected that. It was too obvious. Did the man honestly think he would get away with it?

Cade clenched his jaw. "I still don't understand why he'd goad me like this. Taking the dead girl to the very place I was going to be. Tying her right under my sign. Why?"

"He's a novelist, remember? He makes things up. Acts things out. In some ways, he becomes his characters. And his characters are killers. Staging the bodies so they'll be discovered is part of their thrill."

"Was there anyone set up in the book's murder? Did it describe the killer going there knowing someone else would be there?"

"No, that part wasn't there. I think that was just icing on the cake for Gibson. Or maybe it *was* all a coincidence."

"It wasn't." Cade got up and leaned over the table. "No way. Whoever put that girl's body there knew she would be discovered that very afternoon. He came after I was there and timed it just right."

"The girl's time of death was estimated at one or two a.m. this morning."

"So Gibson could have killed her after he was released from custody. Any way he evaded surveillance? Got away without being seen?"

Smith shook his head. "I don't think so. We had cameras mounted around his house. Even if one of our guys fell asleep, the cameras would have shown him leaving. He didn't leave the house."

"We need to find out who he knows on the island. Someone he could have paid to hide the girl there."

"We're looking. So far, we haven't found any witnesses who saw anyone but you going out there."

"You need to interview everyone I told about the proposal. See who *they* told. See if you can make any connections to Gibson. Maybe he overheard somebody in my department talking about it when he was there. The walls are paper-thin."

"By the way," Yeager said, "Gibson was right about his first draft being bad. We're talking amateur. Hack stuff, just like he warned us. I would have thought he had some command of the language. He was an English professor, after all. And he talks like Sherlock Holmes. Weird that he'd write something that would flunk him out of an English class."

Cade had to admit he was curious. "Can I have a look?"

"Sure, I have a printout." He handed Cade a stack of pages. Frowning, Cade scanned the scene. How had the man ever passed an English class, let alone taught one? He supposed that was what editors were for.

Maybe he had people to clean up all of his messes—the books, as well as the murders.

CHAPTER

23

It was 7:00 p.m. when Cade got home from the GBI office. The phone was ringing when he walked in. It was Chief Grant of Tybee Island's police department. "Cade, I need you to come over here to Tybee. There's somebody here I want you to see."

"I can be there in a few minutes. What's up?"

"I've got a couple of parents here from Brunswick who think the body you found today might be their daughter. They drove here as soon as they heard it on the news. Some of what they have to say might interest you."

Brunswick. The town was about ninety miles away.

"All right," Cade said. "I'll be right over."

A knot formed in Cade's gut as he headed across the island to face another set of parents. He could only imagine what they were going through right now, hearing that a body was found, that the girl fit their daughter's description.

He crossed the bridge and reached the Tybee police department, a building much more modern than the

Laundromat housing the Cape Refuge police department. He went in and asked for Chief Grant.

Grant was waiting for him in one of the interview rooms. As soon as Cade stepped into the doorway, he saw the grief-stricken couple. The woman's foot jittered as she sat clutching her chair, white-knuckled. The father was sweating as he paced from one side of the room to the other.

They both wore wild, panicked expressions. Uncertainty about their daughter was clearly killing them.

When Cade stepped into the room, they froze.

Grant got up and introduced them. "Cade, this is Bob and Lana Roarke. They drove here this afternoon from Brunswick, after hearing about the girl you found."

Cade shook the father's hand.

"What did she look like, Chief Cade? The girl you found . . . we have to know."

Cade cleared his throat. "She had blonde hair. Brown eyes."

"Oh, no." Lana pressed her mouth into the palm of her hand and shut her eyes as if that could mute Cade's voice.

"You'll have to identify her in person," he said quietly, "but if I could see a picture of your daughter, maybe I could tell if she looks like the girl we found."

Lana dug into her purse for a wallet-sized photo. Cade took the picture and studied it. Was it the girl? He wasn't sure. Hadn't the girl in the cave had a darker shade of blonde hair? Or was it just that it was wet?

"I can't honestly say."

Hope lifted both their faces. "Then you think it might be someone else?"

He didn't want to get their hopes up—but there was no point in destroying it either. "She looks different, but the girl I found was wet, and . . . I just don't know. Mr. and Mrs. Roarke, is your daughter a runaway?"

Lana started to cry. "If you can call it that at nineteen. She and her best friend Jamie Maddox vanished three days ago. It took us awhile to trace her steps, but we're pretty sure they were coming to Cape Refuge."

Bob rubbed his mouth roughly. "Chief, was there a mole on her left temple?"

Cade shook his head and handed the picture back. "I don't remember seeing one, but that doesn't mean there wasn't. Why do you think she came here?"

Bob's voice was raspy. "Our daughter is adopted, and she's been on a crusade to find her birth mother. We kept discouraging her. We've given her a good home, and we couldn't understand why she wanted another set of parents, especially when they didn't want her to begin with. We've had her since she was a week old."

"A year and a half ago, she tracked her mother down in prison," Lana added. "She was crushed that she was there, and we thought that was the end of it. But she started checking her out again in the last few weeks and found out she was released a year ago. She kept it from us."

"How did you find out?"

Bob sighed. "We weren't able to get in touch with her, and we got concerned and called one of her suitemates at school. She told us Amelia and Jamie had been gone since Wednesday."

"Did she know where they went?" Grant asked.

Lana got her purse and dug through it for a tissue. Swabbing her nose, she said, "She told us they went to Atlanta to find her mother. I guess she thought she could get a forwarding address from the prison or one of her former neighbors."

"We tried to retrace her steps and found out that this woman had moved to Cape Refuge."

Cade frowned. "What's the mother's name, Mrs. Roarke?"

"Sheila Caruso."

Cade felt the blood draining from his face. Grant noticed his expression. "You know her?"

"Yes, I know her. She lives at Hanover House."

Grant's eyes narrowed, and he sat down. "Hanover House? That halfway house?"

"Yes. Sheila's been there about a year. Grant, she's the one who works for Marcus Gibson." He saw the words registering on Grant's mind and knew what he was thinking. Could Sheila be implicated here? Was the connection mere coincidence?

Lana stood up. "I want to talk to this woman."

Grant turned back to Cade. "Doesn't your fiancée own Hanover House?"

He didn't bother to remind him she wasn't his fiancée yet. "Blair's family owns it. I'm sure I would have heard if your daughter contacted her."

"Unless Sheila didn't want anyone to know," Lana touched his arm. "Is it possible she's dangerous?"

"Sheila? No."

"But she's an ex-con." That fear deepened in her eyes. "How do you know?"

"She was in prison for drug violations, Mrs. Roarke. Not for anything violent."

Grant leaned on the table, arms crossed. "Cade, you think you should approach her first?"

That was a good idea. If Sheila had seen this girl, he needed to drill her about what had happened without her parents listening to every word. Their emotions might get in the way. "Good idea. After I interview her, then you can talk with her. For now, Mr. and Mrs. Roarke, you need to go to the morgue. That's the only way you'll know for sure if the girl we found is your daughter."

Lana pressed the wadded tissue against her eyes and wilted into her chair.

"Yes," Bob said weakly. "That's what we need to do."

Cade stood up. "I'll take you. That all right, Grant?"

"Sure. Call me the minute you know."

"I will."

The couple were quiet as they got into Cade's squad car. As he drove them to the Chatham County Morgue, he prayed it was all a big mistake, that the girl he'd found in the cave was someone else. Not Sheila's daughter. Not Sadie and Caleb's lost sister.

But then there would be other parents who had to come and identify their child's remains. Other broken hearts. Other lives destroyed.

But he was here, with *these* people, who braced themselves for a nightmare—and with all his heart, he hoped their daughter was still alive.

Cade hated the morgue. He always had, though coming here was often part of his job. He'd been present at more autopsies than he wanted to remember, and stood at too many people's sides as they identified their loved ones. He'd even had to come here when his own mother was killed in a car accident when he was eighteen. His father was out of town, and there'd been no one else to identify the body.

He'd been in denial as he and Jonathan strode down the long, dark, cold hall next to the clerk who called him "Hon." Even now, so many years later, he remembered how badly he'd wanted to tell her she didn't have to be so nice to him, because it probably wasn't his mother, just some other woman in a white LeSabre . . . who just happened to have his mother's ID.

Jonathan had been at his side, and when they showed him the woman's body, Cade stared for a moment. It *looked* like his mother. The same curve to her lips, the same laugh lines etched next to her eyes, the same silver streak that highlighted her black hair. But the vacancy in her eyes, her features, made her seem like someone else. He clung to that hope, his eyes searching her for clues that it wasn't her after all . . .

Then next to him, he heard his best friend's soft, broken sob. "Aw, no . . . it's her, man. I'm so sorry."

Cade hadn't shed a tear. Not then. He just stood there, staring at her and trying to make his mind grasp the truth.

Shaking off the memories, Cade looked at the couple walking next to him—hand in hand—down that same hall he'd followed all those years ago. Their faces were ashen and stark, controlled terror shadowed their features.

Were they believers? Would they be able to lean on the only One who could comfort them? Or would they lash out at God, blaming Him for the death of the child they must have considered such a perfect gift?

They reached the room with all its drawers, each containing bodies from Savannah or Wilmington or Tybee or Cape Refuge or any of the other towns that made up Chatham County. The girl's drawer was 316. The clerk led them to it and pulled it open.

The body was covered with a sheet. Lana wobbled, and Bob held her up.

The clerk peeled back the sheet, revealing the girl Cade found in the cave. He searched her face for the mole . . .

Lana caught her breath and put her hand over her mouth, and long, crushing moans came out of her throat as she wilted against her husband.

"It's not her!" Bob's voice was raw, hoarse. "It's not Amelia."

Cade almost didn't believe them. Was it denial, the same kind he'd had? Or was it truth?

Lana turned back to the body. "It's her friend, Jamie. Oh, dear God, if she's dead, where is Amelia?"

So they weren't in denial. They had given the girl a name. "Tell me Jamie's last name again?"

"Maddox. Oh, her poor parents! We have to call them, Bob."

Bob wasn't thinking about calling the girl's parents. "Amelia could still be alive, Chief Cade. She's somewhere around here. You have to find her. You *have* to. Please, I'm begging you."

Cade nodded to the clerk, who covered the girl back up. "I'll do everything in my power. You have my word on that."

CHAPTER
24

It was getting dark as Cade took the couple back to the Tybee police station, where they agreed to wait until the GBI agents came to question them about their daughter. Meanwhile, Cade needed to break the news to Sheila and see what she knew.

Grant walked him out to his car. "Are you sure you've never seen that girl before?"

Was Grant doubting his story? "No. We've already been over this. I'd never laid eyes on her. Look, Grant, I know it looks bad, with my having been at the cave and all. If I were investigating this crime, I'd probably consider myself the prime suspect. But this was as much a surprise to me as it was to anybody."

Grant sighed. "You let me know if the Caruso woman sheds any light on things. And find out if she has an alibi."

"I will." Cade started to get into his car, but Grant kept him from closing the door. Leaning in, he said,

"Cade, is there anybody you can think of who would want to set you up? Any enemies? Somebody you might have sent to prison?"

"There are always enemies. It's an occupational hazard. But your guess is as good as mine."

He drove across the bridge back to Cape Refuge, his mind racing through all the people he'd helped convict over the years. Which one would want revenge enough to kill for it? And if murder wasn't too high a price, wouldn't they have killed *him* instead of an innocent girl?

If Gibson was the killer, then who had he gotten to move the body? For the right price, he probably could have hired any stranger on the docks. Or someone he already had on his payroll.

Sheila Caruso's connection to one of the dead girls was disturbing, in light of her connection to Gibson. Did she know more than she was telling?

For the life of Amelia Roarke, he had to find out.

He called Joe McCormick as he rounded Ocean Boulevard. "Hey, Joe. I need you to meet me over at Hanover House to talk to Sheila Caruso."

"Okay, I'll be right there. Something wrong?"

He told him about Amelia Roarke and her connection to Sheila.

"You don't think Sheila was involved in the murders, do you?" Joe asked. "Because I just don't see it in her."

"I don't know. But I want you there to help me judge whether she's telling the truth."

McCormick paused for several seconds longer than necessary. "Okay, Cade. I'll see you there."

CHAPTER
25

Jonathan was on the front porch changing a light bulb when Cade pulled into the driveway. Cade got out of his car.

Jonathan peered down at him. "You okay, buddy? Blair told us what happened."

"Yeah, I'm fine. Jonathan, I'm here on police business."

"Yeah?" His friend came down the steps. "Is it about the girl you found today? Do you know who she is yet?"

"Yeah, her name's Jamie Maddox. She's from Brunswick."

McCormick's car pulled into the driveway, his headlight illuminating the front of the house. Jonathan's frown went deeper. "Wow. You brought your detective. What's going on, buddy?"

"It's a long story. I need to talk to Sheila right now. Is she still up?"

"I think so. She's not in some kind of trouble, is she?"

Cade evaded. "We just need to ask her a few questions."

Jonathan wiped the sweat off his brow with the back of his arm and set his hands on his hips. "Come on, man. If Sheila's done something, I need to know."

"You will," Cade said. "Just let us talk to her first."

Jonathan led them into the house. Morgan came out of the kitchen. "Cade, Joe, I didn't expect to see you. Blair told me what happened. How horrible."

"Yeah, it was a surprise, that's for sure."

Jonathan went halfway up the staircase. "Sheila! Can you come here, please?"

After a moment, Sheila came to the stairs and started down. She caught sight of Cade and McCormick and brought her hand to her hair. "Hey, guys."

"Sheila, Cade and Joe need to talk to you," Jonathan said.

"Sure. About Marcus Gibson?"

"Not exactly," Cade said. "Can we step into the parlor and talk?"

"Okay." She looked back at Morgan and Jonathan. "Can they come too?"

Cade looked back at his friends. "It's okay, if you don't mind."

Morgan gave Jonathan a concerned look, and they followed her in. It was one thing to give a resident privacy when she needed it, but another when there were police involved. If Sheila was somehow involved in this crime, the directors of Hanover House needed to know.

They all sat down, and McCormick set his serious eyes on Sheila.

She looked from him to Cade. "Okay, you're scaring me. What's going on?"

Cade started. "Sheila, I just came from meeting a couple who thought that the girl I found today was their daughter. It turned out not to be. It was her best friend, who was traveling with her. Their daughter is still missing."

"Uh-huh."

McCormick took it from there. "Their daughter was headed to Cape Refuge. To search for her birth mother."

Sheila seemed to wait for more.

"She's nineteen," Cade said softly. "Born October 29 . . ."

Sheila's face shifted, changed, and Cade saw that she understood.

"She's . . . *mine?*"

Morgan frowned at Jonathan, not quite following.

"Wait a minute," Jonathan said. "Is *Sheila* this girl's birth mother?"

Cade nodded, and Sheila sprang up. "My *daughter?*"

"Amelia Roarke," Cade said.

Sheila started to cry. "Amelia," she whispered. "What a sweet name. She came looking for *me?*"

Morgan stood up with her. "Sheila, I didn't know . . ."

Sheila wiped her eyes, then rubbed her hands against her jeans. "I had a baby when I was fifteen. I gave her up for adoption. It almost killed me. A few months later, when I got pregnant with Sadie, I made up my mind to keep her. I couldn't let go of another one."

Cade pulled the girl's picture out of his pocket and handed it to Sheila. Morgan looked at it with her. "She's beautiful," Sheila whispered.

Morgan agreed. "She looks like Sadie."

Sheila looked up at Morgan. "I never told Sadie. I guess I need to now." She held the picture to her chest and turned back to Cade. "Where is Amelia?"

"No one knows."

"And her best friend . . . the one she came here with . . . she's *dead?* What . . . what in the world . . . ?"

"Sheila, we need to know if Amelia has contacted you."

"No, she hasn't. How long has she been here?"

"She went missing three days ago." Cade leaned forward. "Sheila, I need you to think. If she came here looking for you, she would have meant to contact you. Maybe she didn't identify herself. Is there a time over the last couple of days that you might have seen her?"

"No! I would tell you if I had. I've wondered about her all these years . . . wished I knew where she was so I could just get a look at her . . ."

Cade leaned his elbows on his knees and locked his eyes on Sheila's. "I have to ask you this, and I need you to answer me very thoughtfully and carefully. What were you doing yesterday, from the time you got up until the time you went to bed?"

Sheila's face went pale. "You don't think I—"

Morgan broke in. "Cade, she was here all day, taking care of Caleb. I don't think she went anywhere."

"I didn't," Sheila said. "It was my day to work in the garden. I planted begonias in the backyard and came in off and on to help with housework."

"What about Thursday?"

Sheila shrugged. "I went to work at Marcus Gibson's, then came and talked to you at the station. After that I didn't leave the house."

Morgan's nod confirmed it.

Cade looked at McCormick and noted the "I told you so" in his eyes. He didn't have to question Morgan's word . . . but he had to consider the possibility that Sheila might have left after Morgan went to bed. It seemed implausible, however, that she would have sneaked out, met up with the girls, killed Jamie Maddox, then arranged to have her body moved to the cave.

Maybe her alibi was genuine.

Sheila looked at him, eyes wide. "You've got to find her, Cade. Please, she has to be all right."

"Everything's being done to find her," he said. "But we wanted to let you know in case she comes here. Her parents are frantic. Please, if you do hear from her, let us know immediately."

"Of course."

"Her parents are staying at the Frankfurt Inn, if you'd like to get in touch with them. Their names are Bob and Lana Roarke. They'd like to talk to you."

Sheila nodded. "I want to talk to them too. I'll call them as soon as I tell Sadie."

Cade and Joe got up and started for the door. Cade turned back before going out. "By the way, Sheila, have you still got a key to Marcus Gibson's house?"

"No, I've never had it. I just know where he keeps it. He puts it under the doormat for me. I don't know if he keeps it there all the time, though."

"Have you been back there since you told us about his books?"

"No, I was afraid to."

"Have you spoken to him at all?"

"Of course not. Why would I do that?"

Cade didn't answer but searched Sheila's face for any sign of deceit.

"You work for him, so I just thought he might have called you."

"No, he hasn't. If he did, I'd hang up. I'm scared of him."

"Rightfully so," McCormick said.

Satisfied that he'd gotten all Sheila would give him, Cade thanked her and promised to keep her updated.

Jonathan followed them out to their cars. "Cade, do you think the girl is alive?"

"I sure hope so. The state police are working hard to find her, and I'm doing what I can to help."

"What did you think about Sheila's reaction? She looked surprised, right?"

"Did to me," McCormick said.

Cade reserved judgment.

"So you don't think she had anything to do with it?" Jonathan asked.

The worry was clear on Jonathan's face. The past year had built his trust for Sheila, but he never *fully* trusted his residents. Drug addiction was a deadly master, and it always had the potential to lure them back. People whose minds were set on drugs would do almost anything for a fix.

"If her alibi is real, I don't see how she could have done it," Cade said.

McCormick looked as relieved as Jonathan. "My thinking too. And it wouldn't make sense for her to do anything to those girls. What would she have to gain?"

Jonathan shook his head. "No, I think we can trust her on this."

As McCormick got into his car and drove away, Jonathan looked into Cade's face.

"Hey, man. I'm sorry about your proposal not working out."

Cade just shook his head. "I couldn't believe it. Who would have ever dreamed?"

"So when are you going to try again?"

"When things blow over, I guess. I just want it to be memorable, you know? Something we can tell our grandkids."

Jonathan glanced back up at the door, making sure Morgan hadn't come out. "You sure Blair doesn't suspect?"

"Positive. She has no idea."

"You know, the *way* you do it is not as important as just doing it."

"But she deserves romance. A knight in shining armor, sweeping her off her feet. I want her to feel like the luckiest girl in the world."

"She will, buddy. Trust me, she will. Just ask her. You've got the ring. Put it on her finger."

Cade blew out a heavy sigh. "When the time is right. But I promise. I won't take much longer."

CHAPTER

26

I have a sister and you never told me?" Sadie felt as if the floor had just opened beneath her, threatening to swallow her whole. "How could you keep a thing like that from me?"

Sheila sat down on the edge of Sadie's bed and looked up at her through her tears. "What good would it have done? She wasn't a part of our lives. I didn't know where she was. I didn't even know her name."

Sadie gaped at her mother, searching for a way to tell her how she felt—that her past, her identity, seemed unbalanced now. Her mother had withheld vital information about who she was and who had come before her. She had a sister. Someone who could have shared the burdens, lightened the load, made her less lonely . . .

She leaned back against her bedroom wall and just stared at Sheila. Her mother had been crying when she came into the room and closed the door, and she was still upset. Sadie was torn between comforting her and railing at her.

"She's only a year older than me?" Sadie's question came out hollow.

"That's right, baby."

The bitter taste of her mother's deceit twisted her face. "I always wanted a sister, Mom. I would love to have known. Even a half sister . . ."

Sheila shook her head. "Oh, no. Not half, baby. Whole. You have the same daddy."

Sadie didn't know why that made it even worse, but she straightened now and took a step toward her mother. "I can't believe you kept this quiet!"

"What was the point in telling you? The records were sealed. There was no way for you to find her. At least, that's what I thought until this." She wiped her face and drew in a deep breath. "Baby, you have to understand. I gave her up because I was fifteen and pregnant, and Mick was no help. He was a musician, in and out of town, and the last thing he wanted was a commitment."

"But you stayed with him and had another baby?"

"Not really. I met him when he was in town doing a gig at this club I wasn't even old enough to get into. He happened to come back a few months after I gave her up, and like a loyal groupie, I did it all again. You know I've always been stupid with men. But when I got pregnant with you, I decided I wouldn't give you up. I might have to raise you alone, but at least I'd know where you were."

What kind of man was her father to take advantage of a kid, not once, but twice? There'd been times in her life when she'd longed to meet him, but when she'd learned of his early death from a drug overdose, those dreams had died.

Now she knew she was better off.

She slid down the wall and sat on the floor, trying to imagine the different paths she and her sister had taken. She looked down at the picture, amazed at how they resembled each other. They wore their hair the same, and looked the same size. Yet Amelia looked more polished, more privileged. Had she gotten parents like Morgan and Jonathan? Had they doted on her and protected her? Had they read her to sleep at night, tucked her into bed, wakened her with kisses?

She'd dreamed of all that as a child. "Mom, if they find her, do you want a relationship with her?"

Sheila didn't hesitate. "Well, of course I would. I've always wondered about her. I knew I'd done the right thing, that she would get a good home, but I felt so guilty and so mad at myself. I hope they took good care of her. I hope she didn't run off looking for me to get away from them." She took the picture back. "What if she's dead, Sadie? What if something happened to her because she came to look for me?"

"She can't be dead," Sadie whispered. "She just *can't* be. They'll find her soon."

"I have to go talk to them." Sheila got up and went to the mirror, began wiping the mascara out from under her eyes.

"Talk to who?"

"The parents. I have questions for them." Sheila turned back to Sadie. "Baby, please don't be mad at me. I'm sorry I kept it from you, but this is a crisis, and I need you now."

Sadie wanted to cling to her anger, nurse it for a while. It was righteous anger, and her mother deserved it. But her tears were real, and her remorse seemed genuine.

Sadie accepted her mother's hug. "I'll go with you. I'll see if Morgan will let us use the car."

Sadie thought the Frankfurt Inn looked like a German chalet, transplanted from the mountains to the ocean. The marquee out front welcomed the Georgia Nurse's Association and the Caliburt wedding party.

They had called ahead to see if the Roarkes could see them now. Though it was 11:00 p.m., the couple had seemed anxious to see them.

Sheila pulled into a space next to a car with Alabama plates, but she didn't get out. Instead, she looked in the rearview mirror, straightened her hair, and dabbed some lip gloss on her lips.

"Can't imagine what they already think of me, knowing I've been to prison and all. I want to look respectable."

"You look fine, Mom."

Sadie followed her mother out of the car and they went inside. They were both trembling as they got onto the elevator to ride to the fourth floor.

Lana Roarke was waiting at the door when they got off. The pain in her eyes was even more intense than that in Sheila's. "Oh, my! You look just like her. Your eyes, your hair . . ."

Sadie stood back, letting the couple look her mother over.

Sheila put her arm around Sadie's shoulders and drew her forward. "This is Sadie, my other daughter. She was born a year after Amelia."

They invited them in, and Sadie followed her mother to a couch by the window. The air was tense, and she felt awkward. Clearly, Sheila did too. There was a legal pad on the bed, with pages full of scrawled notes torn off. Stacks of posters with the girls' pictures and a plea to call with information sat all over the room—on the dresser, the desk, in a chair, on the floor. Maybe they'd let her take a stack.

Bob Roarke moved one of the stacks off of a chair and sat down to face them. "Sheila, have you had any contact with our daughter at all?"

"The police asked me that. I told them I hadn't. I wish I had, though. All these years . . ." Her voice broke off, and tears rushed to her eyes again. "This is all my fault. She came here looking for me, and now look what's happened."

Sadie looked down at her feet, wishing for something to say to ease the awkwardness. "Those posters . . . do you think we could take some? We could put them up . . ."

"Yes, of course." Lana sprang up and got Sadie a stack. "This picture was taken on her last birthday. We took her and Jamie down to Florida. It was a good time. Kinko's got them printed fast tonight."

Sheila cleared her throat. "You seem like such nice people. Why would she have run off looking for me?"

Lana slid her hands into her pockets and turned her sad eyes to Sheila. "She was curious about you. I think it had a lot to do with her being an only child. She always wondered if she had siblings. What her mother looked like. And she wondered why she was given up. She romanticized you, Sheila. We told her from the time she was little that she was adopted. We wanted her to know that we chose her, that we considered her a special gift from God. But instead, I think it made her feel more lonely as she got older."

"What about her friend?" Sadie asked.

"Jamie's been her best friend for years. They brought her car." Bob paced across the room as he spoke. "Jamie's parents hadn't been that involved in her life since she went to college. They didn't even know she was missing."

"They must be in shock."

"We all are." Bob went to the window. "If Amelia was all right, I know she would have called us by now. She wouldn't keep hiding out, knowing her friend was murdered."

"Maybe she doesn't know," Sadie said. "Maybe they got into a fight or something, and split up."

"Maybe," Lana said. "I've thought of that. They didn't always get along."

"Someone's seen them." Sadie was doing her best to sound definite. "Someone knows where they were. They'll come forward. They have to."

Sheila stood. "The man they arrested for the first girl's murder . . . I worked for him a couple of times last week. I've been thinking. It's far-fetched, but what if they somehow found out where I worked? Went there to find me and ran into him?"

The wheels in Sadie's mind started turning . . .

Could that, indeed, have happened? There were a few people who knew where Sheila was working. Everyone at Hanover House knew. Others in town had known through word of mouth. There was no reason for secrecy.

If Amelia had gone to Marcus Gibson's, then he might have had something to do with her disappearance . . . and Jamie's murder. Dread shivered through her, and her mind wandered away from the conversation. She started making a plan.

Tomorrow morning she would enlist Blair's help. Together, they could find her.

CHAPTER

27

Sheila retreated to her room as soon as they got back to Hanover House. Sadie hoped she would get some sleep. Sadie tried, but rest was far from her mind. Instead, she lay in bed, praying for her sister. When morning light softened the shadows in her room, she got up and got ready to search for Amelia.

She took the stack of posters and some tacks and walked to the newspaper office, stopping at every pole to put up a sign. When she finally reached the office, she found Blair on the phone with her friend at the Chatham County morgue, trying to get information about Jamie's cause of death. Sadie sat down in her office, listening and trying to glean what she could about what might have happened to the girl. But there was no new information.

When Blair hung up, she leaned on her desk and looked into Sadie's eyes. "I guess your mom told you."

She nodded. "Yeah, she did. Did Cade tell you?"

"Yes. Are you all right?"

She didn't want to cry right here in front of Blair. It would just slow them down. "Can we work on this story, Blair? With your help, I know we can find Amelia, maybe in time to save her."

"That's just what I was thinking. I already have some ideas, honey. We can work on it after church."

"I can't go to church today," Sadie said. "I'm too distracted, and time could be running out for Amelia. Mom and I met Amelia's parents last night. And it occurred to us that Amelia and Jamie might have found out where Mom worked. Maybe they went to Marcus Gibson's instead of Hanover House. We could go and ask him—"

"Whoa, wait a minute." Blair shook her head. "No way we're doing that. Cade is interviewing Gibson. Let's leave that to him."

Sadie's hopes deflated. "Then what's your idea?"

"I was thinking we need to put ourselves in Amelia's shoes. If she and her friend made it to Cape Refuge, where would they have gone first?"

Sadie thought for a moment. "Hanover House?"

"If they knew she lived there. But her parents didn't think she did. They thought she only knew that Sheila lived in Cape Refuge. So first they'd have to ask questions, find out where she was. Who would they ask?"

Sadie closed her eyes and tried to think like Amelia might. "Well, they'd come into town over the Tybee bridge. The first thing they'd see would be that Texaco station and its convenience store."

"Right. They might have gone in there and asked."

They stared at each other for a long moment.

"Let's go," Blair said.

They hurried out to the car, and Blair drove across town. Sadie looked out the window, struggling not to cry. Her sister had been here somewhere on this island, looking for her mother. Something horrible had happened to her and her friend. Had she wound up dead, like Jamie, and just hadn't yet been found? Was she lodged in another cave, tethered to a stone wall, and floating in the salt water?

Or was she alive somewhere, held hostage by a madman? *Lord, let me find her alive.*

In moments they'd made their way around the island, to the line of businesses Amelia and Jamie might have seen coming into Cape Refuge. They pulled into the Texaco station at the intersection, a block down from the bridge.

They got out of the car, and Blair looked at Sadie as they went inside. "You ask the clerks, and I'll talk to the customers."

Sadie headed to the cash register. The clerk was talking on the phone and ringing up the customer in front of her, taking her time as if a girl's life didn't depend on her speed. She thought of moving up to the counter, and explaining her dilemma: *"Excuse me, but my sister could be dying while you take your time ringing up a Mountain Dew and Snickers bar."* Instead, she stood there, waiting her turn. Sweat broke out on her lip and trickled down her temples as the minutes passed.

Blair worked the busy store, showing pictures of the girls to the customers, asking if anyone had seen them. Sadie strained to hear what they were saying, but finally, the clerk finished with the customer. Sadie handed her a poster. "I'm Sadie Caruso with the *Cape Refuge Journal.* We're looking for two girls who might have come in here in the last few days. One of them is the girl who was found murdered yesterday."

Fascinated, the woman took the picture and stared down at it. "Which one was killed?"

Sadie pointed to Jamie. "This one. Did you see either one of them in here?"

"I ain't seen 'em. Pretty girls too. I think I'd remember."

"Could you show it to the employees on other shifts? Maybe they saw her."

"Sure." The woman took the picture and studied it. "Do they know who killed her?"

"No. That's what they're trying to find out."

"And this other little gal? Where is she?"

"We're trying to find that out too."

"Sadie, over here!"

Sadie turned. Blair had found another clerk in the back of the store. Sadie hurried over.

"This gentleman says he was in here the other night when they came in. They were asking him if he knew a woman."

"Sheila Caruso?" Sadie blurted.

"Yeah, that's prob'ly who it was, but I can't say for sure. Told 'em I'd never heard of her, and they left. You say one of 'em was that murdered girl?"

"That's right." Blair handed him her card. "Please, will you call me if you think of anything else? Maybe someone else saw them talking to someone. Keep the picture and ask around."

"Will do."

Blair took the man's name down so she could give it to Cade for follow-up.

Sadie was encouraged as she put two posters up on the store's windows. "Let's go next door to the Burger King. At least we're on the right track."

Blair pulled her car around to the Burger King parking lot, and Sadie got out before the car even stopped. She went in and saw some of her schoolmates decked out in BK uniforms, stressed from flipping burgers and thrusting fries out the drive-in window. At least these weren't the snub-nosed group, who thought they were better than Sadie. These were common kids from common families, trying to scrape up money to buy rusty sedans and keep gas in the tank.

Steven Pratt—a tall, skinny kid who was two years her junior—stood straighter as she came in. Apparently self-conscious about his baseball cap, he turned it around to the back of his head and shoved his thick glasses higher on his nose. "Hey, Sadie. What can I get you today?"

"Nothing, Steven. I'm here as a reporter." She looked around for Blair and saw that she was outside talking to a kid who was taking a break to smoke.

"Yeah? Look, I don't know anything about how that bug got in that woman's food, but she's got a lot of nerve calling the newspaper about it."

Sadie smiled. "Uh . . . no, I don't know anything about that." She handed him a poster. "I need to know if you or anyone here has seen these two girls in the last few days."

He took the picture, and shoved his glasses up again. "Oh, yeah, I saw them. Musta been Friday. I remember because I thought one of them was you until she got up close. Real cute." His cheeks flushed, as if he hadn't meant to say that.

Sadie didn't tell him that they were sisters. "Did you talk to them?"

"No, I was just getting off work. I think they talked to Sam, though." He turned around and yelled back to the kitchen. "Hey, Sam. Come up here."

Another kid from school came dragging up. His hair was long and greasy, with a piece of a goatee that looked like a smudge beneath his lip. "Yeah?"

"You remember these two coming in here?" He handed him the picture.

The kid looked up at Sadie. "Yeah. Why?"

"Did they talk to you?"

"Yeah, they were asking me if I knew where some woman lived."

"Sheila Caruso?"

He shrugged. "Man, I don't remember. I'd never heard of her, so I couldn't help."

"Is Sheila a relative of yours, Sadie?" Steven asked.

"She's my mother."

"Man, wish they'd asked me. I could have told them where you live."

Sadie wished it too. "Keep the poster, okay? And is it all right if I put some on the door?"

"Sure, no problem. Who are they, Sadie?"

"This one was the girl found dead in the cave yesterday. The other one is missing."

"No way." Both guys stared at the picture with new interest. "You mean they might have left here and got killed?"

"We don't know. But if you learn anything, please call me. It's very important." She took the picture and wrote her cell phone number on the back. "Okay? You promise?"

"Sure. We'll ask around. Do you think one of them might have killed the other one?"

That thought had never even crossed Sadie's mind. "No. That's impossible."

"Why? Do you know them?"

"Well, no. But I don't think—" The very idea started an aching in her temple, and she felt a little sick. If *he'd* thought of that, surely the police had. Did Cade think her sister was a killer? "I have to go."

She hurried out and joined Blair. "Anything?"

"Nothing."

Sadie gave her the names of the guys inside who'd seen them, to add to Cade's list, then put the posters up on the doors. "The next stop is Clara's Trash and Treasures. If they went in there, I know they found out something. She even knew about Mom's job."

"We should have started there," Blair said. They drove a block down the road and pulled into the shop's parking lot. The shop was closed today, but they found Clara in her house behind it, getting ready to leave for church.

"Did you come here to buy that crib for your sister, Blair? It would make a darling baby gift. A family heirloom too."

Blair frowned. What was the woman talking about? "No, I'm not here to buy anything, Clara. I'm here about the girl that Cade and I found murdered yesterday."

Clara's face changed, and she suddenly looked interested. "Oh, yes. What a horrible thing to have happen on such an important day."

Blair frowned. Why did Clara always seem to talk in riddles? She started to ask Clara why she thought it was an important day, then stopped. No point getting bogged down in conversation. "We think this girl and her friend might have come in here."

Sadie handed her a poster. "They might have been looking for my mother. Did you see them?"

Clara took the picture and stared down at it. "Well, yes, I did. They came in here Friday afternoon, I think. And now that you mention it, they *were* asking for your mama. Are you telling me one of these is the dead girl?"

"That's right," Blair said. "Clara, we need to know everything they said."

Clara looked distraught. "They didn't say much. Just came in, acted like they were looking around, then when I came to help them, they asked me if I knew a woman named Sheila Caruso. I told them I did. One of them—this one—" she pointed to Amelia—"told me that Sheila was an old friend of her mother's, and she wanted to look her up. So I told them she lived at Hanover House. Gave them directions and a phone number. Then they asked me where she worked, and I remembered that she was working for Marcus Gibson."

Sadie felt as if the wind had been knocked out of her. She looked at Blair.

"Clara, did you tell them where he lived?" Blair asked.

"Well, yes. I knew he'd bought Gabe Stone's beach cottage, so I gave them directions there too." She stopped and swallowed. "Oh, my! You don't think they went there. Do you think he hurt that girl?"

Sadie couldn't answer. She groped for a chair and sat slowly down.

"Clara, is there anything you can tell us about them?" Blair asked. "What they were wearing? Anything?"

"Well, let's see. They were real cute girls, both wearing jeans. Vague about where they came from. I walked them out to their car and noticed a Glynn County tag. It was a blue Focus. The dead girl was the one driving. Oh, and when they started the car, they were listening to a Christian music station. That 'Who Am I' song. I remember 'cause it's my favorite. And I think the one girl had on a red shirt. One of them stretchy ones with part of the belly showing. Sadie, why were they looking for your mama? Do you think she had something to do with this?"

Sadie fought valiantly not to cry. "No. They never found her. She didn't see them at all."

"But she could be lying. I'm sorry, honey, but you know your mama does have a criminal history. I mean, when something like this happens, you can't hardly help but look at the ones with records."

The urge to cry fled, and anger set Sadie's cheeks burning. "You know my mother has changed. You go to church with us."

"Well, it does seem that way, but we have to be realistic, don't we?"

"Let's go, Sadie." Blair nudged her toward the door before Sadie could respond. "Clara, call me if you think of anything else, will you?"

"I'll be racking my brain, hon."

Sadie marched out to the car, and Blair got in next to her. "Sorry about that, honey. Clara says whatever comes to her mind."

"Is that what everyone's going to think?"

Blair sat there for a moment, looking down at her steering wheel. "I don't know. They might."

"You don't like my mom. Do you think that too?"

Blair looked at her then. "No. Your mother and I haven't always gotten along, but I know she's not a killer. And despite her background, I do believe she's changed."

Sadie's eyes filled with tears. "Thank you."

"Yeah." Blair started the car, and dug her cell phone out of her purse. "I'm going to the station to see Cade. He needs to know what we've found out."

As she rode, Sadie tried to picture the two girls heading to Hanover House. Had they come and found no one home? Or had they gone straight to Marcus Gibson's? Had they checked into a motel?

"Blair, what if they went to a motel for the night, planning to get an early start the next day? Something lower priced. We need to check out the motels. Maybe we'll find her holed up in a room, scared to death. Or the car . . . it's got to be somewhere."

"All right. We'll work the motels next, as soon as I brief Cade. He won't be too happy about us questioning witnesses without him, so I'd better tell him what we found out. And we have to tell him about the car, in case he doesn't already know it." She glanced over at Sadie. "Honey, maybe it's all right. Maybe Amelia's safe and sound somewhere. Maybe she'll see these posters and call her folks. Plus Cade told me they had released her picture to the television networks, and they'll be putting it on the news tonight, asking if anyone has seen Amelia. They'll get calls. Lots of leads. And maybe Marcus Gibson will tell them something."

A sob rose up in Sadie's throat. "He won't tell anything. The stupid judge should have kept him locked up. Why did Mom have to take a job with him?"

"How could she have known? And think about it. If it weren't for her, they might not have made the connection so soon."

Urgency pulsed through Sadie. She couldn't just sit still while Blair talked to Cade. "Stop the car. I want to get out and walk along the Boulevard putting up posters. You can come and get me when you're finished at Cade's."

Blair agreed and let her out. Sadie stood on the side of the road with an armload of posters as she drove off. She looked back up at the long string of hotels and motels along the beach. Amelia and Jamie *must* have checked into a motel when they'd arrived. According to Amelia's parents, they had about a hundred dollars between them, so it was doubtful that they'd had to sleep on the beach like she had that first night here. But where would they stay?

Not anywhere along the beach. Those were too pricey. She put herself in Amelia's place again. As they came off of the bridge, which motels would they have seen? If they'd asked for the lower-priced ones, they would have been directed to some of the places on Mimosa Street. Sadie crossed Ocean Boulevard and made her way to the first hotel they might have come to. The Flagstaff.

If the girls asked anyone decent, they would have told them to avoid that place. It was one of the worst places in town, a magnet for crime and drug deals. Every week in the police column of the *Journal*, seventy-five percent of the arrests made were at this hotbed of drugs and prostitution. Sadie once heard Cade say that if he could do one thing to lower crime on the island, it would be to shut down that motel and run its residents out of town.

But if Jamie and Amelia checked in during the daytime, they might not have realized what the place was like. All the worst activity there happened at night.

Dread weighed down on her as she approached the parking lot and saw that already some of the drug dealers congregated there, loitering and waiting to make their next deal.

She spotted the office and went in. The clerk, who looked like he'd spent the last three days lying unconscious in a gutter somewhere, was waiting on a man.

"I lost my key," the biker-type was saying. "Musta fell outta my pocket."

The manager got another keycard and programmed the code. "No problem. This oughta do it."

Sadie bit her lip. Instead of doing the reporter's spiel, what if she pretended to be Amelia? Everyone said they looked alike. Maybe she could pull it off.

She stepped up to the desk. "I lost my key too. Amelia Roarke."

"What room?"

She leaned over the counter, as if too weary to stand upright. Rubbing her eyes, she said, "I don't remember. I've been in so many motel rooms in the last few weeks . . . and I had a rough night. Could you look it up for me?"

He looked through his registration book. "Could it be under another name?"

She cleared her throat and tried again. "Oh, I forgot. We put it under Jamie Maddox."

He looked and she waited, holding her breath.

"Here we go." He turned around and got her a key, programmed it, and slid it across the counter. "Room 218."

"Thanks." She took the key and stepped back outside, her heart pounding so hard she thought it might come through her chest.

With every fiber of her being, she knew she should call the police. But she had the key, and she could go in the room. If Amelia was there, she would find her. If she wasn't, she could look around before the police cordoned the place off.

She went up the steps and found room 218. Her hand was trembling so badly that she dropped the key. She picked it up and started to jab it into the slot. But what if Amelia was in there, oblivious to the search? She hesitated, then knocked.

No answer. Inside, she could hear a television. Did that mean someone was there?

She knocked again, harder this time. "Amelia? Please open the door."

No response. The window was open slightly, but there was no sign that anyone was there. Finally, she stuck the keycard into the slot, and eased the door open.

One lamp shone in the corner of the room, and a golf tournament played quietly on the television. The bed was unmade, and two suitcases lay on the floor, clothes spilling out of them. Outfits considered and discarded lay scattered across the room, wadded on the bed, tossed over a chair, dropped on the floor. Makeup cluttered the sink area.

They clearly intended to come back.

She looked around for any clue, any item that might give her some idea what could have happened. And then she saw a purse with a cell phone sitting on top of it.

A cell phone, connected to its charger plugged into the wall, lying at the center of a rumpled bed. Sadie picked it up and checked the call history. Pulling out her notepad, she jotted down each number from which a call had come over the last three days, and each call that had gone out.

At the sight of one number, she felt her throat constrict. They'd called Hanover House. The call was short—only a few seconds. Either they'd asked for Sheila and been told she wasn't there, or they'd hung up before asking.

The last call went out two days ago. Friday, the last day they were seen.

She finished writing down the numbers and quickly scrolled through the list of favorite numbers, jotting down each one, in case she needed it later.

Then she set the phone down and went into the bathroom. The tub was dry, as were the towels on the floor. No one had been there this morning.

She went back out to the dresser and saw some change lying there, along with the keycard envelope, and some papers. She looked through them and saw the birth certificate with her mother's name, copies of Sheila's prison release papers, and a Xerox of her mother's mug shot.

Had Amelia figured out she had siblings?

Sadie went back to the door. It was time to call the police. They'd be able to read a million more messages into the mundane things lying around her. She looked down at the styles of clothes and the colors and the shoes abandoned next to the bed . . . some of these were her sister's things. She and Sadie were alike. She could tell by the things Amelia wore, the size of her feet, the colors of her makeup.

Oh, please, Lord. Give me a chance to know her.

Finally, she went back out, sat on the concrete walkway outside of the room, and pulled her own cell phone out. She dialed the number of the police station and asked for Cade.

He answered after a few moments. "Hey, Sadie. How ya doing?" His voice was soft, compassionate.

"Fine." She swallowed, trying to steady her voice. "Cade, I thought you'd want to know that . . . I found my sister's room."

There was a slight pause. "*What?*"

"Her motel room. They checked in two days ago at the Flagstaff on Mimosa. I went in. Her stuff is still here."

She could hear the controlled excitement in his voice. "Sadie, don't touch anything."

"Hurry, Cade. Maybe there's a clue here."

"We'll be right over."

She hugged her knees and waited right outside the door until she heard the sound of the sirens. Her phone rang. The caller ID showed it was Blair.

"Hello?"

"Sadie, Cade just called me and told me you found Amelia's room. Are you sure it's hers?"

"Absolutely. I even saw her birth certificate. They intended to come back, Blair. The television is still on, and all their clothes are here. She even left her purse and cell phone."

"You went in? Sadie, are you crazy? How did you manage that?"

"I told them I was Amelia and that I'd lost my key."

Blair huffed out a huge sigh. "Look, I'm coming over. Don't leave, okay?"

"I won't. But, Blair, before you come, can you go back to the office and do a quick search? I need to know who belongs to the number 555-1289."

She knew Blair had jotted it down. "Why?"

"Because it was on her cell phone's call history. It's a local number and it might be a clue."

"Sadie, you *know* better than to touch her things before the police can go through them!"

"Please, Blair. Just tell me whose number it is."

Blair hung up, and she heard the sirens getting closer. The men loitering in the parking lot vanished, and she heard doors closing.

Her phone rang, and she clicked it on. "Hello?"

"It's me," Blair said. "I found out whose it was."

"That fast?"

"I know somebody at the phone company. You'll never guess who that number belongs to."

Sadie closed her eyes. "Tell me it's not Marcus Gibson."

"Bingo."

Sadie thought she might throw up. She clicked off the phone and managed to hold herself together as Cade's car and the others filled the parking lot. She got up and went to the rail. Scott

Crown was there, and he started up the stairs behind Cade and McCormick.

"I have a key," she told Cade as he approached.

"How did you get—?"

"I lied. Told the clerk I was Amelia."

Cade sighed. "Sadie, you shouldn't have gone in."

"I didn't touch anything except her cell phone. She tried to call Hanover House and Marcus Gibson. But the calls were short. Maybe she hung up when they answered. I left everything else just as it was."

Cade clearly wasn't happy about her detective work. "We'll talk about this later. But I think you knew better than to do that." He opened the door, and McCormick went in and started his perimeter search.

Scott lingered back. "You okay, Sadie?"

She nodded, distracted as she watched. "Yeah, I'm fine."

"Don't let him bother you. He jumps down my throat all the time. Even when I found Emily Lawrence the other night, you would have thought I'd destroyed any chance of solving the crime. He gets all bent out of shape, but I guess he means well."

Sadie didn't need reassurances. She didn't much care what Cade or anyone thought of her right now. She just wanted them to find her sister.

CHAPTER

28

Sadie called the Roarkes and let them know of her discovery while the police searched Amelia's room. They arrived there moments later, pulling their car haphazardly into the parking lot and running toward the stairs that would take them to the room where police were clustered. Several officers stopped them, refusing to let them pass.

Sadie crossed the parking lot and headed toward them.

"She's our daughter!" Bob shouted. "We need to see what's in there."

"I'm sorry, sir, but I can't let you go in. I'm sure the detective will fill you in when he's finished searching the room. You need to wait here until they're finished."

Sadie touched their shoulders, and Bob and Lana swung around, their faces wild with panic. "Sadie!" Bob grabbed her arms and looked into her eyes. "Did you go in? Did you see anything?"

"Yes. I went in before I called the police. I didn't see any sign that anything had happened in that room. Their

suitcases and clothes are still there, and the television was on."
She decided not to tell them about the cell phone.

"Were there notepads that they might have written their
plans on? Her laptop?" Lana demanded. "Amelia's a note taker.
She writes everything down, and she keeps a detailed journal."

"Yes, the laptop was there, but I didn't touch it. I didn't see
any notes, but if there's anything the police will find it. They've
already found the car. It's over there, but the police won't let
anybody near it."

Lana turned and peered at the activity centering around the
Focus. "Could you tell how long it's been since they were in the
room?"

Sadie shook her head. "I'm sorry, but I couldn't. We just
have to wait for the police to finish, and I'm sure they'll be able
to tell a lot of things that I missed."

"Sadie!"

She turned and saw her mother trotting toward them, her
eyes swollen and red. Sadie ran into her mother's arms.

"You shouldn't have come here!" Sheila cried. "What's the
matter with you? You could have been walking into danger. I
couldn't take it if something happened to you too!"

"I'm okay, Mom. And I did the right thing, because I found
what I was looking for." She filled her mother in until she saw
Scott Crown coming down the steps. "Wait, Mom." She met him
at the bottom of the stairs. "Have they found anything?"

"Can't say. But I can tell you they just picked up Gibson."

"Was there any sign of Amelia?"

"Didn't sound like it. I'm just telling you what I heard on
the radio."

Bob stepped up. "Where are they taking him?"

"The GBI are taking him to our station to question him
again."

Bob spun around and grabbed Lana's hand. "Come on.
We're going over there."

"Can I have a ride?" Sadie asked. "I want to go too."

"Sure. You can come too, Sheila."

Sheila looked back up at the open door of the girls' room, as if she could imagine her daughter alive there better than at the police station. Sadie understood. Amelia did seem alive there, with her clothes scattered on the floor and her makeup containers left open. Death—or news of death—seemed to wait at that police department. But they might not get any answers here, and Sadie felt certain Gibson knew where her sister was.

"All right. I'll come too." Sheila slid behind Sadie into the backseat.

Bob sped out of the parking lot, and headed across town. "I'll get that man to tell me where my daughter is," he said through gritted teeth.

Lana turned her pleading face to his. "What are you going to do?"

"I'm going to choke it out of him."

Sadie knew they wouldn't be able to get near Gibson, but she didn't say so. Bob seemed determined. Maybe by the sheer force of his will, he would be able to get some results.

They reached the police station and hurried inside. Bruce Baker met them at the door.

"Has Gibson been brought in yet?" Bob demanded.

"No, sir. They're on their way here now. You can have a seat if you'd like."

None of them could sit. Instead, they all stood at the glass front of the building, pacing and watching for the car to arrive.

When they finally saw the car turning in, Sadie thought Bob might explode. But instead of bolting out as she expected, he stood inside, seething until they brought the writer into the building.

Maybe he wouldn't erupt. Maybe he just talked big.

But the moment they brought Gibson over the threshold, Bob flew at the man. Three officers grabbed him and wrestled him back.

"Tell me what you did with my daughter! Where is she? *Where is she?*"

Gibson only croaked out, "I don't know!"

Bob struggled to break free of the officers holding him. "Tell me where she is! Is she dead or alive? Did you kill her?"

Gibson's gray hair frizzed and stuck out from his head, giving him the look of a mad scientist. He caught sight of Sheila then, and his expression changed. "You!" He pointed a skinny finger. "You're responsible for all of this. You were snooping in my house, weren't you? You told lies about me, started rumors. I'll sue you when this is all done."

"You can't sue me," she screamed back. "Because you'll be sitting on death row!"

"I didn't kill anybody!" His wild hair flopped into his sweaty face. "I *write* about murders, I don't commit them!"

The police dragged Gibson into the interview room, but he kept yelling. "I've never even seen those girls! Not even once!"

"Just tell us where she is!" Lana sobbed so hard she could barely speak. "Please, she's precious to us."

Everyone was screaming at once—Bob threatening, Lana begging, Sheila accusing, the police warning. In the chaos, one of the GBI agents shouted for someone to get them out of the building.

Bruce tried to herd them out. "Please, you'll have to leave."

Bob began to weep. "You've got to find her! Time could be running out. She's just a little thing. She's in trouble, and she needs us."

Lana pulled away from Bruce's outstretched hand. "We'll be quiet. Please let us stay."

Bruce softened then and led them to some chairs. "You can sit here if you'll be quiet. I'll update you as soon as I get information."

"He knows." Bob wept more quietly, and Lana put her arms around him. "He knows where she is. I don't care about protocol or legalities or whether he has some hot-shot attorney. They can get that information out of him if they want to. Beat it out of him if they have to. If they can't do it, they should let me."

Lana shook her head. "They can't do it. You know that."

Sadie's chest was so tight she could hardly breathe, so she stumbled to the door and stepped out into the heat. Sheila followed her. "Baby, you okay?"

Sadie leaned back against the glass and slid down to the concrete. "I had to get out of there. I feel sick."

Sheila lowered to the pavement next to her and stroked Sadie's hair.

Sadie drew in a deep breath and looked up at her mom. "I'm okay. I'll get through this."

Sheila nodded and leaned her head back on the glass.

"I've been praying so hard," she whispered. "But I don't know if God listens to my prayers."

Sadie wiped her eyes and sucked in a sob. "Of course He does, Mom. He hears everyone's prayers."

"No, He doesn't. I've been reading the Bible. I found places . . . reasons why He won't hear. Things that I've done."

Sadie looked at her mother. "Like what?"

"Like not forgiving. Mark 11:25 says it real clear. If I forgive, God can forgive me. If I don't, He won't. But I haven't forgiven, Sadie."

"Forgiven who?"

"Lots of people. The ones who turned me in and got me arrested. All the men who did me wrong. Your daddy. My parents."

So much hurt in her mother's life. There was bitterness deep within her, for good reason.

"And Psalm 66:18 has haunted me ever since Morgan showed it to me. 'If I had cherished sin in my heart, the Lord would not have listened.' Well, sometimes I cherish sin, baby. Sometimes I just ache for the old days. A shot of vodka, a snort of coke . . . the dope that made me feel better about all the things I've done, all that I've been through. Until I hate those sins, I can't truly repent. So God won't hear me. I hope *you're* praying, baby. I know God will hear you."

Sadie felt soul-weary, and her mother's self-image gave her new cause for concern. She drew in a long, cleansing breath and wiped her eyes. "You can repent now, Mom. You can get right with God so He'll hear you."

Sheila drew in a shaky sob and shook her head. "There's so much to repent of. All the stuff I've done . . . It didn't just hurt me. It hurt you and Caleb . . . and now Amelia. She was supposed to get the best end of the deal. A decent home, good parents who fight for her."

She looked over her shoulder, through the glass. Bob still wept into his hands. "But *I'm* her mother, and the Bible says the children will be cursed by the sins of their parents. So she comes looking for me, and this happens. All because of me. All because of my own sin."

"What sin, Mom? You didn't do this."

"Didn't I? Didn't I get pregnant with some guy who didn't care anything at all about me? Not once, but *twice,* like some fool who begged to be abused. I gave my baby up because I didn't want the responsibility, but then I went and did it again." She pushed herself up and got to her feet, turned around, and looked down at Sadie. "Things could have been so different. Every wrong I did, I did another wrong to undo it, and things just got worse. My sins piled up so high they were like a mountain I couldn't climb. I was a terrible mother to you, baby. I would have been a terrible mother to her too. Even now, when I haven't seen her in nineteen years, I'm still hurting her. And I can't even pray for her."

Sadie stared up at her mother. If only she didn't feel so spent. Her mother needed her, but she had little to give. "Mom, I think you're where God wants you. It sounds like you do hate your sins. You *can* repent. God will hear that."

A car pulled into the parking lot. Joe McCormick and Scott Crown got out, saw Sheila and Sadie, and came toward them.

"You okay?" McCormick asked.

Sheila didn't answer his soft question. "Did you find anything?"

"Not in my initial scan of the place. The GBI agents took over."

"Do you think she's dead?"

At her mother's question, the detective's eyes softened. He looked at her for a moment. "I didn't see anything to indicate that, Sheila. She could very well be alive."

She crumpled under her grief, and Joe took her into his arms and held her. Sadie saw the man with new eyes. Always before, he'd just been a cop, on the hunt for whatever piece of evidence he needed. Now she saw him as a man—a kind man, who cared that her mother was broken.

Scott came and stooped down next to Sadie. In a low voice, he said, "You okay, Sadie?"

She wiped her eyes and wished people would stop asking her that. "Yes, I'm fine."

"We'll find her, Sadie. I feel like we're close to it already. Now that we have pictures, names, people will start coming forward. We'll fill in the timeline of where they were and what they did and who they were with."

She didn't want to cry in front of Scott, but the tears wouldn't stop. He put his arm around her and pulled her against him, kissed the top of her head.

"It'll be all right, Sadie. You'll see."

His touch calmed her fears and gave her hope—and for a moment, she almost believed he was right.

CHAPTER
29

Sheila knew the questioning of Marcus Gibson would prove to be as unproductive as his first interview had been.

After a couple of hours, police convinced the Roarkes to go back to their hotel room and wait for an update. Blair came to pick Sadie up to take her back to the newspaper office, and Joe offered to take Sheila home.

As they walked out to his car, Sheila let her mind revisit the thought of death. She'd been suicidal many times in her life, but lately things had been going well. She'd had a better self-image, felt she could accomplish some things with discipline and hard work.

But now she wanted to walk to the Tybee Bridge and take a dive over the side.

McCormick seemed to read her thoughts. "You've got to have faith, Sheila. You can't think the worst."

She stopped before getting into his car. "Joe, do you believe in God?"

He nodded. "Yes, I do. I don't know as much about the Bible as Cade and Jonathan do, but I do know God is watching over us. He's watching over Amelia too, Sheila. Just like He's watched over Sadie and Caleb." As he spoke, he set his elbow on Cade's truck bed.

"What are the statistics? Of finding missing people alive, I mean?"

"I don't know. But it doesn't matter. All that matters is that we find *her*."

She propped her own elbows on Cade's truck bed and dropped her face into her hands. "But what are the chances? From your experience, when a friend winds up dead . . ."

"I've never been through this before." He put his arm around her and rubbed her arm. "I could make something up, Sheila, tell you what you need to hear . . ."

She looked up at him. "I don't want that."

His blue eyes were soft, sad. "I didn't think you did."

He looked down into Cade's truck, as if searching there for the right thing to say. His eyes locked onto something there, and he frowned and straightened. "What is that?"

She followed his gaze. It was a girl's sandal, pink with a yellow daisy on top. He climbed into the truck, stared down at it. "I don't believe it."

"What is it?"

He just shook his head, but urgency filled his voice. "Go back inside and get them to call Cade. Tell them it's an emergency."

Whatever was going on, she knew not to stall. "Okay." Sheila started into the building. What was the big deal about a sandal? Maybe Blair left it there, though it didn't look like something she'd wear. She had the officer inside radio Cade at the motel and heard him say he was already on his way back in his squad car and would be there in a couple of minutes.

He was pulling into the parking lot when she went back out. He got out and saw McCormick at his truck.

"What's up, Joe?"

He pointed to the sandal. "Recognize this?"

Cade froze. "Jamie Maddox was wearing one just like it."

Sheila gasped. "Are you sure?"

"Yeah, I'm sure." Cade looked at McCormick. "Where did you find it?"

"Right where it is."

Cade's eyes shot up. *"In my truck?"*

Joe nodded. "That's right, boss. It was in your truck. Maybe somebody tossed it in when they got her back to shore."

Cade stared at the dead girl's sandal. "If that's been in my truck since Jamie was found, how did I not see it? No, I know it wasn't there this morning."

"Then somebody planted it."

"Just like he planted the body." Cade's features were tight, drawn. "Don't touch anything, Joe. Leave it right where it is. I have to tell Yeager."

Sheila stared after Cade as he went inside, dumbfounded at the new development.

"I can't take you home now, Sheila," Joe said. "I have to stay here."

She turned back to Joe. "That's okay. I want to stay."

"No, you can't. I have to clear the parking lot. This is a crime scene now."

"A crime scene?" What was he talking about?

"That isn't just the dead girl's shoe, Sheila. It's a key piece of evidence." His gaze came back to her. "I'm sorry, but you have to leave."

Her heart sank. "All right, then. Will you . . . will you let me know if you learn anything new?"

"Sure."

But she knew he was distracted and probably wouldn't. She crossed the busy road and stepped onto the beach. The sun was beginning to set, and Amelia was still missing.

The oppression of helplessness hung like a metal coat over her shoulders, and she walked along the beach under the weight of it, the soft breeze blowing her hair.

With each step, her own self-loathing grew, choking her with its poison. Sins old and new passed through her memory, flooding her brain with that same venom, stabbing through her with deadly aim. She had laughed about them in jail, swapped war stories with her cell mates, tried to one-up them with accounts of near-death experiences brought on by those sins.

But now they made her sick. The drugs, the men, the choices . . . she hated them all with as much passion as she'd loved them. The very thought of them made her feel filthy.

Yet she still had the capacity to go back to them. Even as she drowned in the misery of those sins, part of her mind still whispered lies, that one drink would drown her sorrow, one snort would chase away this grief, one needle would solve her woes. If she let herself, she could believe them.

She was so weak. So incredibly weak.

Feeling that weakness deep in her muscles and bones, she dropped to the sand, just beyond the reach of the waves, and stared out at the water rolling up onto the shore at high tide, then hurrying back from where it had come. She wept at the sheer absurdity of her condition, the paradox of her thoughts, the division of her loyalties.

Hatred, vile and putrid, for herself and her actions—past, present, and future—forced more tears from her eyes. She had never cried so much in her life. She had never wanted death more.

"Just kill me, Lord! Just strike me dead, like I deserve. I don't want to live with who I am anymore."

She sobbed, letting her weeping carry on the wind, hoping that God would forget her sins for the moment and answer this one prayer, if no others.

"I'm so sorry. I'm so, so sorry."

She realized as she said the words that she really was. For the first time, she knew that deep, cutting sorrow, that piercing anguish, that true authentic hatred of her sins.

She looked up at the sky, overcast with thick clouds. "Make me new. The old me needs to die."

She'd heard Jonathan talk "of dying to self" so many times, and she'd pretended to understand what that meant. Being unselfish, putting others first, doing unto others . . .

But that wasn't it.

Now she finally understood. It meant putting the past behind, stepping out of that old, sinful self, leaving it to rot in the grave where it belonged. Emerging new, fresh, whole.

But she couldn't do it herself.

"I need your help!" Instead of beseeching God again to kill her, she found herself crying out, "Save me!"

She imagined herself wearing a dead, decaying skin, darkness on the outside, filthy slime dripping off of her. And God's hand reached down and unzipped that skin, allowing her to step out of it like a new, regenerated, newly born baby, emerging from its womb.

Born again.

She closed her eyes and lifted her face to heaven. "Can You wash me clean, Lord? Is that really possible?"

A warm, wet wave came tumbling over her, soaking into her clothes, her skin . . . She started to laugh through her tears.

God had answered her.

Not only *could* He do it, but He'd already done it.

The crushing weight of her sin lifted, and she felt lighter, freer than ever before. God seemed just a breath away, His ear against her lips, waiting for her whispered prayer.

30

I know how this looks." Cade sat in his office with Yeager and Smith, aware that he'd just been promoted from person of interest to prime suspect. "Whoever did this is trying to set me up. You've got to see that."

"The sandal isn't all we found in your truck bed, Cade."

Cade gaped at Yeager. "What do you mean, that's not all?"

"There was blood."

Cade sprang out of his seat. "*What*? No, there wasn't blood. There *couldn't* be. I didn't see it."

"It was there. The Luminol showed it."

Luminol was the chemical reagent used to detect bloodstains, even after attempts to wash them away. If it had shown blood . . .

Closing his eyes, he brought the heels of his hands to his forehead and leaned back hard in his chair. "It's part of a pattern. I found the body. I have the other shoe. There's blood in my truck bed . . ."

He dropped his hands and looked hard at the detective. "Do you even know that it's her blood . . . or human blood for that matter? It could be from fish, for Pete's sake."

The two agents exchanged looks. "We're waiting for the lab report."

Cade knew he was in trouble. "Look, just take my truck. Anything you need . . . search it, run tests. I had nothing to do with this. Anyone could have dropped that sandal in my truck. It's been parked there all day. Gibson may have done it himself. Maybe there are fingerprints."

"We're dusting, Cade."

"Good. Give me a polygraph. I want to take a polygraph."

"We'll have to take you to our offices. You can take the test there."

He closed his eyes, nodded. Of course they were taking him in for questioning. What else could he expect? "All right. Let's go. I'm ready to clear my name and get to the bottom of this."

Blair drove up just as the tow truck came and lifted Cade's truck to take it away. The parking lot was still cordoned off, but she parked her car across Ocean Boulevard and hurried over.

Scott Crown stood on the edge of the parking lot, holding back traffic as the tow truck pulled out.

"What's wrong?" Blair demanded. "Why are they taking Cade's truck?"

"A piece of evidence was found in it."

"What evidence?"

Scott looked from side to side, as if he didn't know whether to say or not. "I probably shouldn't say."

She grabbed his arm and looked up at him. "Off the record. I'm not asking as a reporter but as someone who cares about Cade. Please, Scott, what's going on?"

He turned to her then and lowered his voice to a whisper. "They found Jamie Maddox's shoe in his truck."

She caught her breath. "Who put it there?"

He just looked at her. "Apparently they think Cade did."

"No! I was with him when he found the body. She was only wearing one shoe!"

Scott didn't answer, just turned away. Television crews were set up across the street and were filming the tow truck. Finally, a group emerged from the front door, and she saw Cade being led out.

Blair ducked under the yellow tape. "Cade!"

He looked back at her but couldn't answer before they put him in an unmarked car. Though he wasn't cuffed, he was clearly not in charge. He waved through the window, as if to tell her that it was okay, that he would be all right.

She wasn't buying it.

She turned to Scott. "Where are they taking him?"

"To the GBI Branch Office in Savannah. They have to question him."

Blair ran back across the street to her car, dodging traffic as she did, determined to follow them all the way to Savannah.

When they arrived in Savannah, Blair watched as Cade was led into the state police office past the reporters that had already gathered like vultures. As she got out of her car, she heard a remote broadcast from in front of the building.

" . . . just bringing Chief of Police Matthew Cade in for questioning in the murder of Jamie Maddox, the girl found yesterday in Breaker's Reef Grotto off the coast of Cape Refuge. Chief Cade admitted to having written Will You Marry Me on the wall of the cavern where the body was found."

Blair caught her breath. Cade hadn't written that. It was already there! She took a step forward, ready to run onto their makeshift set and set the woman straight.

"Sources tell us the girl was murdered with a .40 caliber revolver, the same gun used by police forces across Georgia. Until the sandal was found in his truck bed, police were wondering if Cade had simply been in the right place at the wrong time, but now it's clear he's being questioned about the murders.

Meanwhile, Amelia Roarke, the dead girl's best friend, is still missing."

When the broadcast was over, Blair rushed forward and grabbed the reporter. "You got that all wrong! How could you report those things? I was *there*. I was with Cade when he found the body. He didn't write that on the wall. It was already there!"

"Oh, you must be Blair Owens."

She hadn't expected the reporter to know her. "Yes, I'm the publisher of the *Cape Refuge Journal*."

"And his girlfriend. My sources tell me that Cade admitted going out to the grotto early that morning to write *Will You Marry Me* on the wall. He wrote it for you, Blair."

She stood, mouth agape, as the reporter took off to join the other cluster of reporters waiting for a statement. Could Cade really have written that? Why wouldn't he have told her? Her heart raced, and she couldn't catch her breath. Her eyes strayed to the door, and she swallowed back the tightness in her throat.

She had to get in there and find out how much truth there was in the reporter's claim. If Cade *had* written the words, it meant he wanted to marry her. Hope fluttered up in her heart.

But then she realized that the proposal itself would implicate Cade further. No wonder they suspected him.

She shivered as she understood the complexity of the killer's scheme . . . and his fearless execution of it.

CHAPTER

31

Blair knew she had no chance of getting into the police station as a reporter, so she kept her press credentials in her purse and found a back entrance. She slipped inside and hurried to the front desk. The place was a war room full of perpetrators and complainants, the chaos barely controlled by irritable cops.

"May I help you?"

"Yes," she said. "My fiancé was brought here. I need to know if he's been arrested." The word had tumbled so freely from her lips—a lie she hoped Cade wouldn't hear about—but she knew nothing less would get her information.

"What's his name?"

"Matthew Cade."

"Oh, yes." The female officer looked her over. "There hasn't been an arrest. He's just being questioned. Are you the one who was with him when he found the body?"

"Yes."

"All right. Wait here just a minute."

She waited as the sergeant left the desk and disappeared into another room. A drunk man who reeked of body odor and Jack Daniels stumbled into her, and the cop behind him grabbed the man's collar and pulled him back. "Sorry, ma'am."

"It's okay." She looked past the drunk and saw the sergeant coming back.

"Miss Owens, could you come with me? Agent Yeager would like to talk to you."

She went willingly, hoping to be taken to the same room where Cade was, but instead, they took her to an empty room. Two GBI agents and a transcriber came in with her, and she realized she had plunged herself into an official interview.

She started to protest but then realized that anything she told them could help vindicate Cade. So she sat down, trying to be submissive, and went through the whole story again.

Agent Yeager took copious notes as she recounted what had happened in the cavern. When she finished, he looked up at her, his small eyes boring into her. "What did Cade say to you about the writing on the wall?"

She tried to think. "Nothing, really. There was chalk there, under the writing, and I suggested that it might have fingerprints on it."

"Then you weren't aware that he'd written it?"

There it was again. She caught her breath and stared across the table at them. "No. The first I heard of that was a few minutes ago when one of the reporters was broadcasting it." She leaned forward on the table. "Is that true? Did Cade say he wrote that?"

"Yes, he did. And frankly, I'm a little confused, Miss Owens. Didn't you tell the sergeant at the front desk that you were his fiancée?"

Busted. She let out a long sigh. "I exaggerated, okay? I didn't think being his girlfriend would get me in. I needed to be here for him. I had to make sure everything was all right."

"So the two of you haven't discussed the writing on the wall since the body was found?"

"Cade's been busy ever since. We haven't had much chance to talk." She sat there, staring down at the wood grain on the table, trying to think. If Cade wrote those words on the wall, then he had planned to ask her to marry him. A sense of loss poured over her, mingled with that fragile joy.

He was going to ask her to marry him . . .

"Has there been any discussion of marriage before?" Yeager's question shook her out of her thoughts.

She swallowed. "Not in so many words . . ." Tears came to her eyes, as she thought back over that day. He'd been so insistent about their taking that day off and going out to the grotto. It had seemed important to him. And when he picked her up that day, he'd had a glisten and a grin in his eyes. He'd been nervous, and very gentle, and enchantingly attentive.

She thought of the struggle they'd both had to keep their relationship Christ-centered, the way he always pulled away when their feelings pulled them together, the way he would kiss her good-bye at night with that look that told her he wanted to stay. *You're so hard to leave at night*, he'd whispered a few nights ago.

How could such good intentions have gone so terribly wrong?

She struggled to steady her voice. "I don't know for certain what his intentions were that day, but I know Cade better than anyone else. He was as shocked as I was to find that body." She held Yeager's gaze and leaned in toward him. "Agent Yeager, you're questioning him. I can understand that, given the circumstances. But you need to be asking the *right* questions. Who wanted to set Cade up? Who knew he was going to be out there that day? Who are his enemies?"

Yeager didn't respond. Maybe they were already doing that. If they weren't, surely Cade was getting those things out in the interview. He wouldn't be taking this passively.

"Is he going to be arrested?"

Yeager looked noncommittal. "I can't say. It depends on what we find."

When they were finished with her, they let her wait in the waiting area. She jittered and paced and tried to fight off the headache clamping on her temples. Two hours went by, and finally, Cade came out. His face was tense, exhausted, pale. She knew the work of deciphering every thought he'd had and every move he'd made in the last few days had worn him out.

When he saw her, his face changed. She saw a visible softening and a smile in his eyes. He was glad to see her.

She went to him, and he slid his arms around her. "How long have you been here?" he whispered against her ear.

"Since they brought you."

"I'm sorry it took so long." He stroked her hair and tipped her face up to his. "Take me home."

"They're letting you go?"

"I told them everything I knew. Passed the polygraph."

Relief flooded through her. "I thought they were going to arrest you."

"So did I. I guess my record and my service count for something. They're letting me leave, but it's not over yet."

They got into her car, and as she drove, he stroked her hair and rubbed her neck, as if she was the one who'd been in the hot seat all afternoon. She wanted to ask him about the writing on the wall, but the words got caught in her throat.

"Cade, who do you think did this?"

He shook his head. "I don't know. I've been racking my brain. I gave them a list of everyone I could think of who we might have arrested in the last couple of years, people who might have it in for me."

"Do you think you're in danger?"

"It's hard to say."

She knew that meant *yes*.

He got quiet as she drove home, and she wished she could take the pain from him. "Are they giving you back your truck?"

"Not yet. Guess I'll drive a squad car until I get it back." He saw that she was heading to the station. "You can take me home. I need to eat something, and I'd love to get a shower before I go back to work. It was hot in there. You'd think they could afford better air-conditioning."

They got to his house, and she sat in the car for a moment, not wanting to say good-bye with so many questions hanging over her. But how would she ask them?

"Come in with me. You're the only bright spot in this day."

He did it to her every time. Made her feel as if she was the most important person on earth to him.

She went in and busied herself making sandwiches as he took a shower. When he came out, he was wearing jeans and a white Henley shirt. His feet were bare, and his hair was wet.

He came to the counter where she'd laid out the food, and he slid onto a stool. Instead of grabbing his sandwich, he took her hand, and pulled her to him. His kiss made her weak, and she felt as if she would melt right into him, merging body and mind.

She could hardly breathe when she pulled back.

He stroked her hair back from her face. "I love you, Blair."

She could never hear those words enough. "I love you too." Tears came to her eyes then, and she started to cry. She wasn't sure why, but it had something to do with a thwarted proposal, a chance that had been lost, a question never posed.

"What's wrong?" he asked.

She shook her head, and touched his lips with her fingertips. "Nothing."

"Something," he whispered. "Tell me."

She drew in a deep, shaky breath. "There are rumors."

He didn't seem surprised. "Which ones?"

She swallowed and wished she could stop the tears. "About . . . the writing in the cavern. They said that . . . they said you wrote it."

He gazed into her eyes, and gently he wiped away the tears from her face. "That's because I did."

She breathed a laugh through her tears, and he took her hand and kissed it, brought it to his face and held it there.

"It was a good plan. I was going to make it the most romantic proposal in the world, because you deserved that. I never expected it to end the way it did."

She drew in a sob. "Cade, it's the question that matters. Not the method."

He nodded. "I know. I just wanted it to be so memorable. I wanted it to be something we could tell our children, our grand-children . . . I wanted it to be a love story, not a murder mystery."

"It *is* a love story. It's romantic, and beautiful. Right here and now."

His eyes misted over. "You're right." He stood and led her to his couch, sat down and pulled her onto his lap. "Blair, you mean so much to me. I've loved you for years. I don't even know how long."

The words were crushing in their honesty, blinding in their beauty.

"I can hardly stand to leave you at night anymore. I want more of you. I want you beside me every day for the rest of my life. I want to wake up and see your face every morning."

She hadn't expected to fall apart, but the sobs racked her throat and her body. He held her, strong and secure, in his arms.

"I don't know what the coming days are going to hold. This whole thing could spiral downhill. I suppose I could even be arrested. It could be a very stressful time."

Blair stroked his face. "We've been through stressful times before. We've fought battles together. God has always been with us."

"Yes, He has. And I know He's with us now, telling us that He created us to be together."

"And He looks at us, His creation, and it's good."

He nodded. "It's very good." He nuzzled against her hand, kissed her fingertips. "Blair, if you would marry me, I would consider myself the most blessed man on the face of the earth, and I would spend my life trying to make you feel as special as you are to me."

She could hardly speak. She nodded her head, trying to say *yes*.

He reached into the drawer of the end table next to them, pulled out an oyster shell. She watched him turn it over in his fingers. "That day, when we were at the cavern, I was going to let you find this."

She took it in her trembling hands. "An oyster?"

"Open it." His eyes were on her as she pried the shells apart.

And then she saw it. A diamond solitaire, radiant and white, catching the light in every facet, and sparkling like his eyes. "Oh, Cade."

He got the ring out and took her hand. "Say you'll marry me, Blair."

She sucked in a sob. "Yes, I'll marry you."

He slid it on her finger, and a symphony crescendoed in her heart. Dreams long unspoken had come true. The man she had longed for would be her husband.

He kissed her again, a long, lingering kiss that told her miracles do happen. God does hear. And when the kiss broke, Cade moaned against her lips. "One condition."

"What?"

"We'll have a short engagement. I'm talking real short. I want you to have the wedding that little girls dream of . . . but I'm asking you to plan it as fast as you can."

That was one request Blair was delighted to honor.

CHAPTER

32

Don't let me die.

Amelia Roarke's silent prayer rose up into the black night, but she feared it hit the ceiling sixteen feet above her, no more able to escape than she was. She longed for morning, when the first rays of light would ease the darkness and make her prison less of a terror.

She was weak . . . so weak she couldn't fight him off any longer when he came for her. She hadn't eaten in . . . how long? Two days? Three? She'd lost track. She'd had nothing to drink in all that time, either. Thank God for the brief rain yesterday, when the rain drizzled through the trap door overhead. She lay on her back, mouth open, desperate for hydration.

She *was* going to die, right here in this pit. She would grow so weak that she'd fall asleep and never wake up. If he didn't kill her first. Would he shovel dirt on top of her? Would this be her grave?

Why had she and Jamie eavesdropped on that conversation outside their window? Why had they answered the door that night? She'd never had a gun pointed at her before, never had two men threatening to kill her if she didn't walk with them to their car.

She should have taken her chances and screamed. Made a run for it.

Then Jamie would still be alive, and Amelia would be able to go home, not to some illusive birth mother, but to the parents who loved her, the parents who were probably insane with worry.

Why had she gone off looking for some woman who'd played such a little part in her life? She knew it had hurt her parents when she'd started looking. They feared losing her, even though she promised them that they wouldn't, that she was still their daughter and always would be.

Her disappearance must have broken their hearts. They had to be worried for her safety, physical and emotional.

And they should be.

They were probably searching for her, tracking her steps. She wondered if they realized she'd come to Cape Refuge. Maybe there had been clues left, witnesses who saw them getting in the car that night. But she doubted any of those people who loitered in the parking lot and lurked in the doorways of the Flagstaff Motel would tell the police anything. Even if they did, would they be able to trace her to this remote farmhouse so far out of town?

No one would ever find her, in this pit someone had built into the ground, a forest basement too deep to be a tornado shelter, too damp to be a wine cellar. Had there been others held here? Were their bones under the dirt beneath her?

She closed her eyes, trying not to see the faces of those two men as they'd bound her and Jamie's hands and feet with duct tape, and sealed up their mouths. One of them smelled of whiskey, sweat, and smoke. His greasy hair hung into his wild eyes, and she saw the excitement there, as if the mere act of taking them had given him a high no chemical substance could produce.

The other one was cleaner cut—he was the one she'd heard cursing through the window, ranting in a harsh whisper about the other's temper. "She was just a kid, you moron, and you killed her!"

"She fought me," the sleazy one said. "I didn't mean to do it, but I lost my temper. It was for the best. She could have ID'd me anyway."

"I'm the one who had to clean up your mess, man! I'm finished with you. That's the last time you'll put me in that position, you hear me?"

"You can't walk away. You're in too deep. They find me out, and I'm taking you down with me."

That was when Amelia knocked a glass off of the table, and it crashed against the air conditioner under the window.

The conversation outside stopped.

Jamie turned to Amelia. "Do you think they know we heard them?" she whispered.

"I hope not. No, they probably don't."

"But they *killed* somebody. We should call the police."

They heard the door next to them close, heard footsteps heading for the stairs. After several minutes, a soft knock sounded on the door.

At first they didn't answer, but then a man's voice spoke. "Manager. I need to talk to you."

Jamie looked out and saw that the man looked clean cut and unthreatening. "It's okay," she whispered to Amelia. "This guy looks all right."

Amelia tried to stop her, but Jamie opened the door.

It was the worst mistake of her life.

He showed them his gun, which he then hid in his pocket. "You two are going to come with me. We're gonna walk real slow. If you make a sound, you're dead."

The men put Jamie and Amelia in the car and drove them to a dark street. There they duct taped their hands and feet, all the while cursing and shouting at each other. Then they drove out here, dragging them out of the car. They cut the tape on their feet so they could walk to their prison.

Jamie made a run for it. It only took one bullet to stop her.

Amelia didn't know why they'd kept her alive, except that her sleazy captor seemed to enjoy her occasional company. No use killing her when he could have a little fun with her first, he'd said. Besides, he liked watching her die. Slowly. He took the duct tape off of her mouth because, he told her, he enjoyed her screams.

She hadn't seen his cohort since that night.

She wondered what they'd done with her best friend, if anyone had found her yet, if Jamie's parents had been notified. What were her mom and dad thinking? Maybe Sheila Caruso even knew about her by now.

Would hers be one of those bodies that someone would discover years from now, dried-out bones with no flesh? They'd search police records and decide that maybe she was that missing girl from all those years ago . . .

She heard something above her, saw a shadow moving across the sunlight through the slats in the trapdoor. He was coming.

She backed against the dirt wall, pulled her knees up to her chest, and started to wail.

The door opened, and the rope ladder came down.

"Hi, honey, I'm ho-ome." His words were lethal, demented. He backed down the ladder, the flashlight illuminating the place.

There was nowhere to hide.

Blair wanted to put out an extra issue of the paper in which to announce her engagement. It deserved fanfare, trumpets, a parade . . .

But two girls were dead, another missing, and Cade was in trouble.

Now wasn't the time to call attention to themselves.

She sat in the driveway at Hanover House, fighting the urge to go skipping in and scream out to anyone within earshot that she was an official bride-to-be, that her prince had staked his claim on her, that her future was thrilling and full of hope.

On a normal day, Cade would have come with her, and they would have surprised everyone with an announcement at the dinner table. She would have carried the ring in her pocket, then slipped it on as the plates were being cleared and desserts were being passed.

But Cade had work to do, so she was left with the choice of waiting for that time, keeping the ring hidden until that grand announcement, or telling them now. Already

Cade's thwarted cavern proposal was making its way on the evening news. Everyone would be wondering what on earth was going on.

It simply couldn't wait.

The house was quiet as she went in. She looked into the kitchen—it was empty. Disappointment rippled through her. And then she looked out on the back porch, saw Morgan and Jonathan sitting out there, deep in conversation. Morgan stroked her round belly as she rocked.

Blair drew in a deep breath, slid her hand into her pocket, and stepped out. "Hey, guys."

Jonathan sprang up at the sight of her. "Blair, what's happening with Cade?"

"They let him go. He's at the station."

"Well, thank goodness for that," Morgan said. "Is it true about the shoe?"

"Yeah, it is. Someone planted it in his truck. And there was blood on the bed of Cade's truck. They're testing it now."

"Man, this is wrong," Jonathan said. "Cade doesn't need this."

"No, he doesn't."

He drew in a deep breath and looked at Morgan. "I'm going to see him."

Morgan nodded. "Go ahead, Jonathan."

He started into the house, but Blair stopped him. "Wait. There's something I need to tell you first."

Morgan stopped rocking. "What is it?"

She pulled her hand out of her pocket as a slow smile crept across her face. "Cade asked me to marry him."

Morgan leaped out of the chair, let out a joyous scream, and threw her arms around her sister.

Jonathan started to laugh. "He came clean about the wall, did he?"

Blair pulled out of Morgan's embrace. "You knew?"

His grin revealed his guilt, so Morgan spun around and hit him playfully. "You *knew* and you didn't tell me?"

"Hey, my best friend asked me to keep it quiet. What can I say?"

"Oh, I'm so excited!"

Morgan lifted Blair's hand and examined the ring, and Jonathan started to laugh softly. "Well, I guess my old buddy is doing all right if he had the presence of mind to propose today. Things can't be too bad." He kissed Blair's cheek and hugged her. "Congratulations, Sis. You're getting a great guy. I think I'll go congratulate him now."

As Jonathan started back into the house, Sadie and Sheila pushed past him and stumbled onto the porch, their faces expectant and hopeful. "Did something happen?" Sadie asked. "I heard screaming. Did they find Amelia?"

Blair's heart sank. "No, honey, nothing's happened like that. I was just telling Morgan . . ." Her words faltered. Maybe she should hide it until a better time. Sadie and Sheila's pain was so intense that it seemed cruel to talk of anything else.

But Morgan spoke up. "Cade asked Blair to marry him, and she said yes."

Sadie caught her breath and looked down at the ring, but the disappointment was clear in her eyes. "Oh. Congratulations, Blair. I knew it must be coming soon."

Sheila just stood at the door. Her eyes were swollen from hours of crying, and tears filled them again. "Thank goodness. I thought you were screaming because . . ." Her voice trailed off, and she rubbed her forehead. "I'm really happy for you, Blair."

Blair shoved her hand back into her pocket. "Sheila, Cade's doing everything he can. They're going to find Amelia. I know they are."

"I know they are, too," Sheila whispered. "I'm just praying she'll be alive when they do."

Sadie couldn't wallow in despair any longer. By Monday morning, she was determined to do something more to help find her sister. She clearly wouldn't get another chance to look around Amelia's motel room, but her hands weren't completely tied. There were still resources she could use to track down information. She went to the newspaper office earlier than usual. Blair hadn't come in yet. She turned on her computer, thankful for the access that could aid her on her search.

The search engine she opened found several hits for Amelia Roarke of Brunswick, Georgia. She scanned a family tree written by some distant aunt, in which Amelia's name was inserted under Bob and Lana's, with the word *adopted* in parenthesis beside it. Nothing helpful there.

She found Amelia's high school yearbook, so she clicked on the link and paged through, stealing glimpses of her sister's life. Amelia was in the choir, had been a chorus member in a production of *Li'l Abner*, and had played the leading role in *Our Town*.

And she was in ROTC. Sadie found her in her uniform, standing at attention in the picture with about twenty others. Interesting. Sadie never would have dreamed that someone so petite and pretty would be interested in something so rigid.

She scrolled through the pages to every mention of Amelia. When she got to the journalism club's page, she saw that Amelia worked on the newspaper staff. She'd won a journalism award her senior year.

So they did have something in common besides their looks.

The phone rang, and Sadie kept scrolling, trying to ignore it. But on the third ring, she glanced at the caller ID. It was someone from the police department, so she snatched it up before it could go to voicemail. "*Cape Refuge Journal.*"

"Hey, Sadie. It's Scott. I just wanted to check on you. Are you all right?"

She sighed. "Yeah, I'm fine. Have they found out anything?"

"Not yet, but they're still looking at the evidence in the room, checking fibers, fingerprints, that sort of thing. Getting phone records, videotape from the stores where people saw them. There's a lot of information to sift through."

"I thought I'd try working on the computer for a while. I found Amelia's high school yearbook online."

"Good. You can get a lot of info from stuff like that."

As he talked, she scrolled through the pages, looking for more pictures of Amelia or Jamie.

"I could come by in a little while and help you, if you want. I'm about to get off work."

She paused on a picture of the two girls, probably at a football game, with their school mascot painted on their faces.

"Sadie?"

"Yeah. Okay, I'll probably be here."

She set the phone back in its cradle and studied the picture. They looked so young, so clueless . . .

Who would have dreamed how things would turn out for Jamie? Sadie's eyes filled with tears, and she suddenly couldn't go any further.

God, please save Amelia.

She heard a car outside in the parking lot, heard the door close. Quickly, she wiped her eyes.

The door opened, and her friend Matt Frazier peeked inside. "Sadie?"

"Hey, Matt. What are you doing here?"

He looked a little embarrassed. "I went by Hanover House and they said you were here. I came to see how you were, what with all the stuff going on. I heard that missing girl is related to you."

"Yeah. Guess news travels fast. We haven't even had an issue of the paper since Cade found the body."

He came in and sat down at the chair next to her desk. "Have they gotten any closer to finding her?"

"Well, they found her motel room this morning. I don't know how helpful that was. I know she had called Marcus Gibson's house. They took him in again, but the judge already let him out once, so I don't know what's going to happen."

"You must be so freaked out."

"Yeah, I have been. My mom's a wreck."

Her throat seemed to constrict as those tears pushed back to her eyes. Matt seemed to have something else he wanted to say, but clearly hadn't made up his mind to say it. "I saw you the other night at Beach Bums."

So that was it. "Yeah, I saw you too. But you were walking away. Why didn't you speak?"

"I didn't want to horn in on things. You looked like you were having a good time." His voice held a note of melancholy.

Sadie didn't quite know what to say. The fact that he seemed sad about her date with Scott flattered her. Maybe he cared more about her than she thought.

He leaned over and set his elbows on his knees, clasped his hands in front of him. "So are you going out with Scott Crown?"

"No. I mean, just that once. We're not an official couple or anything."

The pain in his eyes made her heart ache. Was his interest brotherly, or did he have feelings for her?

He looked at her through his glasses. "Do you like that guy?"

"Who? Scott? Yeah, he's pretty nice. Do you know him?"

He breathed a laugh. "Yeah, he was in my graduating class. I know him a little too well. That's why I was surprised to see you with him. He doesn't seem like your type."

"I didn't know I had a type. What's wrong with him?"

"He's just . . . not the most sincere guy in the world. And he has an ego. He can be a real jerk." He sat up straighter and set his elbow on her desk. "I just want you to be careful. You deserve someone who treats you like a princess."

Their eyes met, and she saw the longing there. Suddenly she knew he hadn't come to give her brotherly advice. A soft smile tugged at her lips. "Do you have anyone in mind?"

He smiled then and looked down at his hands, began trying to rub off a callous. "You know, I've been wanting to ask you out for a long time. The age thing bothered me a little."

"We're not that far apart, Matt. Two years, maybe. I'm eighteen."

"Yeah, but I'm in college and you're in high school."

He had nice eyes. And the glasses gave him an attractive air of intelligence.

"I thought it might be more appropriate to wait." He shrugged. "Until you graduated."

"Another whole year?"

"Seemed like a good idea at the time." He laughed softly. "But when I saw you with Scott, I realized you were old enough to date someone out of high school, and if it wasn't me, it was going to be someone else. Now it's probably too late."

"I didn't marry him, Matt. I just had a burger with him."

His eyes met hers. "Then, you'd consider going out with me?"

"Of course I would. When all this is over, and my sister is found . . ."

The hope in his expression crashed, as if he interpreted that as rejection. "I shouldn't have even brought it up with all this going on. I really didn't come in here to do this. I was worried about you, wondering if you were all right."

"I appreciate that. And I mean it. When all this is over, I want to go out with you. I've been hoping you'd ask."

A slow grin crept across his face. "You have?"

"Yes. Why would that surprise you?"

"I don't know." He leaned back and looked at the ceiling as he drew in a deep breath. "Okay, then. I'll call you when it's all over, and we'll go out."

"Okay."

"Good." He smiled into her eyes, and she wished she could just drop everything and go have a Coke with him right now. But she had to find Amelia.

"I'm just . . . really distracted right now. I'm trying so hard to find Amelia, or to figure out what might have happened to her."

"I can imagine. I'm like that too, always trying to look out for people in my family. It's not always a good idea, you know. Sometimes it gets out of hand. You could get hurt, or in trouble."

"I know. I've been warned. I'm being careful."

"I hope so. You never know who you're getting tangled up with. And you're kind of . . . well . . . innocent. I'd hate to see anything happen to you."

It surprised her that he thought of her that way, given her background. The kids at school who talked about her behind her back considered her anything *but* innocent.

She heard a car in the driveway and stood up to look out the window. Scott Crown was getting out.

Matt got up and saw him too. "What's *he* doing here?"

"I think he came to help me."

The door opened, and Scott stepped in. He looked surprised to see Matt. "Hi. I hope I'm not interrupting anything."

"No, of course not. Scott, you know my friend Matt Frazier, don't you?"

"Yeah. How ya doing, Matt?"

Coldly, they shook hands. "Doing fine. You?"

"Pretty good." Scott looked at Sadie, and she saw he wasn't any more pleased with the situation than Matt was.

"I was just leaving." Matt headed for the door. "Let me know if I can do anything, Sadie. I'll check back on you later."

"Okay, Matt. Thanks for coming by."

He didn't say anything more to Scott as he walked out. Scott waited until the door was closed and turned back to her. "What was that guy doing here?"

"He's a good friend. He just came by to check on me."

"You need a better class of friends." He plopped down in the chair Matt had abandoned. "So have you found anything?"

"Not yet. I just finished going through her yearbook." She backspaced to the search engine and found the next hit for Amelia.

Scott pulled his chair around to sit beside her. "Look, it's a blog."

"A blog? One of those daily journals?"

"Yeah. Never knew why anybody would post personal stuff on a website for all to see."

Sadie clicked the link, and Amelia's journal came up. It looked like she'd kept it for the past couple of years. "It'll take me all night to read all this. I'm going to print it out so I can take it home."

"Good idea."

She clicked *print*, then scanned each page as it came off the printer. Amelia had filled the blog with mundane stuff, ramblings about her teachers and her challenges at school. Still, it fascinated her. It was a glimpse into the person most closely related to her by DNA, a person she might never get to know any other way.

"I'm so afraid she's dead." Her whisper caught in her throat.

Scott shook his head. "I just have a gut feeling she's not."

Sadie appreciated that, even if it wasn't true. "Gut feelings are sometimes right."

"Yeah, they are. It was a gut feeling that led me to look in that boat where I found Emily."

The blog had finished printing, so she pulled the rest of it out. There had to be seventy-five pages or more.

"I'll tell you what you can do to cut through the rambling."
As he spoke, he selected the text on her blog, copied it, then
opened Sadie's word processing program and pasted it in. "Now,
you can do a search for the words *birth mother*. See what she said
about her."

Sadie wouldn't have thought of that, so she watched, fascinated, as the search took her to an entry Amelia had posted just
last month.

> It's not that I don't love my parents. I do. They've
> spoiled me rotten and they mean everything to me. But
> sometimes a girl just needs to know where she came
> from. I have a birth mother out there who might look
> like me. Maybe she's thought about me since she gave
> me up, wondered where I am, and prayed that we
> would meet up someday. And I'm thinking that maybe
> she has children—brothers and sisters of mine. How
> cool it would be to find people who looked like me—
> the same eyes, the same hair, the same shapes of our
> hands . . .
>
> I know all brothers and sisters don't look alike,
> especially if they're halves, but it's fun to think about.
> Sometimes I imagine a big family sitting around a table
> with a place set for me, because there's a hole in that
> family without me.
>
> I know it's probably not that way at all. My birth
> mother's probably kept it secret, never told a soul, espe-
> cially any other children she's had. There wouldn't be a
> hole there. She may have gone out of her way to forget
> me. But maybe if I showed up, she'd be glad I did.

Sadie couldn't stop the tears coming to her eyes. She pursed
her lips together and bit the inside of her cheek. Scrolling to the
next entry, she saw more thoughts on her mother. "I wonder if
this might be helpful to the police."

Scott nodded. "I was just thinking I need to call my uncle
Joe's attention to this. It's crazy to put stuff like this up on a public

website. Predators can use it. Maybe someone did, and that's why she's missing. If she talked about where and when she was going to look for her mother, someone could bait her and be waiting for her. Maybe there are emails from someone. They could be clues."

"They confiscated the laptop in her room. I'm sure they're looking into that." She sighed. "I wonder if I should show this to my mom."

"How is she?"

"She's been in the room crying her eyes out ever since this happened. I can only imagine how she feels."

"So how old was your mom when she had Amelia?"

"Fifteen. She had me at sixteen."

"Slow learner, huh?"

Sadie didn't appreciate the slam against her mother. "I guess so."

"You know, we have a lot in common, you and I."

Sadie frowned. "What do you mean?"

"I mean, I came from a teenage pregnancy too."

"Really, how old was your mom?"

"A little older than yours. Around seventeen."

"Did she ever marry?"

"Three times." His face hardened. "To the meanest jerks you could ever imagine. In fact, my mother had a knack for attracting men like that. She was weak."

"Mine was too."

He backed off of the blog and went back to Google. "So who do you think was better off? You or your sister?"

She watched the screen as Amelia's list came back up. "How could I know that for sure?"

"Well, did you have a good life?"

She didn't want to speak ill of her mother. She loved her. But the truth was that she had not had a particularly good childhood. It had been tough and dangerous and stressful.

Scott read her hesitation. "You don't have to answer. I can tell you I didn't. I would have been a lot better off if my mother had put me up for adoption instead of dragging me around like a ball and chain, working two jobs to keep food on the table. Her life would have been better, too."

"Maybe from a financial standpoint. But I know my mom's life wouldn't have been better without me. She loves me. I'm sure yours loves you too."

He didn't answer.

"You don't think your mother loved you?"

He stopped typing and looked up at the ceiling, as if thinking that over. "Whether she did or not doesn't make much difference to me. It doesn't change anything about my life."

"Of course it does. She loved you enough to keep you, even though she got off to a bad start. I mean, what if she'd chosen the alternative? What if she'd had you aborted?"

He sighed and looked into her eyes. "That's the thing I don't get. Abortion."

Sadie agreed. "Yeah, I don't get it, either."

"I've always thought that instead of killing the babies, they should kill the mothers."

She caught her breath. Was he serious? He went back to typing, then broke out in a grin. "Look, here's something." He typed a few keys, and she saw a database coming up.

"What's that?"

"Driver's license records."

"How'd you get those?"

"I use them all the time at the station," he said.

"Yeah, but that's the police database. You can't just sign on to it here."

He grinned and laughed under his breath. "That's what they think." While he spoke, his fingers worked on the keyboard, and finally, up came Amelia Roarke's driver's license.

Sadie leaned in and studied the picture of the girl who looked so much like her. Amelia had probably fixed up the day she'd gotten her license, had curled her hair and applied her makeup perfectly, as if she'd been going for a photo shoot instead of the line at the DMV. Her smile was all teeth, as if she giggled deep in her throat at having passed her driver's exam.

Sadie remembered feeling that giddy too, even though she hadn't gotten her license until last year. Morgan and Jonathan had taught her to drive and taken her down to the driver's license office themselves. But she had felt just as giddy that day. Her sister's stats read that she was a blue-eyed blonde, 5'5", 120 pounds, with 20/20 eyesight. And she was an organ donor.

Those tears ambushed her again. Scott looked over at her, surprised.

"Hey, what is it?"

She put her hand over her mouth and shook her head. "Nothing. Can I print it out?"

"Sure. Just don't let on where you got it. In fact, don't show anybody. I don't want anybody knowing I can do this. I could get in a lot of trouble."

She waited for it to print, then took it out and gazed down at it.

"Are you sure you're okay?"

"Yeah, fine. It just hit me all of a sudden."

"What did? That she's your sister?"

She suddenly wanted to be alone. Glancing down at her watch, she said, "Oh, gosh, look at the time. I really need to go check on my mom." She got up and looked down at him. "Thanks for coming by, though. You've been a big help."

"I'll keep working on it, Sadie." He got up and slid his hands into his pockets, and she saw the sympathy on his face. Matt was wrong about him, she thought. He was sincere.

Any other time she might have been flattered by his attention, even excited that he wanted to spend time with her. But now was not the time. She had important things to do, and working on her love life was not among them.

"Well, I guess I'll see you later, then, okay?"

"Okay," he said. "Call me if you need me? I have a few other tricks up my sleeve. I'd be willing to use them if the price was right."

She didn't want to ask him what the price was, but when she gave him a strange look, he laughed. "I meant the pleasure of your company over a milkshake or something."

She smiled then. "When this is over, we'll go do that."

When he left, she locked up the place, then took off walking the perimeter of the island to Hanover House. As she walked, she tried to figure out what to do next.

CHAPTER

35

Sheila was still locked in her room when Sadie got home, so she knocked on the door and pushed it open. She saw her mother, scrunched up in a chair, hugging her knees and looking out the window. "Hey, Mom. I just wanted to see if you need anything."

Her mother's eyes were swollen and red, and her nose was crimson. She reached out. "Come here, baby."

Sadie came and sat down on the arm of her chair.

"I'm sorry I fell apart like this. Surprised even me. I go for such long periods of time without even thinking about her. You would think this would just roll right off my back."

Sadie just looked at her.

"Does that disappoint you, baby? That I wouldn't think of her every day, every hour? I did that first year, you know, until I had you. And then it was almost like you replaced her—like you were her. That little baby I'd held one time and had to give up was back in my arms, and I kind of pretended to myself that you were the same person."

It wasn't what Sadie had expected to hear, and yet it sounded like her mother.

"Did that work for you, Mom?"

"Sometimes. Most times. But then there were other times, when I would get down and I would think about the pain I went through that day, and all the agony leading up to that decision, and I would imagine where she was and what she was doing. I would tell myself that some rich billionaire had adopted her, and she was jetting off to Paris, dressing in the nicest outfits, with servants at her beck and call, getting ponies and cars for birthdays. I would convince myself that she was so much better off."

"She had nice parents, Mom. She was pretty well off."

"And then there were the times when I was at my lowest, when I would sit there and think how lucky that little girl was that I wasn't the one who raised her. I would look at myself in the mirror and see the lines and the paleness and the bags under my eyes from a hangover or a four-day high, and it was you I felt sorry for. She was the lucky one."

Sadie's throat tightened. "That's not true, Mom."

"You're sweet," Sheila said through trembling lips. "You always let me off the hook. He's in you, Jesus is. All the forgiveness, all the love." She got up, went to the window, turned back with tears in her eyes. "He's in me too, baby. I repented yesterday. I did what you said, and I gave it all to Jesus. Asked Him to save me, and I know He did."

Sadie caught her breath, and her mother's face twisted as her emotions overcame her. She pulled Sadie into a hug. "The greatest peace came over me, baby, and I felt clean for the first time. I knew He broke that cycle of curses on my children for my sins. I can pray now, for her protection. Maybe God will give us a miracle, if it's not already too late."

Sadie wept with her mother, gratitude mounting up to equal her despair. "It's not, Mom. She's not dead. I know she's not."

"How do you know?"

She thought of telling her about Scott Crown's gut feeling, but then she realized she had it too. "I can feel it." She let her mother go and looked out that window, into the sunlight. "It's just something inside of me, Mom. I don't think she's dead."

"Baby, we're not immune to this kind of tragedy just because we're Christians."

She couldn't believe her mother thought she had to say those words to her. "I know tragedy, Mom. Do you really think I don't know that?"

Sheila stood behind her and put her hands on her shoulders. "I know you know it. Maybe I just needed telling myself. I'm trying to look at things in a new way, baby. Trusting God, no matter what He does. The old me would have ranted and raved and run to a bar to drown my sorrows."

Sadie turned around. "The old you. But you're new now, Mom."

Sheila nodded. "I guess that's what being on the other side of salvation does for you. It shows you that there's nothing for you but to keep moving through the pain. Feeling it, every nerve-prick of it, because if you numb it, it waits for you and ambushes you as soon as you come down. Dealing with it is your only hope of coming out clean on the other side."

She smiled weakly. "Don't worry, baby. I'm not going back to the bottle, or to a needle or a pipe. That person is dead. And now that she is, I can do what a good mother would do. I can pray for my daughter."

"That's *all* you can do, Mom. That's the most important thing."

"The thing is, I don't know her well enough to know how to pray for her. I don't know the first thing about her."

"I do." She reached into her bag and pulled out the stack of pages she had printed out from Amelia's journal. "Look what I found today. It's her journal. She had it posted on the Internet on a blog. I printed it out. We can read it now, Mom, and find out all about her."

Sheila grabbed the first few sheets, sat down on her bed, and began skimming the pages. "This is her? She wrote this?"

"That's right."

"We've got to read it, baby. It might have clues. Here, you take this part, and I'll take this one."

Sadie did as she was told. She'd really wanted to read it alone, curled up on her own bed, but her mom needed this. So she took her part and lay beside her mother on her bed and started reading where she was told, in the middle of the journal.

After several pages of mundane stuff, Sadie decided to skip to the end. She turned to one of the last few entries and almost caught her breath when she saw that it was dated June 2—the day of Amelia's disappearance.

Sadie started to show her mother, but something told her to keep it to herself until she could process it.

I don't know why I thought it would be easier than this. I always pictured myself riding into town, looking her up in the phone book, and knocking on the door. But it wasn't that simple. Soon as I found out that Sheila Caruso was out of prison, it took a lot of doing to locate her. And now that she's in Cape Refuge, I'm not sure what good that knowledge does me. I plan on starting at some of the businesses on the strip, and find out if anybody here has ever heard of her. Meanwhile, we're having to sleep in this two-bit motel room with dead roaches all along the floor. The clientele here is pretty low class. There might even be some illegal activity going on in some of these rooms. We couldn't afford better. Besides, even if we could have, everything seemed to be booked up.

The guy next door is playing his music too loud, but I'm afraid to knock on the wall and ask him to turn it down, for fear he'll come through the wall and shoot me or something.

Sadie frowned. Had the police questioned whoever it was next door?

The air conditioner is broken and it's hot in here. Maybe when we get back we'll open a window and air the stench out. Meanwhile, we're going out to see what we can learn. I'm almost wishing I had never come. There has to be a better way to do this.

She dropped the last page, picked it up.

"You find anything yet, baby?"

"Not yet." Sadie wasn't ready to share this with her mother yet. She wanted to read to the end before the pages were taken away from her.

We're back now. Got the information I was looking for. This nice lady at an antique shop told me my mother lives at a place called Hanover House. She told me where it was, but then she mentioned that she lived there with her daughter and son, and all of a sudden I got cold feet. I wondered what they would think if I showed up at the door and told them I was their long-lost sister, and I started feeling pretty cruddy, as if I couldn't go through with it. So we came back here so I could get my bearings. I don't think I can do it like that. But there is one other option. She told me where she worked. She's typing for some writer guy that lives on the beach, and she told me where he lives, too. I'm thinking that I might be waiting there when she shows up for work tomorrow. Maybe then I'll catch her alone, and I won't have to disrupt her family if she doesn't want them to know.

Sadie sat up, her heart wanting to scream out, "No! Amelia, don't go there!" But it was too late. If she'd gone, and encountered Marcus Gibson . . .

She kept reading.

Meanwhile, we're stuck in this place, and I keep trying to get Jamie to go out, but she's fascinated listening to the conversation outside. We've got our curtains closed, but the windows are open, and she's engrossed in a conversation going on outside our window. Two

guys, chewing each other out in harsh whispers, thinking no one hears. One of them has the room next door.
Why they don't fight in there is beyond me. They
apparently don't know we can hear. Guess I'll go tune
in, see what we can find out. It's better than any other
entertainment we've got.

Sadie sat up, and her hands began to tremble as she clutched
the pages.

I'm thinking I might call my parents tonight, let them
know I'm okay. I really miss them and want to hear
their voices. After I see how things go with my mother,
I might look my sister and brother up, just to see what
they look like.

That was the last entry. Sweat drops trickled on Sadie's hairline, and she put the paper down and stared at the window, trying
to think what she should do. She should call the police—let them
handle this. But then she'd never have the chance to look into that
neighbor's eye and judge whether he was capable of murder. And
she *had* to know. Just as she'd had to see the inside of her sister's
motel room.

She would call the police after she found him.

Only then would she tell her mother.

She folded those pages, stuck them under her shirt. "I just
remembered, Mom. I was supposed to meet Blair. She had a story
she wanted me to work on."

Sheila was engrossed in her reading. She waved at Sadie.
"Okay, baby. Don't worry about me. I'll be okay."

"Are you sure?"

"I'm sure. I'm gonna read this whole thing."

Sadie slipped out of the room and went to her own room
and read back over the entries again.

Dropping the pages onto her bed, she headed for the stairs,
hoping no one would stop her before she got out the door. Then
she took off as fast as her feet would carry her to the Flagstaff
Motel.

CHAPTER

36

The Flagstaff Motel was not a place for a woman to be alone, day or night, but Sadie didn't care. She strode across the parking lot, past the two men she supposed to be drug dealers and the women pacing outside their doors, cigarettes in their hands, as if awaiting their next clients.

How in the world had her sister decided to stay in this place?

The room Amelia had occupied still had crime scene tape sealing it off. Sadie stood and looked at it for a moment before going up the stairs. If men had been talking outside of Amelia's door, it was likely they were next-door neighbors. Maybe they were still here. If she could piece together what had happened right after Amelia wrote that last entry in her journal, maybe it would lead her to some clues about where Amelia was.

Her feet clanked on the metal and concrete steps. A couple of people stepped out of their open doors to see who was coming, and she felt self-conscious. Did Amelia and Jamie get the same stares as they'd made their walk to their room?

Her gaze went beyond the room with the tape to the one next door. She knocked and turned back, and saw her observers stepping back inside their rooms.

After a moment, the door opened, letting out a smoky draft of air. A man of about twenty, with long, greasy brown hair and gray red-rimmed eyes came to the door. "Yeah?"

"Hi, I'm Sadie Caruso, with the *Cape Refuge Journal.* I'm working on a story about the two girls who were in this room next door."

"Yeah?"

"I was wondering . . . were you here when they checked in?"

He hesitated a moment. "No. I checked in right after all of it happened."

"All of what?"

"The whole police thing. The girls disappearing. That tape was up when I checked in a couple of days ago."

He was high and wasn't making much sense. The tape hadn't been up a couple of days ago. It had only been yesterday that the room was discovered. "Are you sure? Because I was thinking maybe you'd remember something about them. Anyone they were with, anyone you saw them talking to, that kind of thing."

"Nope. Sorry." His tone was defiant.

"Well, okay. Thank you." She started to walk away, then turned back before he shut the door.

"Can I ask what your name is?"

"For what?"

"I'm just trying to keep up with who said what. For my story."

"Name's Nate."

Clearly, that was all she was going to get out of him, so she jotted his name down as she started away. She stopped at the door on the other side of Amelia and Jamie's room, and knocked. No one answered.

She thought of going from room to room, poking her head in those open doors, asking questions of the people who lived and worked there. But she would do that later.

For now, she hurried down the stairs into the motel office, where a grubby man with one rotten front tooth greeted her. "Help you, honey?"

Thankfully, he wasn't the same man she'd conned yesterday. "Sadie Caruso, with the newspaper. I'm working on a story about Amelia Roarke and Jamie Maddox, and I wonder if I can ask you a couple of questions."

"Sure. I'll tell you what I told the police."

"Could you tell me about the man named Nate in the room next to the girls? How long has he been there?"

"Couple of weeks. He's a regular. Comes and goes."

Then he *had* been lying to her. She wondered if the police had questioned him. If so, did they pick up on his contradictions? Her heart began to hammer as she tried to decide what to do.

"It's a terrible thing, what happened. I try to run a decent establishment here. Hurts business when stuff like this happens."

His comment shook Sadie out of her racing thoughts. Did he really think this was a decent establishment? How on earth could the kind of business that took place here be hurt? Were the hookers finding another place to hang out? Were the drug dealers looking for classier corners?

"We all been talking about it, piecing stuff together," he drawled on.

"Oh, yeah? What kind of stuff?"

"Like the girl who saw them with two guys, and that Gibson dude hanging around here."

Sadie caught her breath. "Marcus Gibson was here?"

"Yeah, a couple of different times. Hung out in the parking lot talking to people. Asking about their families, their dope, how much they use a day, how they shoot up . . ."

Sadie wondered if Cade knew this. "Did Gibson ever threaten anyone?"

"Nope, most of 'em just laughed at him. Weird dude. Couple of 'em followed him when he left, saw he was sleeping in the woods like a homeless guy."

"Who followed him? Can you give me their names?"

"No, hon. I didn't get names. Just heard some of the gals talking about it. Everybody was real surprised when it turned out he was a famous writer. Who woulda thought? And why would a dude like that go around killing people? You'd think he had it made. Money, fame . . . Unless he was just cracked in the head from the start."

Sadie thanked him for the information, then stepped outside and pulled her cell phone out of her pocket. She dialed the number of the police station, and got Cade on the phone quickly.

"Yeah, Sadie. What is it?"

"Cade, I was just at the Flagstaff talking to the manager—"

"Sadie, get out of there! You don't have any business there!"

"But listen. He told me Gibson was hanging around up here. That he—"

"We know all about that. We're on top of it."

"You do?"

"Yes. We know what we're doing, Sadie. You need to get out of there and let me handle the police work. Will you do that? Will you leave right now?"

She sighed and looked around. She had come here to find out about the tenant in the room next to Amelia's. She still needed to know. "Okay, okay. I'm leaving right now, as we speak."

"What made you go there in the first place? Does your mother know where you are? Do Morgan and Jonathan? I know Blair didn't send you there."

"I was reading Amelia's journal. I found it on the web. She talked about hearing a conversation outside her window, a conversation between two guys. That was her last entry. Have you talked to the guys in the room next to hers?"

"Yes, Sadie, we have. And I know the journal you're talking about. We found it too."

"Well, don't you think it's important?"

"Everything is important. Now I want you to get out of there right now!"

She didn't want to lie, but she wasn't ready to leave. "I'm already a block away."

She could hear the relief in his voice. "Good. Keep walking, and don't turn back."

"I won't."

She hung up and looked back up at the room. Maybe she should just keep her word and leave . . . but there were still too many questions. The manager had mentioned a girl seeing Jamie and Amelia with two guys.

She pushed back into the managers' office.

"Excuse me."

"Yeah?"

"You were saying a girl saw Amelia and Jamie with two guys. Who were the guys? What were they doing?"

"She said she saw them getting into their car. I don't know who they were."

"She saw the girls getting into someone's car? Did she tell the police?"

"Yep, she told 'em. I heard her myself."

"Did she know the guys?"

"She didn't know. Said she only saw them from behind, and it was getting dark. Got into a car she didn't recognize. Couldn'ta been the girls' car, since the cops found it here."

"Were the girls going willingly, or were they being forced?"

"Lady, I don't know. Why don't you ask her?"

"I will. Which room is she in?"

"212. Name's Tina."

Sadie hurried upstairs to 212 and found the door open. A girl who couldn't have been older than fourteen lay on the bed watching *Lizzie McGuire*. She looked as if she hadn't bathed in days and nursed a weeklong hangover. Her hair was greasy, and black makeup was smeared under her eyes, as if she'd just awakened and hadn't bothered to look in the mirror.

Sadie knocked on the door casing, and the girl sat up. "Excuse me, are you Tina?"

"Yeah. Why?"

"I'm Sadie Caruso, from the *Cape Refuge Journal*. I was just talking to the motel manager about the two girls who disappeared."

"Yeah, freaky, huh?"

Sadie stepped into her room. "Listen, he said you saw the girls the night they disappeared, talking to two guys."

"I thought I did. But now that time has passed I think I may have got it wrong."

Sadie's heart fell. "Got it wrong? How?"

"Well, I don't think it was them. And the nights are all blurring together. Might have even been somebody else before they checked in."

Sadie came into the room. "Look, I know you've probably gotten cold feet about talking to the police—"

The girl sprang off of the bed and pushed past Sadie to the doorway. She looked out in both directions, checking to see if anyone was listening. "I didn't talk to the police, okay? And I'm sure not talking to no reporter."

Sadie reached for the door. "Can we close this and talk where we won't be heard? I promise I won't print anything you tell me."

Tina shook her head and peered out again. "No. I have to leave it open."

"Why?"

"Never mind. I'm not talking to you anyway, so it doesn't matter."

Sadie stood there a moment as the girl went to her bathroom mirror and leaned in, examining her face. "Man, I look awful." She grabbed a used tissue and wiped under her eyes.

Sadie came further into the room and stood behind her, meeting her eyes in the mirror. "Look, I don't know what you're afraid of, but in some ways I've been where you are, and I can understand how real that fear is. I'm not here as a reporter, okay? I'm here because one of those girls—the one who's still missing—is my sister."

The girl turned around then and looked fully into Sadie's face. She looked even younger now, with the smeared black makeup gone. "Your sister? Oh, yeah. You do look like her."

"Then you did see her?"

Tina looked toward the door again, as if certain someone was listening. "We all saw her. You couldn't miss those two. They looked like little preppies bopping up in here, perfectly innocent, like they expected to order room service and go for a swim."

Sadie lowered to her bed. "Did you talk to them at all?"

"Yeah, once." The girl's voice lowered almost to a whisper. "I kind of passed out in my doorway, and they got me a glass of water."

Sadie's heart twisted. "They helped you?"

"Yeah, sort of. The one did, the one that looks like you. The other one acted like she was afraid she'd catch a disease just standing on my carpet."

"What did they say?"

The girl's eyes glazed over as she stared at her memory. "The one—Amelia—said she'd get me some food or take me somewhere. I told her I was fine. I told them they didn't belong here, that it was dangerous for somebody like them. They just went on to their room. They should have listened."

"Why were they in danger?"

Tina laughed then. "Are you *blind?* Haven't you seen the people who live here? They were targets in the first ten minutes after they got here. They went to their room, all stiff, like they were scared to death. These dudes who live here, they smell fear, like animals." She walked to her doorway, looked out. "Oh, man, what are they doing here?"

Sadie stood up and looked past her. She saw a police car pulling into the parking lot. She might have known Cade would send someone to make sure she'd left. She stepped back into the shadow of the room. "I think they're looking for me."

Tina turned around. "You in trouble?"

"No. They just didn't want me here. Chief Cade is my friend. He's a little protective."

Tina watched out the door. "He's gone now. Just drove through and looked around."

Sadie peeked out the window into the parking lot below. She saw the squad car pulling back into traffic, and relaxed.

"Must be nice to have people looking out for you. Even if they are cops."

Sadie supposed that was true . . . most of the time. "Listen, the manager told me Marcus Gibson was here, snooping around."

"Yeah, talk about a weirdo."

"Was he here that day? Did you ever see him talking to the girls?"

"No, not that day. But the way he crept around, he could have been here without my noticing."

"Did he ever threaten anyone or hurt anybody?"

"No. He seemed harmless enough, until all this happened."

"You said *they* smelled fear. Was he one of the ones you meant?"

"No, not him. People who live here."

"Who? I need names."

She grunted. "I'm not giving you names."

"Is it the men who are out there right now?"

The girl turned away. "You're crazy. You should go now."

Sadie touched the girl's arm and tried to turn her back around. "Tell me about the girls getting into the car with two guys. What did you see?"

Tina jerked her arm away and went to get a cigarette out of a glittery handbag with Audrey Hepburn's face on the side. "Okay," she said on a whisper. "I'll tell you what I told the cops. I saw them with these two guys walking out to a car and getting into it. I didn't see their faces, just the backs of their heads. Could have been anybody around here."

"What kind of car did they get into?"

"Hey, it was dark. I didn't see. Little boxy car, four doors. Dark colored, I think. I remember it rattled when it pulled away."

"Did you see which direction they drove?"

"No, I didn't think much of it, so why would I watch?"

Sadie got up and went back to the doorway, peering out over the rail to the parking lot below. "Can you think of anybody else that was out that night, anyone who might have seen them? Somebody who might have gotten a look at the guys' faces?"

"No. We've all been talking ever since. I haven't heard of anybody else who saw that."

Sadie wanted to write it down, but she didn't want Tina thinking of her as a reporter again. She looked up at her, and noted the look of hopeless vacancy. "Can I ask you one more question?"

Tina shrugged. "Not like I can stop you."

"Do you know the guy Nate who lives on the end down there, next to where Amelia and Jamie were staying?"

She turned away and put her cigarette out. "Yeah, I know Nate."

"What can you tell me about him?"

"He's just another doper," she said in a low voice. "It wasn't him."

"How do you know? You said you couldn't see their faces."

The girl pulled open a drawer, began searching through her wadded clothes for something. "It wasn't him, okay? He has a walk."

Sadie watched her. Why was Tina so nervous talking about Nate? The girl finally found what she was looking for—another pack of cigarettes. She pulled out the cigarette and lit up as she looked Sadie over.

"You ever get high?"

Sadie thought of those days when dope was readily available in her own home, when methamphetamine was going out as fast as other drugs were coming in. She'd experimented a couple of times, trying to escape the life in which she was trapped.

She hated the memory of it.

"No, I don't get high."

"Smart girl." Tina leaned back against the wall, blowing her smoke up toward the ceiling. "I used to be like you."

Sadie just looked at her feet.

"You're all clean and prissy and probably think you're so much better than me. But if you came from the kind of place I came from, you'd be where I am right now."

Sadie *had* come from such a place. "We all have choices. It's not too late for you, Tina. You can still turn around. I know some people who would take you in if you didn't have a place to go."

Tina laughed and brandished a hand across her room. "And leave all this? Are you kidding me? No thanks."

Sadie thought of walking out, but something about the girl's demeanor made her stay. She pulled her notepad out, jotted down her own name and the phone number for Hanover House. "Look, if you need help or decide that you want to turn your life around, call me at this number, okay? If I'm not there, talk to anybody who answers. Tell them I gave you the number. They can help you. I promise they can. I came here a lot like you—my mom was in prison and her boyfriend had taken over our house with his meth lab. I came to Cape Refuge all beaten up with a broken arm and bruises all over me . . . and Morgan Cleary found me and took me in. I was underaged too, but she didn't send me back home. I've lived there for a year and a half now, and they've helped me change my life. It's what they do. Most of the people who live there are right out of prison, all of them have drug problems—"

"I can't afford a rehab program."

"There's no cost. Christian people donate money to keep the house going. God uses them to rescue people like you all the time."

"I'm a crack addict." The girl lifted her chin almost proudly as she said it. "You don't know what that's like. You can kick it, think you're over it, that you've got it under control. But then your mind tricks you into believing that you can't do without it or you'll die, and when you get like that, you'll sell your grandmother's pacemaker to get a fix. In fact, you'll sell whatever you've got."

Sadie knew the girl had been peddling herself for that fix. She handed her the paper. "Take it. Call them if you ever feel like you want a hand out of here. Or call me. I'll help you."

Tina stared down at the number, and tears came to her eyes. She turned and stuffed it into her drawer. "You two are a lot alike, aren't you? You and your sister?"

Sadie wanted to tell her that she didn't know, because she'd never met her. "Why do you say that?"

"You both want to help me." She closed the drawer, drew in a deep breath. "Thanks for the number. I don't happen to need it, but—"

"Keep it anyway. One day you'll find yourself crying out to God for help, begging Him for an escape, and He'll remind you of that number. You'll call, and you'll find Jesus there. And that'll be the beginning of your new life. Don't lose it, okay?"

Tina leaned back against the wall again. "I won't."

Sadie left her room, feeling like she'd left a part of herself behind. She started down the stairs, as a wave of smoke drifted up to her. Someone was waiting down below. She slowed her step as she came down and saw a shadow of a man leaning against a car, right at the bottom of the stairs. She reached the bottom, stepped around the wall, and saw him. Nate leaned against a beat-up old Volvo, staring up at her with dull, impatient eyes.

"Want to tell me why you're asking around about me?"

She stopped cold. "I wasn't asking about you. I was asking about the girls—"

"I heard you ask about me by name."

She knew there was no point in lying. If he'd heard the conversation upstairs, then she couldn't deny her way out of it. "Okay, I *was* asking about you. I think you know something about my sister."

His eyebrows shot up. "Your sister?"

"Yes. The girl Amelia. The one who hasn't been found."

He let out a long stream of smoke and grinned. "Shoulda known."

"Are you the one she left with that night?"

He started to chuckle.

Sadie's heart began to race. "I'm not trying to accuse you of anything if you were," she said, keeping her voice level. "Just because she got in the car with you and went somewhere doesn't mean—" The words caught in her suddenly dry throat. "Look, I'm just trying to retrace her steps. The more I know, the closer I'll get to finding her. It *was* you, wasn't it?"

He drew in a deep breath and took a step toward her. She stepped back against the brick wall.

He came closer, until she could smell his breath—that hungover, didn't-brush-your-teeth smell of whiskey and smoke. He reached into his pocket, pulled out a switchblade.

With a flick of his wrist it came open, and she jumped.

He stepped closer, the sharp point on that blade pressing against her throat. She closed her eyes and swallowed.

"Don't . . . please . . ."

"I think you and me need to go for a ride."

"No! I'm not going anywhere."

He moved the blade up, breaking skin. He'd kill her right here, in this parking lot. Maybe someone would see and tell, but it would be too late for her. Where was that police car? She prayed it would come back. "Please . . ."

He put his arm around her shoulders and moved the knife down to her side. "In my car. You and me, we're gonna get real close, and I'm gonna walk you to my car. You're gonna go like you're willing, because you'll know that if you don't, you'll have a knife through your ribs."

He started to move, pulling her beside him. She touched the nick at her throat, smeared the blood beading out. As they walked, she could feel the blade at her ribs. It had already drawn blood there too. One move could cost her life.

Nate was in the mood for another murder.

He put her into the car on his side, shoved her over, and got in behind the wheel. His car rattled as he pulled out of the parking lot.

CHAPTER 97

Where are you taking me?"

"You'll see."

"Please . . . you can let me out. I won't tell anyone."

He laughed as his car picked up speed, heading onto Ocean Boulevard, toward the Tybee bridge.

She tried to inch over to the door. If she could get it open, she could jump out. Whatever injury she sustained from jumping from a speeding car had to be better than certain death at his hands.

"I wouldn't do that." He let her go long enough to reach under the seat . . . and come up with a gun.

Her heart caught in her throat. She tried to calculate whether he'd be able to shoot her if she flung the door open and threw herself out. They'd crossed the bridge, and he was only able to go about forty in traffic. If she jumped, could he drive and hit a target at the same time? And if he did, wouldn't he have police surrounding him in seconds? A gunshot on Tybee Island wasn't likely to go ignored, especially on such a busy street.

"Be still now, or I'll kill you the same way I killed the others."

Terror made its screaming ascent in her head. Amelia *was* dead. Dear God, her sister was dead. Rage exploded inside Sadie, and suddenly she didn't care if he killed her or not.

She went for the gun, trying to wrest it out of his hand.

He kept one hand on the steering wheel as he fought her. The car yanked to the right. He cursed, grabbed her by her hair, and jerked her back, getting control of the wheel again. She reached for the door, but he jerked her again, ripping her scalp.

"Let go of me!"

"You wanna mess with me?" he grated through his teeth. He turned left, off of the busy street, and drove to the center of Tybee, where there wasn't as much traffic. He kept up his speed as he flew through a residential section. "Nobody messes with me and gets away with it."

Sadie kept fighting. "You killed her! You *murderer!*" She fought him for the gun or the steering wheel, and when he had to loosen his grip on her to get control of the car, she threw herself to the other side and got the door open.

He was going fifty, at least, down a shady neighborhood street. She hesitated, and he grabbed her hair again, trying to hold her back. She clawed at him, tearing her fingernails into his arm, trying to make him let go.

The car screeched to a halt, and Nate grabbed her arm, yanking it up behind her back. Sadie arched, feeling the strain on the same bone that had been broken before, the ripping of tissue in her shoulder. He shoved the gun up under her chin, its nose threatening to puncture her skin and come up into her throat.

"I'll show you what it costs to fight me, just like I showed the others."

He opened his glove box and got out a roll of duct tape. With his teeth, he peeled back the end, then slapped it over her mouth and wrapped it around her head.

Sadie fought with all her might, praying that someone would come out of their house to get the paper and stop this madness. She felt the binding of the tape as it came around and around her face, and then he ripped it with his teeth again and bound her hands behind her. She bucked and kicked at him, trying to get her footing so she could get out the door, but he grabbed a foot and wrapped it with tape, then grabbed her other one, pulling her to her back, and bound her ankles together.

He stank with sweat as he reached across her and slammed the car door, sealing her fate. She tried to scream, but the tape muffled her voice, rendering her efforts useless. He sat there for a moment, catching his breath, watching her with those bloodshot eyes. She bucked and writhed, trying to break free of her bonds, but to no avail. Clearly satisfied that she was restrained, he slid back behind the wheel and drove the car to the end of the street where a grove of trees gave a little more privacy. He got out, and she prayed he would leave her there to be found.

But he walked around the car, opened her door, put one arm under her knees and the other behind her back.

As he lifted her, she jerked and kicked and twisted, sending out muffled screams into the tape.

He threw her into his trunk, and she fought to break her hands free or separate her feet or scream out for help.

"Who's in charge now, baby?" he asked through sneering lips. The trunk slammed, encasing her in darkness, and Sadie squealed, trying to be heard. The car started again, the engine rattling . . .

Sadie closed her eyes. Was this it? Was this how it had been for Emily and Jamie and Amelia? Would he murder her too and walk away free?

She tried to reel her thoughts back from her panic and focused instead on the possibilities. God knew where she was. Maybe He'd orchestrated things so that someone saw the struggle on Ocean Boulevard or on Butler Avenue on Tybee. Someone in one of these quiet homes might have heard the screaming and screeching and looked out the window . . .

Scott or Cade would come after her, bringing a brigade of police to surround Nate's car and stop him. He wouldn't get far.

But that was unlikely.

Her hopes flattened into despair again. If no one *had* called them, would anyone even know she was missing for another hour or so? Realistically, it could be hours before anyone grew alarmed.

What had she done?

Why had she taken such stupid chances for a person she'd never even met? And now she knew Amelia was dead, so it was all worthless. She'd never meet her, never see how much alike they were, never know the pleasure of having a sister like Morgan had Blair.

Oh, God, help me!

Where was Nate taking her? Would he kill her wherever they stopped? Would he terrorize her first?

How would her mother ever survive this? Two daughters killed by the same hand. She would go back to drugs for sure, wind up back on the streets and go back to prison. Poor little Caleb would be abandoned once again.

Morgan and Jonathan would grieve for years. Blair would blame herself.

Oh, *why* had she done such a careless thing? So many people would be hurt.

Please, God, my refuge and my strength . . .

He would help her fight. He had to. Nate might kill her, but it wouldn't be without cost.

Sadie felt the car turn off of a paved road onto an unpaved one. Rocks crunched under the wheels, and the car bucked and bounced, as if it weren't meant to take such a path.

He was going to kill her and leave her body out in the middle of the woods. Or would he pose her like the others, in a boat or a cave? Was it all a game to him, or was there some sinister motive she couldn't even imagine?

She felt the car come to a halt, and she held her breath, waiting for the worst. Several moments passed, and nothing happened, then finally the trunk swung open. Light bore down into her eyes, and squealing into her tape, she looked up at Nate.

He was holding rope, and before she could fight him, he began tying the rope around her waist. It was too tight, but she couldn't stop him. She fought the bindings on her hands and feet, wondering if he intended to hang her. But wouldn't it go around her neck if he did?

He lifted her out of the car, dropped her down hard on the ground. She groaned.

He got the switchblade out of his pocket, clicked it back open. She squeezed her eyes shut as he bent over her.

She felt him slashing the tape at her ankles, nicking her shin as he did.

"Get up," he said. "I'm not carrying you. You can walk."

Her feet were free! She pulled herself up, thinking that she could escape if she could just get far enough away from him. If she pretended to cooperate, to go where he told her . . .

He tugged on that rope around her waist. "Come on. This way."

She looked around and saw a house a couple of acres away. Maybe someone there would see this and come to her aid. Maybe they would have a gun. *Please, God.*

He dragged her beside him, using the rope, jerking on her and chafing her ribs and her waist. She fell down and he jerked her back up.

Finally, they came to a door in the ground that looked like the opening to a tornado shelter. He threw the door open and turned back to her.

"Get in there."

She wasn't sure which she feared more—staying with him or going into that dark place. And what if he came in with her?

She didn't move, so he jerked on the rope, knocking her forward. She fell to her knees at the opening and looked in. There were no stairs, and it looked like a deep dark pit, too deep to be a shelter.

She turned back to him and looked up, her face pleading.

He kicked her then, knocking her off her knees. Bending over her, he grabbed her shirt, lifting and dragging her.

She fought as he got her over that hole, trying not to let him push her in, but her hands were still bound, and her feet weren't enough.

Suddenly, she lost the fight and fell into the hole. She screamed in the back of her throat as she free-fell into the darkness . . .

The rope caught her before she reached the ground, jerking her to a stop before she shattered at the bottom. Her ribs cracked with the sudden halt. She hung there for a moment, terror radiating through her limbs, bolting through her like lightning.

"I ain't going to kill you just yet." His voice drifted down from the opening several feet above her. "There might be another use for you before that." He laughed long and hard and let go of the rope. She fell the remaining few feet, landing flat on her face, her hands bound beneath her.

His laughter rang cruel and piercing above her. "You wanted to find your sister, didn't you? Well, there she is."

Sadie scrambled to her knees. Light from the opening kept the darkness at bay. She turned around, searching the dirt hole he had thrown her in.

And then she saw her.

A girl, bound hand and feet just like Sadie, hunkering in the corner, her eyes wide with rabid fear.

C H A P T E R

39

The girl screamed, and Sadie's abductor laughed harder, then dropped the door shut. Sunlight razored in through the slats, providing a dim light in the hole.

The girl kept screaming, her heels digging into the dirt as she tried to back as far into the dirt wall as she could to get away from Sadie. Her face was scraped and bruised, and lines of scabs scarred her cheeks, as if duct tape had been ripped off of her.

Amelia! It had to be her. She had blonde hair and a small frame like her own.

She was alive!

After a moment the screaming stopped, replaced by a terrorized whimper. Amelia's bound hands balled under her chin. Sadie grunted through her tape and crawled closer, trying to make her see that she was no threat. Finally, the girl cried out, "Who are you?"

Sadie made a noise through the tape and raised her bound hands to try to work it free. But it was wrapped around her head, and she couldn't find the seam.

She crawled across the floor to Amelia, and the girl pulled her knees up to her chest, trying to back further away. "Leave me alone! Get away!" She was crazed, terrified, and Sadie didn't know how to calm her.

Sadie stopped, her hair stringing into her eyes and sticking to her wet face. The girl looked weak, pale, as if she was near collapsing, and Sadie wondered if she'd had anything to eat in all this time. Had he left her here to starve to death?

Sadie shook her head. If only Amelia would understand that she was as helpless as she, that she wasn't going to hurt her. She held up her bound hands, pleading with her eyes for Amelia to help her.

Finally, Amelia seemed to calm down, and she sat there, staring at her. A vein strained against the skin in Amelia's forehead, and she sucked in sobs, mucus running from her nose and tears streaking through the dirt on her face. She'd clearly been through a scuffle before being thrown into this place . . . or since. She'd been beaten, broken.

Sadie wanted to help her, but she couldn't even help herself. She inched closer, careful not to set Amelia off again. Reaching her bound hands out, she touched the tape on Amelia's wrists. Amelia seemed to understand and held out her hands. "Yes . . . p-peel me loose."

The girl's hands trembled harder than Sadie's did. Sadie dug her fingernails into the seam on the tape and began to work it free. It had been there too long and resisted being peeled, but slowly she pulled it from Amelia's wrists.

When her hands were unbound, Amelia rubbed her chafed wrists. "Thank you," she whispered. She looked at Sadie then, her eyes assessing her. "I'll . . . I'll do yours." She reached for the tape across Sadie's mouth, wrapped around her head, and started to peel it off.

Despite her weakness and the tremor in her hands, she was careful as she peeled it from Sadie's skin. When Sadie's mouth was free again, she started to cry. "You're Amelia, aren't you?"

Amelia stared. "How do you know me?"

"Everyone's looking for you."

"Then they know I'm missing?" Her mouth trembled.

"Your parents are in Cape Refuge. They're frantic."

Her face twisted and reddened, and that vein on her forehead bulged even more. Weakly, she said, "Why did I do this to them? They don't deserve it. I should never have come. My friend . . . she was taken with me, but they shot her. Has anyone found her?"

Sadie didn't know if Amelia could take the truth. She thought of lying, saying she hadn't heard anything about her, but the words got caught in her throat.

Her hesitation was answer enough. "They have, haven't they?"

Sadie swallowed hard and nodded. "They found her body a couple of days ago."

Amelia wilted back against the wall. "Oh, no. I was hoping I was wrong. That she wasn't really dead. That she got away somehow."

Sadie sat there quietly, watching her sister cry. She wished she knew how to help her, but they were both in such a mess that she saw no way out. Amelia wept, and Sadie sat still, waiting.

Finally, Amelia wiped her face on her shirt and got a look of resolve on her face. She reached out for Sadie's hands and began unpeeling the bindings. "So how did you wind up here?"

Now that the dirt was wiped from her face, Sadie could see her sister's delicate features. She had her mother's eyes, just as Sadie did, and her nose was pretty and delicate, her lips full and shaped just like her own.

"I was looking for you and I got too close to the truth. I guess he had to get rid of me."

Amelia got Sadie's hands free. "You were looking for me? Why?"

Sadie stared at her for a moment, wondering if she was dumping too much on the girl all at once. Finally, she said, "Because I'm your sister."

Amelia's eyebrows came together, and she sat back, staring at Sadie.

"I'm Sadie Caruso."

Amelia drew in a breath so hard that Sadie thought she might choke. "Caruso? Sheila's daughter?"

Sadie nodded.

"My birth mother? She knows about me?"

"When they found your friend . . . the police came to my mom and told her that you had come there looking for her. I didn't know I had a sister. I'm a year younger than you."

Amelia seemed disoriented again as she stared at her, taking it all in.

"I can't believe this. When they said my birth mother had two children, I expected them to be ten or twelve years old. Not practically my own age."

"We have a little brother, Caleb. He's only two and a half."

A look of awe came over Amelia's face. "Caleb . . ."

Sadie got up and inspected her own injuries. She had heard her ribs crunch when she'd fallen in, and pain stabbed through her. Her knees were bloody, and her shoulder ached. The rope still hung from her waist. She tried to undo the knot, and an urgency suddenly took hold of her. "We've got to find a way out of here."

"There's no way. I've been trying to figure one out for days."

"I don't understand why he's holding us here," Sadie said.

"He's waiting for something. He told me he fully intends to kill me when the time is right."

"What time?"

"I don't know. But every now and then he comes down here, and . . ." Her voice trailed off, and Sadie knew what she was going to say.

"Has he hurt you?"

Amelia couldn't answer that directly. "He's a monster."

Sadie looked up at the door. "The next time he comes we'll overpower him. He can't handle us both."

"What if he has his friend with him?"

Sadie looked at her. "What friend?"

She looked too weak to answer. "The other guy who was with him when he took Jamie and me." She leaned her head back against the wall. "We heard them talking outside our motel room, about some girl that one of them had killed. The other one was furious at him, telling him he'd gotten him into all sorts of trouble. That he'd made a mess of things. He told him to leave town and never come back."

"Emily Lawrence! She was found in a boat, and the police said she was dead before the killer put her there."

"We were listening to their conversation, and all of a sudden, I knocked a glass off the table and broke it. They realized we were in there, and that we'd heard them."

"Oh, no."

"Yes. We heard them go back into their room, so we waited for a while, then decided to leave. Then somebody knocked on the door. Jamie answered it, and there they were. They had a gun. They forced us to go with them and get into their car, and they brought us here. Jamie fought them with all her might and tried to make a run for it, but they shot her. Then they threw me down here."

"Who was the other guy? Was it a flaky middle-aged man?"

"No. He was my age. I never heard his name. He was cleaner cut than Nate. Light brown hair, about five-ten."

That described dozens of guys. "Well, we'll just have to find a way out before they come back." She looked fully at Amelia now. "Are you all right? You look really weak."

"I haven't eaten in four days. I wouldn't have had anything to drink except that it rained a couple of times." She wrapped her arms around herself. "We're going to die here, you know."

"No, we're not."

"We are. They're never going to let us go. We can identify them. They have to kill us."

"That might be what they think." Sadie got the rope off of her waist, wincing with the pain in her ribs. "But they don't know me. I've had a lot of experience fighting for my life. They just may have met their match."

CHAPTER
40

My birth mother occupies a special place in my mind, a channel in the sea of my existence, leading me to where I am today. I wonder about her sometimes. Was she an unmarried teen when she gave me up? Did she agonize over the decision? Did she hold me when I was born? Did she weep for days—months—afterward? How did it change her life?

I know that it may not have been significant at all. Maybe it didn't faze her. Maybe she hasn't thought about me in years.

I can't explain why it matters so much to me, except to say that I need to know the first chapters of my life story. I need to understand who I came from so I can understand who I am now, and maybe even why I'm here.

Sheila put down the stack in her hand, and stared at that entry. She'd cried more today than she'd cried in years—even more than the day she was taken to prison, leaving her children in the hands of a violent, selfish man.

But the tears were useless. They did nothing to help her daughter.

She heard Morgan coming up the stairs. She was rubbing her belly and looked tired as she came to stand in her doorway. "Sheila, did Sadie say anything to you about not coming home for supper?"

"No. At least, I don't think so. She might have said something that didn't register. I was a little preoccupied."

Morgan had that look she got when she was worried but trying not to show it. "I can't decide whether to wait for her or go ahead and eat."

"I'll call her and see." She picked up the phone on her bed table and dialed Sadie's cell phone. No answer. "Maybe her battery died. She's always forgetting to charge her phone. Or maybe she's in a noisy place and can't hear."

Morgan looked worried as she came in and sat down on her bed. "Try the newspaper office. See if Blair knows."

Sheila dialed that number. Blair picked up quickly. "*Cape Refuge Journal.*"

"Blair, this is Sheila. Is Sadie there, by any chance?"

"No, I thought I was going to see her late this afternoon, but she didn't come in."

Sheila drew her eyebrows together and looked up at Morgan. "Not at all? When she left here earlier she said she was going to the office."

"Nope. She didn't come at all."

A sense of sudden dread tightened her chest. "Well, if you see her, would you tell her I'm looking for her? Ask her to come home or call? She's not answering her cell phone."

"Sure thing."

Sheila hung up and turned her troubled eyes to Morgan. "Where could she be?"

Morgan's gaze locked on hers. "Maybe she just got a lead on a story and took off after it."

"Yeah, that's what I'm afraid of."

As the next hours drifted by with no word from Sadie, Sheila began to get more concerned. Jonathan was pacing on the front porch, watching for signs of her, and Morgan was on the phone calling everyone who might have seen her. Sheila sat on the back porch, begging God to bring Sadie home soon. But something in her heart told her Sadie hadn't simply neglected to call. She was sure Sadie was in trouble.

By ten o'clock, Sheila had had enough. "I have to go look for her. Something's happened. Sadie wouldn't do this."

Jonathan agreed. "Take the car and my cell phone. If we hear from her, we'll let you know."

When her search around the island turned up nothing, Sheila thought of Scott Crown. Maybe Sadie had run into him, and he'd taken her out. It wasn't like her to go out on a date and not let anyone know, but with all that was going on today, who knew where anyone's head was? As far-fetched as it sounded, she wanted to believe it.

She drove to the police station, hurried inside. Joe was there, even though it was late. He seemed glad to see her.

"Joe, I need your help. We're looking for Sadie, and I wondered if she'd been in here to see Scott or something."

"I haven't seen her. Scott's on duty, but he's out in the squad car." He stood up and called across the room to the dispatcher. "Hey, Myrtle. Radio Scott and ask him if he's seen Sadie Caruso."

Sheila kept standing and watched Myrtle as she made the call. Finally, the woman turned back to her. "He says he hasn't seen her since this morning, Joe. Said she didn't say where she was going."

Sheila wilted, and tears burned in her eyes. "*Where* could she be?"

Joe sat back in his chair. "You're really worried, aren't you?"

"Yes!" She raked her hand through her hair and bent over his desk. "I've already got one daughter missing. What if something's happened to Sadie too? What if she's been taken—" Her voice broke off, choked by a sob.

Joe came around his desk and pulled her into a hug, and she melted against him and wept into his shirt.

He stroked her back as he held her. "Sadie's okay, hon. I bet she ran into some friends and just forgot to call."

She drew in a ragged breath and looked up at him. "Could you look for her, Joe? Could you radio the other cars and ask them to look for her?"

"Sure, I can." He let her go, handed her a box of Kleenex from his desk, and headed for Myrtle.

Sheila blew her nose and tried to calm down. But fear was like a fog around her, and she couldn't see through it to the light that might wait just beyond it. *Sadie, where are you?*

When Joe finished radioing his patrol cars, he came back to her. "I'm sure she's fine, Sheila. Maybe she just ran into some friends. Any minute now she'll check her watch and realize how late it is."

She wiped her tear-streaked hands on her jeans. "Do you think so?"

"I sure do. Sadie's got a level head, but she's still a kid. And you know how kids can be sometimes. She's probably home already."

Sheila pulled Jonathan's phone out of her pocket, checked the display to make sure she hadn't missed a call. "No, Jonathan said he would call if she came home. The thing is, Amelia's disappearance was heavy on her mind. Whatever she's doing, it has something to do with her, I guarantee you. What if she found her and got into trouble herself?"

"If we haven't been able to find Amelia yet, I doubt Sadie could. No, I'm sure she's okay. Just go home and relax. One of our guys will find her soon. I'll have them bring her right home."

Helpless, Sheila drove back home. Jonathan and Morgan hadn't heard a word from her.

When Cade pulled into the driveway a few minutes after Sheila got home, she saw the concern on his face.

"Sheila, Joe told me Sadie's missing," he said as he got out of the car.

So Joe was more worried than he'd indicated. "Yes. Have they found her?"

Cade shook his head. "No, not yet. But I thought I should tell you that I heard from Sadie earlier today."

"You did?"

"Yes. She was at the Flagstaff, poking around."

Sheila gasped. "No! She wouldn't do something that crazy!" She took a step toward him. "Cade, please tell me you're kidding."

"I'm not, Sheila. She was there. I told her to leave, that we had it under control. Before she hung up, she told me she was already a block away. Just in case, I sent a squad car to make sure. They didn't see her, so we assumed she'd gone."

"Oh, dear God, why didn't someone tell me this earlier?" Sheila's voice was frantic as she started into the house. "I have to get the keys. I have to go there."

"To the Flagstaff?" Morgan tried to stop her. "Sheila, you can't go there!"

"Why not? *Somebody* has to! My daughter is missing!"

"But let the police handle it!" Morgan cried. "Please, Sheila—"

"The police *aren't* handling it! They knew she was there and they just took her at her word!" She turned on Cade. "You should have known she wasn't going to leave until she found what she was after! You should have known!"

Cade took Sheila's shoulders, trying to calm her hysteria. "Sheila, you have to trust me. I'm going to go back to the station and put out an APB that'll extend to the Tybee and Savannah police and the sheriff's departments."

"Marcus Gibson is free," Sheila cried. "What if he sensed her getting closer and came after her?"

Cade looked as if he'd considered that possibility already. "He's been under surveillance, Sheila. He couldn't have done anything like that without being spotted."

"You don't know him," she said. "He's slippery. If anyone could slip out of surveillance, he could!"

"Well, if he has, we'll find out tonight. You can mark my word."

CHAPTER

41

When Cade left Hanover House, he called Yeager at the GBI office and told him Sadie Caruso was missing.

"She has a cell phone with her," Cade said. "I need you to trace the Global Positioning chip in her phone and see if you can locate her."

Yeager got back to him in minutes with the exact coordinates of her phone. It was in a seedy area in Savannah, not a safe place for a teenage girl to be. "I've sent some men over there. Hold tight, and I'll get back to you."

It was nearing midnight. What could Sadie possibly be doing in that part of town? Had she been taken there against her will? He turned his car around and headed there. If they found her, he wanted to be the one to bring her home.

His phone rang when he was halfway there.

"Bad news, Cade."

Cade's heart sank. He wasn't sure he wanted to hear it. "What, Yeager?"

"They found Sadie's purse with her cell phone in it, but it was in the backseat of an old Volvo at a bar called Rover's. Car was abandoned. No identification. When we ran the tag, we saw that the car was reported stolen last month."

"Are they interviewing the people in the bar?"

"As we speak. But it's a popular place, and there are a lot of people to question. They're also running prints. Meanwhile, it looks like we've got another missing girl. Maybe Sadie's with her sister."

Cade slammed his hand against the steering wheel. Why hadn't he gone to the Flagstaff himself when he heard from her today? Sheila was right. He should have known Sadie was stubborn enough to stay there until she got what she wanted.

What had she told him? His mind raced back through their conversation. She'd learned that Gibson had been seen hanging around at the Flagstaff.

His jaw popped as he ground his teeth together and headed to the DA's house. He would wake him up and convince him to issue another search warrant for Gibson's house. The DA gave him one without a fight.

Cade found the GBI agent, who had Gibson under surveillance, sitting in his dark car on the street in front of Gibson's house, his windows rolled down. He'd already been warned that Cade was coming and gave him a quick rundown on Gibson's activities throughout the day. The man hadn't left home at all since yesterday. He hadn't so much as poked his head out the door, and the "lifeguard" who'd been posted on the beach said he hadn't come out the back way, either.

Cade knew better than to rest on that. Gibson was sneaky, and his imagination might prove useful as he tried to find ways to evade the authorities. It was possible he'd gotten out of the house without their notice.

Armed with the search warrant, Cade led the way as they went to Gibson's door. Scott Crown, Alex Johnson, and Joe McCormick scattered out around the house, while the GBI agent came with him.

Cade knocked on the front. "Open up, Gibson! Police!"

He heard footsteps through the house, the bolt being unlocked. The porch light came on, and Gibson stuck his head out, squinting as if he'd been snatched from sleep. "You could have rung the bell, gentlemen. Less dramatic, I realize, but certainly as effective."

The man's smugness made Cade want to spit. "We have a warrant to search your house again, Gibson."

"For what?"

"For Sadie Caruso, another teenage girl who's come up missing."

"And I'm supposed to know where she is? Tell me, gentlemen, how do you suppose I abducted a girl when I've had police guarding my house day and night?"

Cade went in and looked around. The place was still a chaos of clutter. Joe headed through the house, searching for any sign of Sadie.

"You're not going to find anything." Gibson watched them go from room to room. "I haven't been out of the house. I've written fifty pages longhand over the last twenty-four hours. Here it is." He brandished the yellow legal pads with his scrawl all over them. "You're welcome to read it. And surely you have my phones tapped. You must know I haven't even made a phone call in the last day. I'm clearly being set up for this. Chief Cade, you must see that, especially now, since you were set up too."

Cade turned back to him, wondering what he knew about that. "How do you know I was set up?"

"I heard them discussing it in your police station. It isn't difficult to eavesdrop through those walls." Gibson shook his head. "I'm telling you, we're both being played. In fact, I thought of proof—something that might help you find the real killer if you'll just listen. But I'll need my computer to show you."

Cade shot him a disbelieving look. "I can't give your computer back to you. The state has it as evidence."

"Yes, of course they do. They took it because of some incriminating file in which they claim that I described the last murder in my work in progress. However, I maintain that I did not write that scene. Someone else either came in here and altered my work, or they hacked into my computer and did it. And if it was the latter, I think I can prove it."

"We're not going to let you alter the evidence, Gibson, so you can let go of that idea right now."

Gibson's expression revealed his rising agitation. "Chief Cade, there's a feature on Microsoft Word called 'Track Changes.' Writers and editors use it all the time, so that we can see the changes the editors make on our work. After the editor sends me my edits, I'm able to see what was altered. When that feature is turned on, it records every change that's made. I had that feature turned on, so it might hold a clue as to who got into my work and changed it."

"How could it show that?"

"When it's on, it makes my work come out in blue. My editor's changes are in red. I can see every single change that's made in a document. And in case I ever wonder which editor did what, I can click on the change and see whose initials are beside it."

Cade laughed. "I doubt seriously if there was a hacker that he would have signed his initials on his work."

"He might not have realized he did it. When you get a new computer, one of the first things you do to set it up is to give it profile information about yourself. One of the things you give it is your initials. The computer provides that in Track Changes. I don't have to tell it it's me, it just knows because I'm on my computer."

"So if, by some wild stretch of the imagination, you were telling us the truth, and someone else inserted that stuff into your book, how do you know they didn't break in and use your own computer to do it?"

"That's possible. And if that's what happened, then it would seem to be my work, with my initials. It would be more difficult to prove, other than the fact that it's so obviously not my style. The grammar was terrible, the punctuation was awful . . . I would never have produced anything that poor."

"You told us your first drafts were terrible. You said that you burn them."

"I do, but they're not *that* bad! Even my *worst* effort is better than that." He thrust the legal pad back at Cade. "Read that. It's not what I'd consider publishable, but for heaven's sake, it's better than the average drivel. The person who inserted that scene didn't know how to construct a simple sentence. I'm a university English professor, for heaven's sake."

Cade realized that made sense. He'd wondered why a professor of his magnitude would have written something so amateurish.

"You see, it would have been so easy to hack into my wireless computer. All someone would have to do is park outside my house with their own wireless computer, and they would be on my server. I have file sharing enabled, so they could tap into my files and change them. My colleagues have warned me about this for years, but I never got a firewall, never took any measures to protect myself. I thought I lived a secluded enough life that no one would do such a thing. But clearly, this is a game, and whoever the killer is, he wants me to take the fall. And perhaps he's trying to take you down as well, Chief Cade."

Cade thought about that shoe in his truck. There obviously was someone out there trying to throw the police off. But how did he know it wasn't Gibson? The evidence was too strong.

Gibson's face seemed less preoccupied and more intense than it had been since Cade met him. "All I'm asking is that you examine the evidence you have. The Georgia Bureau of Investigation must have a computer person on staff, someone who knows what he's doing. It might be a way to identify the killer."

Joe came back, shaking his head. Cade and the GBI agent stepped to the side with him. "Nothing," Joe said.

Cade might have known. He looked at the agent. "Did you check on phone calls?"

"Sure did. He was telling the truth. No calls in the last twenty-four hours, and my men are certain that he never left the house."

"The DA's going to pull the plug. If he's got a confirmed alibi, then we don't have probable cause."

McCormick looked at Cade. "Maybe we are barking up the wrong tree."

"But he's been living in the woods. He wrote the scene . . ." Cade glanced back at Gibson, who was sweating profusely, his gray, Einstein hair looking as if he'd come out of a wind tunnel. Maybe . . . just maybe, the man was telling the truth.

"All right, let's go check out his computer story, see if it turns up anything."

McCormick nodded.

Cade drew in a deep breath and walked back over to Gibson. "We're going to be watching you, and you won't make a move that we don't see. Got it?"

"I'm being set up, Chief Cade, just as you were when you found the body in the grotto."

"Why would someone set both of us up? That doesn't even make sense. It makes a lot more sense that one of us is guilty and is trying to pin it on the other."

"But I don't believe you're guilty, Chief Cade."

Cade almost laughed. "I wasn't the one of us I was talking about, Gibson. But thanks a lot for that vote of confidence."

"Perhaps your perpetrator has a God complex. Just wants to have power over two powerful men." Gibson didn't look all that powerful, sitting there with that demented hairdo. "Maybe he wanted to hedge all his bets. Make sure that one of us took the fall in case it wouldn't stick on the other one. Or maybe it's all part of some game."

As Cade left Gibson's house, he drove to the GBI office. He'd get them to examine the computer file and see if any of what Gibson had told him was true. As eccentric as the man seemed, he did make sense.

But if Gibson didn't have Sadie, who did?

CHAPTER

42

It finally occurred to Sheila to look in Sadie's room. Maybe she would find a note, if she looked hard enough. Maybe something Sadie had jotted on a piece of paper would tell her that she hadn't done something stupid.

She stepped into her daughter's room. It was clean, as Sadie often kept it. That was her way of keeping some order in her life when her family was in turmoil and everything else was out of control.

But on her made-up bed, Sheila saw the pages of Amelia's journal. Sheila had finished reading what she'd had, but hadn't realized Sadie had more. She picked up the pages and started to read.

> Meanwhile, we're stuck in this place, and I keep trying to get Jamie to go out, but she's fascinated listening to the conversation outside. We've got our curtains closed, but the windows are open, and she's engrossed in a conversation

going on outside our window. Two guys, chewing each other out in harsh whispers, thinking no one hears. One of them has the room next door. Why they don't fight in there is beyond me. They apparently don't know we can hear. Guess I'll go tune in, see what we can find out. It's better than any other entertainment we've got.

She dropped the page as if it had burned her. "*Morgan*!"

Morgan came running up the stairs, Jonathan behind her. "What is it?"

Sheila thrust the page at them, and Morgan read. "Oh, no wonder she went there!"

"I'm going there now!" Sheila pushed past her and started for the stairs.

"No, Sheila, you can't. Please!"

Sheila pulled away from Morgan's grasp. "It's my fault. It's all my fault! I have to go!"

"How is it your fault?" Morgan demanded.

"If it hadn't been for my actions, Amelia wouldn't have come looking for me and she wouldn't have gotten kidnapped. Then Sadie wouldn't have gone looking for *her*."

Jonathan tried to block her. "Sheila, I need you to calm down and just listen to me. If you go to the Flagstaff, something could happen to you, and then you'd be of no help at all to Sadie or Amelia."

"I should have gone there sooner. It should have been me who found that journal. Me who went out to that motel room and started asking questions. Why does it have to be my children?"

"Because it just was."

She pushed past him and started down the stairs. "Well, it's not too late. I'm going to that motel, and I'm going to find my daughters."

Morgan followed. "Sheila, please don't go!"

"I *have* to. I'm not going to sit here wallowing in self-pity. I'm going to take action. I'll find my daughters. And if they're still alive, I'm going to get them back."

Morgan followed her down and into the kitchen where the car keys were hung. "Sheila, I want you to stay here."

"I need to take the car, Jonathan. Please, I need your permission."

"No, you don't have my permission! You can't go. I won't let you."

"Then I'll take it against your will! *My children's lives are at stake.* Don't you understand?" She started out the door, and Morgan followed her out to the porch.

"Sheila, let us go with you! Please—"

Sheila heard a choked yelp as she reached the car, and she turned back around.

Morgan was bent over, groping her stomach in pain.

Jonathan leaped off the porch and ran to her. "Honey, are you all right?"

Morgan didn't answer, just moaned as the contraction held on.

Sheila stopped, frozen. She couldn't leave Morgan like this.

As the contraction eased, Morgan relaxed. Suddenly water trickled down her leg. "Oh, no! My water broke!"

"She's in labor!" Jonathan yelled. "I've got to get her to the hospital."

Sheila just stared at them, knowing he was right.

"You have to stay here," Jonathan said. "You've got Caleb asleep upstairs. Felicia's sleeping too, and she's not good with Caleb. Let the police handle the search for Sadie."

Sheila didn't say anything as Jonathan took Morgan out to the car. "Pray for us!" he shouted. "The baby's a month early. It's too soon."

She wanted to scream that she didn't have time to worry about Morgan or her baby, that her own children were in much more immediate danger. But she only stood there, crying.

"I mean it, Sheila," Jonathan called from the car. "Stay here!"

Sheila stood on the porch and watched them pull out. When they were gone, she went into the kitchen, grabbed the other set of keys. But she couldn't leave Caleb alone.

She didn't trust Felicia to wake up if Caleb needed her, so she called Karen, who had been a former member of the household until she'd moved out to marry another resident.

Gus answered the phone. "Hello?"

"Gus, this is Sheila Caruso. I'm sorry to call so late, but it's an emergency. Can I speak to Karen?"

"Sure, mon. What's wrong?"

"Morgan's gone to the hospital. She's in labor."

"This soon?"

"That's right. And Sadie's missing. I have to go look for her."

"What?"

"Please, can I speak to Karen?"

Karen came on the line, her voice raspy with sleep. "Hello?"

"Karen, could you come over and babysit for me? It's an emergency."

She heard Gus's voice mumbling softly across the wire, and she knew he was informing her about Morgan. "Of course, Sheila. I'll be right over in just a few minutes."

Sheila was pacing on the front porch as Karen drove up in Gus's ten-year-old Toyota. Karen got out and ran to Sheila, threw her arms around her. "Is Morgan gonna be all right?"

"I don't know. I haven't heard a thing."

"What about Sadie?"

"Sadie's in a lot of trouble." Sheila started to cry again. "Oh, Karen, I've got to go. Please pray that I find her."

"I will. Call me soon as you know something."

Sheila started out to Jonathan's pickup truck, then realized she was going unarmed. She just might need a gun. Morgan and Jonathan had one that they kept in their room. She ran back up onto the porch. "I forgot something. I'll be right back."

Karen nodded and went into the house, turned on the kitchen light, and started making coffee.

Sheila ran up and tiptoed into Morgan and Jonathan's room. Where would she keep a gun, if she had one? Probably right next to the bed, Jonathan's side. She saw his bedroom slippers parked on the right side of the bed, so she went to his bed table and pulled out the drawer. Just as she hoped, the gun lay there. She pulled it out in her trembling hands, checked to see if it was loaded. It wasn't.

She held the weapon in her hand and went through the drawers, looking for bullets. Of course he wouldn't keep the gun loaded. There were ex-cons in this house, former drug addicts . . . He wouldn't be stupid enough to leave a loaded gun where anyone could take it.

But the bullets had to be somewhere. She went through every drawer, found nothing, then tried the closet. There was nothing on the shelves that could have contained the bullets, so she ran to their private bathroom. In the bottom drawer of the vanity, she found his shaving kit, unzipped it.

There they were, in a box, at the back of the kit, next to a new tube of toothpaste. Her hands trembled as she loaded the gun. She double-checked the safety, then tucked it into the waistband of her jeans, pulled her shirt over it, and ran back outside.

She would do whatever she had to do to get her daughters back.

And she didn't care what the consequences were.

The flashing lights from half a dozen police cars lit up the Flagstaff Motel when Sheila pulled Jonathan's truck into the parking lot. A crowd of tenants leaned over the rails on the second floor, watching the activity as the cops went in and out of the room next door to Amelia and Jamie's. She saw Joe in his car with the driver's door open, talking into his radio, so she went over and leaned in.

"Joe, what have you found out?"

He held out a hand as he finished the call, then he turned to Sheila. "We haven't found Sadie, but we're trying to run down all the information we can about this guy named Nate."

"Nate?"

"Yeah, he was the one in the room next to Jamie and Amelia."

"Then he's the one Sadie came here to find." She peered up at the room. "Is he there?"

"Nope. Nobody knows where he is."

"What about Gibson?"

"We don't think he's involved, Sheila. He's under heavy surveillance." She heard someone call Joe's name from the room in question, and Joe got out. "I'll be right back. Looks like I'm needed."

She nodded and stood by his car, watching him run up the stairs and into Nate's room. Had they found any evidence that Sadie was there, that there was a struggle, that her daughter was taken against her will? Did they know what kind of car Nate drove, where he lived when he wasn't in the motel?

Then she looked on the seat of Joe's car, saw a writing pad on his seat. It was the pad he kept in his shirt pocket all the time. He'd been jotting on it as he'd radioed for information, and he'd left it here.

She looked around, hoping no one would see her, and slipped inside the car. She tore the page off of the pad, stuck it into her pocket, then slipped back out of the car. No one had noticed.

She hurried back into Jonathan's truck and looked at the paper. There was an address written there. Sheila started the truck and headed to Hinesville to find that address. If that was where this Nate person lived, maybe it was possible that both of her daughters were there.

She prayed that they were still alive.

CHAPTER

44

Blair raced to the hospital as soon as she got the phone call that her sister was in labor. When she arrived, she couldn't find a parking space. "It's the middle of the night, for Pete's sake! What are they having, a convention?"

She double-parked, ran inside, and bolted up to the information desk. "My sister just checked in. She's in labor. Morgan Cleary."

The elderly woman at the desk took her time typing Morgan's name into her computer. "Yes, here she is. Room 403. The elevators are that way, dear."

Blair dashed toward the elevators, almost taking out a nurse and a man in a wheelchair.

The elevator wouldn't come, so she ran to the exit door and headed up the stairs. By the time she reached the fourth floor, she was dripping with perspiration.

She saw room 426 and took off down the hall, counting down as she went. Finally, she came to her sister's door.

She burst inside and saw Morgan in the bed, soaked with her own sweat, clutching Jonathan's hand as a contraction gripped her.

A doctor and nurse at the foot of her bed turned as Blair shot in. "I'm her sister. Is she all right?"

Jonathan looked up at Blair but kept whispering to Morgan. "Breathe, honey . . . come on, baby, one, two, three . . ."

"She's doing fine," the doctor said in a low voice. "We're about to take her to delivery. She's fully dilated and ready to go."

Morgan came out of the contraction, and Blair could see her relaxing.

"Blair, I'm glad you're here . . ."

She went to Morgan's side and took her hand as the nurse busied herself unlocking the bed so they could move it. "They can't be delivering the baby! Isn't it too soon? Can't they stop it?"

"No," Morgan said. "I'm too far. The baby's coming."

Blair shot Jonathan a distressed look. "It's okay," he said, but she saw the fear on his face. "Babies come early all the time."

"That's right." The doctor smiled as they got the bed moving. "We have an excellent neonatal staff here. And the baby's heartbeat is strong."

Blair waited as they pushed Morgan into the hallway, and then she caught up and walked beside it.

"Are you coming with her?" the nurse asked. "If you are, you'll need to change into some sterile scrubs."

Blair looked down at Morgan. "Do you want me to come?"

Morgan shook her head. "Stay here. I want you to call home and find out if Sheila's still there."

"Why?"

"Because I'm worried about her. She was trying to go to the Flagstaff to find Sadie. She's missing, Blair. We can't find her anywhere, but if Sheila went to that motel, there's no telling what might happen to her."

Blair looked across Morgan to Jonathan. "Is that why Morgan went into labor? Because of the stress about Sadie?"

"No doubt," he said.

Another contraction clamped on Morgan, and she pulled her legs up and moaned. Blair touched her sister's shoulder, wishing there was something she could do to help. But Jonathan was right there with her as they hurried down the hall, talking her through the pain in a calm voice.

When they reached the double doors to Labor and Delivery, Blair hung back. "Take care of her, Jonathan."

"I will, Blair. Pray, okay? Pray hard."

She watched as her sister disappeared through the doors. As they swung shut behind them, she felt as if the world had plummeted out of control again.

Her sister was in labor, Sadie was missing, Amelia might be dead, Cade was implicated, and now . . . Sheila. Blair pulled her cell phone out and called Hanover House. A voice Blair didn't recognize answered the phone.

"Who's this?"

"Karen. Is that you, Blair?"

"Yes, what are you doing there?"

"Babysitting Caleb. Sheila called me—"

"Oh, no. Where did she go?"

"She said she was going to look for Sadie."

Just as Morgan feared. Blair leaned her forehead against the wall. *Now* what?

"How is Morgan?"

Blair tried to refocus her thoughts. "She just went into delivery. Please pray for her. The baby's too early."

"Call me when she comes out, okay, Blair?"

"I will. And do me a favor. If you hear from either Sheila or Sadie, please call me at this number."

"Sheila seemed really upset about Sadie," Karen said. "I wouldn't put it past her to walk into something dangerous. I'll call you if I hear from her."

Blair clicked her phone off, then dialed Cade's cell phone number. She knew he hadn't been to bed yet tonight.

"Chief Cade."

"Cade, it's me."

"Hey, babe. How's Morgan?"

"In delivery. Listen, Morgan's worried about Sheila. She left Hanover House to go to the Flagstaff. She was panicked and desperate to find Sadie. I'm worried she might get into trouble."

"I'm at the Flagstaff right now. Sheila was here for a few minutes, but she left."

"Left? Where did she go?"

"I don't know. She didn't say. I figured she just went back home after she saw that we had things under control here."

"She didn't."

He sighed, and Blair couldn't blame him. The last thing he needed was another missing person. "I don't know, but I'll try to find out. I'll call you back if I learn anything."

Blair hung up and dropped the phone back into her pocket, then stood there, staring at those doors. She started to cry. She should have argued with Morgan and gone in with her. What would her mother have done?

If only her parents were here with her, reassuring her and praying with her. They would have words of comfort and faith. Her mother was supposed to be here at a moment like this. She was supposed to celebrate the news of her grandchild's birth, praying for safe entrance into the world.

Blair went to the waiting area and sat down, trying to trust God. She knew He could orchestrate things perfectly to bring a healthy, beautiful baby to her sister. But He'd allowed Morgan to lose a baby before.

Please, God, let this be a day of joy and not a day of grief.

Those fateful words—"Not my will, but Thine"—hung on her tongue. But for the life of her, she was unable to speak them.

CHAPTER
45

Daylight dawned by the time Sheila found the address in Hinesville, twenty-five miles southwest of Cape Refuge. The address was a route number on a rural road, and there was no way to tell which dirt road to turn down. She'd ambushed a mailman as he loaded his truck out in back of the post office, and she flirted with him just enough to get the information she needed.

She made a few drive-bys first to check out the layout and realized that the moment she pulled her car down the drive, whoever lived there would be alerted that she was there. Instead, she parked her car about half a mile down on the side of the road and walked the rest of the way.

She stayed in the trees as she followed the driveway down to the house. It looked as if there were about five acres here, a little run-down house at the front of the property, and a ramshackle barn at the back. Thick trees covered most of the land, and as she made her way up to the house, Sheila skimmed those trees, staring hard at the buildings.

Were Sadie or Amelia in there somewhere?

The only vehicle on the property was an old rusty pickup truck with grass growing beneath it. It looked as if it hadn't been moved in months, maybe even years.

She tried to decide on a strategy to get into the house and look around, but it was too dangerous. She sure wouldn't do Sadie and Amelia any good if she offered herself up freely to the murderer. But as she came out of the trees, she realized a strategy might not be needed. An old man who looked as if he were pushing a hundred sat rocking on the front porch, staring off into space.

He looked as if a strong wind might shatter his bones into dust. Surely this wasn't the killer! But maybe he knew something. Maybe she should just hide until he went back inside, then peer through the windows, searching out the property . . .

But what if she was at the wrong place, wasting time while her children's lives were ticking away?

There was only one way to know for sure. She had to approach him. And say what? What if Nate was inside, watching through the windows? What if he recognized her as being related to Sadie and Amelia?

It was a chance she had to take. She thought of the story she would tell, about what had brought her here. *My car just broke down, and I was wondering if I could use your phone.* Yes, that might work. If the old man was here alone, then maybe he would believe her.

Slowly, she emerged from the woods.

The old man caught sight of her, and he stopped rocking and stood up.

Sheila's heart pounded so hard that she thought it might beat through her chest. She froze. "Hello," she said in a weak voice.

The old man laughed with delight. "Come right on up here, young lady! I been waiting for you! You look purtier'n your mama. Come give your ol' daddy a hug."

She stood there a moment as his words sank in. Did he think she was his daughter? Wouldn't he realize she wasn't as she got closer?

She forced herself to move and took a few steps toward him. "How are you?"

His eyes glistened as he wobbled toward her, his arms stretched out wide. "Oh, Ruby, you're just a sight for sore eyes!" He threw his arms around her and laughed as he held her.

He was weak and shaky, and he seemed so certain she was his daughter. She let him hold her and realized it wouldn't hurt anything if she hugged him back. There was no emptier feeling than hugging someone who stood stone cold, and he didn't seem the kind of man who deserved that. So she closed her arms around him.

His shoulders shook as he wept, and he pulled back and looked into her face. He would see now that she was not his daughter.

"I got some eggs, Ruby." His raspy voice lilted with delight. He let her go and clapped his hands. "In here, darlin.'" He opened the door and stepped into the dark house. "Mama! You'll never guess who come to see us."

Sheila's heart raced as she followed him into the dark house. She looked around for some sign of a murdering maniac. Instead, she saw a small living room with threadbare furniture and thick dust floating on the sunlight coming through the windows. The air was thick with the smell of mold and urine. She reached for the light switch, turned it on. One of the four lightbulbs in the overhead fixture worked—the others had all burned out.

His kitchen was covered with old, dirty, crusted-over dishes, but a vase of fresh cut flowers sat among them. She peered up the dark hall, wondering if his wife would come bustling out and scream at the top of her lungs when she saw the stranger standing in her house.

But no one came.

He led her into the filthy kitchen and reached into the refrigerator, but there was little there. "Musta ate them eggs. I'll have to make a list for Nate. Mama needs some milk, anyways."

She caught her breath. "Is . . . is Nate here?"

He didn't answer, and she realized he was almost deaf. She didn't want to raise her voice, for fear that Nate slept somewhere in the house.

The old man busied himself moving dishes around, humming a song. He dropped one and it broke on the floor, and he looked rattled as he turned around, clearly looking for a broom.

Sheila backed away and looked up the hall. If she walked through there, looked into the rooms, surely he would think it was a natural thing. Wouldn't his daughter do that?

"Don't know where I put that broom. I'd lose my head if it wasn't nailed on."

As he muttered, she went up the hall. There were only two bedrooms and a bathroom, and she looked into the first one. The bed was unmade, the sheets were dirty, and a lifetime accumulation of junk was piled high. She went to the next room. A twin bed was pushed against the wall. A man's clothes lay over a chair and were strewn across the floor, and several pairs of dirty sneakers lay on a round rug. A book lay open on the bed. She closed it, and saw the cover.

In Cold Blood.

The blood drained from her face. She'd read that book in prison. It was full of graphic descriptions of a horrible mass murder by crazed, sociopathic killers. She thought she might faint. She reached out to the dresser to steady herself. *Think. Maybe Sadie was here.*

She forced herself to move, to go to the drawers and pull them out one by one. There was nothing there to incriminate Nate. Just that book.

No one else was here. No mama . . . no Nate.

She went back to the old man as he started to bend over to pick up the pieces of the plate. "Here, let me! I'll get it."

"You're a good girl."

She picked up the pieces of the crusty dish, knowing that it hardly made a difference with the sticky film of filth on the floor. But it seemed to satisfy him. She raised up and looked around for a garbage can. It was overflowing, so she just placed the pile against the wall. "Where is Nate?"

"At school, I reckon."

School? How old was he?

"Has he been here lately? In the last few days, I mean. Has he brought anyone here with him?"

"He's gettin' so big now. School bus drops him off sometimes, and he comes to see his ol' grandpa. Come over here and I'll make you some eggs."

He went to the refrigerator again, just as he had done before, and as he opened it, he simply stared inside, as if lost in thought. She went to stand beside him and looked at his wizened old face. His mouth hung open, and his eyes looked blank. He'd clearly forgotten what he was doing.

"Sir?"

He looked at her then, confusion clear on his face, and this time there was no recognition, no delight, no awareness at all.

It reminded her of one of her cell mates in prison—Liza, who'd later been diagnosed with Alzheimer's. She would have moments of lucidity, but more moments of confusion. She remembered her childhood but nothing of today, and each time she saw Sheila or the other inmates, she called them by different names.

Maybe this man had Alzheimer's too. Sheila took his arm and closed the refrigerator, then escorted him over to a chair. He lowered to it, that blank look making his eyes look more shadowed, his skin more pale.

She took the opportunity to look around the room. A picture of a boy—about ten years old—sat on the table. She picked it up and took it to the old man, stooped down in front of him.

"Sir." Maybe she could shake him back into whatever fantasy world he'd just come out of. "Sir, who is this?"

He stared down at the picture for a long moment, then whispered, "My boy. Finer grandson nobody ever had. Nate."

Nate. She studied his young face, trying to figure out what he might look like now.

She saw another picture of the boy, but he was older in this one. He looked dirty and greasy and had a cigarette hanging out of his mouth.

She stood up, her eyes fixed on the face of the man she was certain had taken her daughters. He was about twenty in the

picture, with an unshaven face and stringy hair. His eyes had
that hungover, secretive, dangerous look—eyes just like Jack
Dent's, Caleb's father. It was a deadly look, a look that said he
had much to hide, a look that dared anyone to cross him.

"Is this Nate too?"

He smiled. "He's a good boy."

She put the picture back and stooped in front of the old man
again. "I need you to listen to me." His eyes fastened on her, and
she thought for a moment that he might actually be listening.
"Has Nate brought anyone here with him? A pretty blonde girl?"

That vacant look almost sent her over the edge. "Nate's a
good boy."

"Listen to me! I need you to think. There are two girls,
blondes, and I think he brought them here! Where are they?"

He didn't answer, so she framed his face in her trembling
hands. "Where are they? Please, answer me!"

He opened his mouth to speak, and she waited, breath held.

"I'll make some eggs," he muttered.

She started to cry then and got up, looking down at him.
How did he manage here alone, completely out of his mind? He
needed twenty-four-hour care, someone to keep him company.
Someone to watch over him.

Nate could have brought anyone here, kicking and screaming,
bleeding, maybe even dead, and the old man wouldn't remember.

She heard a car coming up the driveway, the rocks crackling
beneath its tires. She ran to the window and looked out. The car
stopped, and she saw the same greasy-haired man get out. *Nate!*
She was certain it was him.

She had to get out of there before he came into the house,
so she slipped out the back door and hid until she heard the man
get out of the car and go inside. Even if his grandfather remembered she'd been there, Nate wouldn't believe him. The old man's
dementia was too pronounced, and Nate probably heard non-
sense from him all the time.

She dashed across the yard and went to the barn. Quietly,
she opened the creaking door and slipped inside. The only light

coming through was the daylight through a window, so she went to the string hanging from the lightbulb and turned it on.

The hay smelled putrid. She walked from stall to stall, searching for her daughters, but no one was here. She looked around at all the farming implements, rusty and covered with cobwebs, leaning against the wall. No, it didn't look like anyone had been here in quite some time.

She abandoned the building through the back way and went into the thick woods behind it. Cutting through the bushes was a beaten path. There were footsteps on it, big ones and small ones. Could they be Sadie's? Amelia's? Sheila's heart hammered hard as she followed the tracks, certain she was getting closer to finding her girls. They could both be dead out here, buried in a shallow grave, and she would stumble on their bodies. If she did, she would want to lie down with them.

But maybe they were alive, waiting to be found. Maybe it wouldn't be too late.

Suddenly she saw it. A trap door in the ground that looked like it could be a tornado shelter, and a rope ladder pulled out of the hole, lying wadded on the dirt.

She went to the door, struggled to get it open, but it was heavy. Pulling with all her might, she managed to pull it up. She looked down into the large dark pit, and shivered with anticipation.

"Sadie?" Her voice came out choked and too loud. "Sadie, are you there?"

"*Mom?*"

Sadie's voice. She was alive! Sheila almost collapsed with relief. Closing her eyes, she whispered, "Thank You, God." She gathered herself and leaned over the hole, trying to see in. "Honey, you're alive! Are you all right?"

"Yes, Mom! Hurry, put the ladder down!"

Sheila reached for the ladder, then froze as she heard something moving behind her. She started to turn, when pain cracked across the back of her skull . . .

And Sheila fell forward.

CHAPTER

46

Sadie and Amelia screamed as their mother plummeted through the hole and dropped flat on the dirt floor.

Sadie scrambled to her mother, who lay facedown in her own blood. "Mom! Mom, wake up, please wake up, please!"

Sheila didn't move, so Sadie turned her over. Her head lolled back, her face scraped and bleeding from the impact. Sadie looked up at the open door, saw Nate's silhouette. "She's dying! She needs an ambulance!"

He just laughed.

"Please! Please, just come and get her, take her to the hospital. You can leave us here. Just get her help, please!" There was no answer, so her screams went up an octave. "You *monster*! You help her! Come and help her now." At his continued laughter, her screams turned into sobs. She closed her eyes and wailed. "Please, I'm begging you. She didn't do anything to you."

He kept laughing—a hard, brittle laugh that chilled her bones. He dropped the door shut above them, and

Sadie knew he was going to let her mother die, right here in this rat hole, and there wasn't a thing in the world that she and Amelia could do.

She felt Amelia's hands on her shoulders, heard her own anguished crying. She tried to pull herself together. "We have to help her. We have to save her somehow."

"She's breathing." Amelia's wet, streaked face was hopeful as she went to touch Sheila's wrist. "She has a pulse, Sadie!"

Blood ran from her mother's nose and mouth, and Sadie tried to see if it was from some internal bleeding or from the impact of her face on the floor. She was bleeding from the back of her skull too, where she'd clearly been hit. How could anyone survive a sixteen-foot fall onto her face?

Amelia's hands were covered with blood as she tried to stop the bleeding on the back of her mother's head. "Her arm looks broken."

Sadie turned her attention to Sheila's arm. It was strangely bent from the elbow, and beneath the skin, she could see the end of the bone. Her leg was unnaturally bent, as well. Had she broken it too?

Sadie went back to her mother's face, held it in both hands. "Mom! Please wake up, Mom. Please tell me you're all right."

There was no answer. Her mother's eyes were closed, her bloody mouth hanging open.

"How did she find us?" Amelia said. "How did she know where we were?"

Sadie looked up at her, her eyes wildly hopeful. "Maybe someone came with her."

"Then where are they?"

She looked up at the door again, praying for help. But she feared there was none.

She touched her mother's good arm, stroking it as she wept over her. She bumped something in Sheila's pocket, and reached in to see what it was. Slowly, she pulled out a gun.

Sadie caught her breath. "It's a miracle."

"Is it loaded?"

Sadie checked. "Yes. Where did she get this?"

"It doesn't matter. It's here now. He doesn't know she has it, or he wouldn't have thrown her down here with it. We can use it."

Sadie nodded. She could almost imagine it—Nate opening that door, putting that rope ladder down. As he descended to terrorize them, completely unaware, she would raise it in the darkness. He wouldn't see it as his eyes adjusted to the light, and he would walk into the trap.

She wiped her face on her shirtsleeve. "I want to do it."

"You don't have to," Amelia said. "I'm not afraid to."

Sadie sucked in a shaky sob and looked down at her mother. "No, it has to be me. He's so fascinated with the sound of bodies dropping. I want to be the one to drop him into the pit of hell."

CHAPTER

47

The moment Joe came back to his car in the Flagstaff parking lot, he knew that Sheila had taken the address on his notepad. His heart sank. Cade was coming toward him as he got out of his car. "I know where she is."

"Sheila? Where?"

"She took that address I got for Nate out of my car. I guarantee you she's headed to Hinesville, if she isn't there already."

Cade closed his eyes. "Surely she wouldn't just go barreling up in there without waiting for us. She's not crazy."

"She's desperate. Who knows what she might do? I don't even know how long she's been gone."

Cade looked back at the second floor, where the room was being searched. The GBI agents had shown up and taken over. Their men had spread out and were talking to the residents from room to room.

Cade found Yeager and filled him in on what was happening. "I'm going to head to Hinesville."

"Yeah, I'll get some of my men out there too," Yeager said.

McCormick was already in his car, starting to pull out of the glutted parking lot. Cade opened his passenger door and got in. "Yeager's sending people."

"We can't wait for them. Sheila's in trouble. We have to hurry."

"Hey, I'm sold, buddy. Let's go. Maybe we'll make it before she does anything stupid."

CHAPTER

48

Cade's distinctive ring startled Blair out of her prayer, and she clicked her cell phone on. "Hello?"

"Blair, it's me." He was out of breath, and she could hear the siren in the background. "We think we know where Sheila is. She took some notes out of McCormick's car, with our suspect's address in Hinesville."

"The suspect? You think she went to his house?"

"We're headed that way now."

"Cade, who is it?"

"A man named Nate Morris. He and a buddy were next door to Amelia and Jamie at the Flagstaff. We have reason to believe Sadie figured it out and confronted him. That's the last anyone's seen her."

She got up, wishing she could run out of there and follow them, but she couldn't leave the hospital. "Please be careful."

He didn't answer. "Has Morgan had the baby yet?"

"Not yet."

"Miss Owens?"

Blair swung around and saw a nurse standing by the swinging double doors, a mask around her chin. "The nurse is here, Cade. I have to go."

"I love you."

"I love you too."

She clicked off the phone and hurried to the nurse. "Has she had the baby yet?"

The nurse grinned. "She sure has. Why don't you go in and let her tell you if you have a niece or nephew? She's in Delivery Room B."

The grin was a good sign, Blair thought as she pushed through the doors. Surely the nurse wouldn't be grinning if something had gone wrong.

She found Delivery Room B and saw Jonathan bent over Morgan. "Morgan!" Blair almost couldn't get her sister's name out.

Jonathan rose up, and Morgan reached for her. She had a smile on her face, and her cheeks were covered with tears and sweat.

"Is it—?"

"It's a boy! Oh, Blair, he's a beautiful, healthy little boy."

"Healthy? Are you sure?"

"He came out screaming bloody murder," Jonathan said with a grin. "The doctor said his lungs sounded fine. They're testing him to make sure."

Blair started to cry and bent down to hug her sister. "Oh, Morgan, I was so scared."

"Me too."

"He's a little small," Jonathan said, "only five pounds, but they think he's perfect."

Blair clapped her hands together and brought her fingertips to her mouth. She looked at her sister. "How are you?"

Morgan laughed. "I've never been better."

Jonathan wiped the hair back from his wife's face. "She was a trooper. Just like she's done it before."

"So did you talk to Sheila?" Morgan asked.

Blair looked at Jonathan, not certain what to say. Should she bring her sister down in her moment of her greatest joy? No, she couldn't do it. Morgan didn't have to know that Sheila was missing.

"I talked to almost everybody." She forced herself to laugh. "Everyone was praying, Morgan. They're all so anxious to hear."

"What about Sadie? Did they find her yet?"

Again, she felt caught in the headlights, and she looked helplessly at Jonathan. She thought of lying, but she wouldn't get away with it. She started to speak, when she heard a baby crying.

She turned and saw the nurse bringing her tiny little nephew in. She covered her mouth at the sight of the screaming infant. "Oh, he's so beautiful."

Morgan raised up to take him. "How is he?"

"He's wonderful. Lungs are fully developed. Except for his low birth weight, you wouldn't know he was a preemie. The doctor wondered if you might have even gotten your due date wrong."

Morgan kissed her son's little cheek. "It's okay, little Wayne, Mama's here."

Blair caught her breath. "Wayne. You named him after Pop." She looked down at the tiny bundle, nestled in Morgan's arms, and tears came to her eyes.

The baby kept screaming, and Morgan pulled him gently up to her shoulder and kissed his cheek as she rubbed his back. His crying settled as his mother whispered and cooed to him, and finally he was silent.

Morgan brought him back down and cradled him in her arm, and he looked up at her with clear, round eyes. "You look like you know everything," Morgan whispered. "Like you're wiser than I am. You came here straight from God. What do you know, little one? What could you tell us?"

Blair watched, awed, as her sister—the proverbial Earth Mother—settled into the role she'd prepared for all her life. The most important role she would ever play.

"Thank You, God." Morgan's prayer was tearful. "Thank You so much. We don't deserve such a precious gift. Make us worthy. Please make us worthy of him."

Jonathan leaned over and kissed the top of Morgan's head, then touched his son's round cheek. "God will equip us. This child's too precious for Him to leave to chance. He has a plan for our boy, and He'll tell us what it is."

Emotions so overwhelmed Blair that she could hardly stand. Would she love a baby of her own even more than this? Could she?

She watched the young family, basking in the glow of the newness of such a gift, and for a moment, she could have sworn she saw her mother and father standing there behind them, bent over this little bundle, proud grandparent smiles on their faces, tears of joy in their eyes.

Her heart ached to reach out for them, to throw herself into their arms, to touch their faces one more time, to take a deep breath of their scents—a breath that would get her through the next year. Just one breath, she thought. Just one touch.

But then she realized her eyes hadn't really seen them. Her heart just felt them near. She squeezed her mouth tight as the tears rolled down her face.

"Look at him, Mama," Morgan whispered. "See how beautiful he is, Pop?" She sucked in a sob and looked up at Blair. For a moment their tearful gazes locked . . .

And Blair knew.

Their parents were here, somewhere, somehow . . . Maybe just the history, and all the years of their watching over their daughters, had brought them to Morgan's and Blair's minds at the same time. Maybe it was the longing. Maybe it was just wishful thinking.

Or maybe they really were here, watching the event and rooting them on. Maybe God let them have glimpses like this that would make them rejoice, and show them that things were turning out fine.

"Want to hold him, Blair?" Jonathan asked softly.

She nodded, hoping she didn't get the baby wet. She watched, amazed, as Jonathan lifted him carefully from Morgan's arms and put him into her own. She held him, squirming in her arms, and he opened his eyes and squinted up at her. "Hey there, little fella." She barely managed the words through the emotion in her throat. "You know, you've got a pretty big name to live up to. I hope you're up for it."

He wiggled, indicating he was, and then he kicked his foot and brought his fists up in the air, and groaned irritably. Not sure what to do, she gave him to his father. Jonathan sat down with him and spoke to him softly until he settled down.

"You'll have to have a girl now," Blair whispered, "so you can name one after Mama."

"Or *you* could." Morgan smiled.

Blair looked down at her, realizing for the first time that she really *could* be next. She looked down at the diamond on her finger. It was real. She was going to marry Cade and have his children.

Unless something terrible happened tonight . . .

When Morgan started to nurse her son, Jonathan pulled Blair out into the hall. "Wanna tell me now what's going on with Sadie?"

Blair tried to find an answer that wouldn't destroy his joy, but he spoke first.

"She's still missing, isn't she?"

Blair swallowed. "Yes, but Cade says they think they know where she is. They're on their way there now."

"What about Sheila?"

Blair moaned. "I'm sorry, Jonathan, but nobody knows for sure where she is."

He looked past her, his eyes vacant as he stared at the air. Then he shook out of it. "Don't tell Morgan. Keep evading."

"I will. But hopefully it'll all be over soon."

CHAPTER

49

Mom! Mom, open your eyes."

Sheila floated down a long black tunnel, groping for something to grab onto, reaching for anything that would give her footing. But she kept floating, unable to land, and the blackness got blacker, deeper, until the darkness came into her, its lethal edges cutting through her flesh, snapping her bones, crushing her skull.

Her brain was exploding, and electric shocks volted through her arm and leg. *Help me.* The plea was half-formed, with no destination, gonging in her head. *Help me.*

"Mom! Please, Mom. Wake up."

Sadie. It *was* her voice, yet it couldn't be. Sadie was lost, hurt somewhere, and she couldn't get to her.

The voltage pulsed through her, and she heard herself moan.

"She's waking up. Mom!"

Dim light slitted through her eyelids, and she tried to lift them. She wasn't in a black tunnel. She was in a black pit.

Her eyes came open, and she tried to focus.

"Mom! Oh, thank God! Mom, can you hear me?"

"Sadie?" She heard the word rip from her throat, yet she didn't believe it.

"It's me, Mom. He hit you, and you fell."

She tried to focus, to make some order of her random thoughts. Sadie was here. She was alive.

"Mom, Amelia's here too. Look at her, Mom. She's right here."

Amelia. My baby. She forced her mind to function, despite the pain assaulting her. She settled her eyes on the faces above her, willed her eyes to focus. She saw Sadie sitting there, whole, weeping over her. And she saw another girl.

Amelia!

Her daughter was beautiful, just as she'd always imagined her. Petite and delicate, though her face was marred with dirt, sweat, and tears.

"Amelia. Oh, baby." She tried to lift her arms to hug her, but excruciating pain shot through one of them.

"Be still, Mom," Sadie said. "You broke your arm and leg, and you have a really bad head wound. But they're coming to help you. I know they are."

Now she remembered. Joe's notes. The old man. That greasy Nate coming into the house.

"No one knows I'm here. No one knows."

She saw Sadie and Amelia look at each other, helpless, defeated. "I'm sorry," she whispered. "I wanted to save you."

"You did, Mom." Sadie lifted something above her. "You brought this."

The gun! "Yes. It's loaded. I made sure."

She looked at Amelia again, reached up with her good arm, and touched her face. "Oh, baby, you're so pretty. Look at you, my beautiful baby."

Amelia touched her hand. "I've wanted to find you all these years. Not like this, though. I'm so sorry."

"No, no. Don't be sorry," Sheila said. "You did right. It just went wrong."

"My parents . . . do they know I'm missing?"

"Yes, baby. They're on Tybee Island, sick with worry."

Amelia wilted as tears filled her eyes. "Dear God, I hope I see them again."

"Mom, how do you feel?" Sadie cut in. "Are you in pain?"

"Only a little," she lied, "but we're gonna be all right, girls. We're gonna get through this. Your mama's here now. I may be in bad shape, but I'll be all right. God is with us, and I know He's gonna take care of us. Look what He's already done. You're both alive, and He helped me find you. Now He'll help somebody else find us."

CHAPTER

50

From the bottom of the pit that held them prisoner, Sadie heard the sound of feet scrambling above them, the trap door being opened.

Sadie backed against the dirt wall and raised the gun above her head.

"Wait for him," Amelia whispered. "He has to put the ladder down, or we'll never get out."

Sadie was shaking as she kept the gun trained on that hole.

"She dead yet?" Nate's voice sang out above them, then he let out a blood-curdling laugh.

Sadie knew she had to bait him. "I think she's still alive. You've got to help her. Please. We'll do anything you say."

"Like you have a choice." He laughed again. The rope ladder fell in, swinging above her head.

She watched as he stepped onto it.

"Not yet," Amelia whispered.

Sadie was shaking so hard that she thought she would drop the gun. Sweat trickled down her temples into her eyes. Slowly, quietly, she cocked the pistol and put her finger over the trigger.

Nate took one step down, then a second, a third.

"Wait," Amelia whispered again.

Sweat ran down Sadie's forehead and into her eyes, and her heart threatened to beat right through her chest. He stopped on the fourth step, swinging on the ladder, and turned to look down at her.

"*Now*, baby!" Sheila cried out.

Sadie squeezed her finger over the trigger, and the gun went off, its percussion so loud that it almost deafened her.

The bullet missed him, and he scrambled back up the ladder. Frantic, Sadie fired again, hitting his leg, and he cursed and tried to keep going.

"Don't let him get away!" Amelia tore the gun out of Sadie's hands and shot straight up, one, two, three times, each bullet hitting home in his hip, his stomach, his chest . . .

Suddenly he let go of the ropes and fell, plummeting toward them . . . and hit the ground with a thud.

Sadie just stood there, shaking, staring down at him. Blood oozed out of his wounds into the dirt floor. He was dead. He had to be dead.

"Check him for a weapon, baby," Sheila said. "Make sure he's dead."

Sadie willed herself to move, but she seemed paralyzed, frozen. Amelia still held the gun pointed at him, every muscle in her body poised and ready to fire if he made a move.

Finally, Sadie swallowed and touched Amelia's hands, made her lower the gun. She moved closer, touching his ribs with her foot, and shoved slightly.

Nothing.

Slowly, she stooped down next to him. She had to check for a pulse . . . make sure he wasn't alive . . . but his neck was covered with blood. He had fallen on his arms, and they lay beneath his body, so she gently worked one of them out from under him, moved her fingers to the wrist . . .

His hand shot out and grabbed her.

As Sadie screamed, he clamped her wrist and came up from the floor, a switchblade drawn in his other hand. He pulled her against him and brought the blade to her throat.

She fought and struggled, watching as Amelia pulled the gun back up, preparing to fire. But she couldn't. She'd hit *her* with him. She'd kill them both.

"Drop it!" Nate yelled through his teeth. He was getting weaker, breathing hard, but he held the blade solid against her flesh. "Put the gun down, or she's dead."

"Drop the gun, Amelia!" Sheila screamed. "Do what he says, baby."

Sadie felt the blade pressing into her skin. He *wanted* to kill her, and she knew he was going to. There was no way out.

Amelia lowered the gun and began to sob, her lips curling up in pain and fear.

The blade against Sadie's throat didn't ease up. He was going to kill her anyway. She felt the slime of his blood seeping into her clothes, the rancid stench of his breath and his sweat, the burnt smell of gunpowder on the air.

Please, God.

"I said drop the gun," he bit out.

"Not until you take that knife away from her throat," Amelia said.

"Drop it, or I'll kill her!"

Sadie squeezed her eyes shut, waiting to hear the gun thump onto the dirt.

"Do what he says, baby, please!" Sheila cried.

A gunshot cracked through the air, and Sadie felt the wind of its bullet whiz past her face. She felt its percussion as it hit home, knocking Nate back. Screaming, she fell with him, then rolled away.

The bullet had hit him right between the eyes.

She looked up at Amelia, saw her trembling, still holding the gun. "I knew I could do it," she said. "I knew I could."

CHAPTER
51

Cade heard the sound of the gunshots, and he abandoned the old man who had answered the door, and ran around the house toward the sound. He heard the sirens of GBI agents turning onto the property, but there was no time to wait for them.

McCormick ran beside him, into the trees and onto the cut path . . .

And then he heard the screams, muffled and distant.

"There!" McCormick spotted the trap door at the same time Cade did, the open hole into a dark pit. And he heard a girl's frantic wailing.

Leading with his gun, he looked into the hole, saw Sadie on the rope ladder, trying to pull herself up.

"It's them!" he cried. "Over here!"

Sadie looked up. "Cade! Is that you? Help me! Please help me!"

He reached down for her hand, pulled her the rest of the way up. She came out of the hole, fragile and filthy, tears and sweat streaking her dirty face. "Who else is down there?"

"Amelia and Mom . . . and Nate. We killed him, I think. Hurry. You have to make sure. He had a knife . . ."

"I need a flashlight," Cade yelled, and someone thrust one at him. He shone it down into the hole, saw Amelia hunkered against the wall, a pistol on the floor at her feet, and Sheila lying flat on the dirt floor, looking as if she'd been in a head-on collision with a bus.

From here, he could see the wound in Nate's forehead, the blood around him.

"I'm going in." McCormick stepped onto the ladder. Cade watched it swing with his weight.

"Sheila, it's me, Joe. Are you all right?"

"Been better, Joe," she said weakly. "I'm glad to see you, though."

"Amelia?" he asked. "Are you okay?"

Cade saw the girl nod her head. She was clearly traumatized, and she looked pale and drawn.

"He pushed Mom in," Sadie said. "She has broken bones, even in her face. How are you going to get her out?"

"The paramedics can do it. What about Amelia? Is she hurt?"

"She hasn't had anything to eat or drink in days. She's really weak, but she might be able to climb out."

Sadie was shivering, so he put his arm around her to warm her. "What about you? Did he hurt you?"

"I think my ribs are broken, and I twisted my ankle. But I'm alive." She burst into tears with the word. "Thank God, we're all alive."

He held her as she wept, pressing her head against his chest. "You're okay. It's gonna be all right now."

"He's got a pulse!" one of the paramedics called up. "He's alive! Help us get him out!"

Sadie caught her breath and went rigid, and Cade saw the fear gripping her. "It's okay. He's unconscious. He can't hurt you anymore."

He watched as they tied Nate onto the basket, then as someone from the top pulled up, they brought him out.

Sadie clung to Cade as they moved Nate past her. His hair strung into his bloody face, and his face looked gray, dead.

She turned her head away.

They went back for Sheila and Amelia, pulling them carefully out. Cade walked Sadie to the ambulance, and she climbed in with her mother and sister.

"What hospital?" the driver asked.

"Candler," Cade said. "That's where Morgan's having her baby."

Sadie gasped. "Now?"

He nodded. "Now. I'll meet you there." He closed the doors, and Sadie turned her troubled face to her mother.

"She went into labor because she was so upset over you, baby. Her water broke and everything."

"Oh, no." She sat down, praying that God would give them one more miracle tonight.

CHAPTER

52

Sadie wished she could bask in her freedom, but a heavy sense of trepidation had settled itself over her. Nate lay just a few beds from her mother in ICU, comatose, but alive. The doctors said he probably wouldn't make it through the night, but she still didn't trust him. Besides, the second man who had helped abduct Amelia and Jamie was still out there somewhere, unidentified. He could come after them at any time to finish the job Nate had botched up. Or to silence Amelia.

When Blair came into Sadie's examining room with Cade, she tried to swallow her fear.

Blair took her in her arms and held her for a long time, as if she'd given her up for dead, only to see her resurrected. "Oh, honey, are you all right?"

"Yeah, I'm good. My lungs weren't punctured by my broken ribs, so I was really lucky. Ankle's sprained, but that's no big deal."

"What are they doing for you?"

"They offered me painkillers, but I don't want them." She had refused them, to the doctor's chagrin. He assured her a few pills to help ease her pain would be all right, but she'd rather have the pain than the fear of addiction.

"Did they give you crutches?"

"I tried them, but the ribs hurt too much." She pointed to the cast on her foot. "They put a walking cast on, but told me to use a wheelchair for the next couple of days."

Cade came up behind Blair and looked hard into her face. "Enough with the physical stuff, kiddo. How are *you?*"

Sadie fought tears. "I'm still scared, Cade. Could you put a guard with Mom and Amelia, to protect them while they're here? That other guy is still out there, whoever he is."

"It's already done."

"But Nate is in the ICU with Mom, just a few beds down. What if he wakes up?"

"Sadie, Nate's struggling for his life. Even if he did wake up, it's doubtful he could move. He's brain damaged beyond repair."

Blair hugged her again, holding her like her mother would have if she'd been able to, like Morgan would if she were here.

"How's Morgan?"

Blair smiled. "Why don't you get in the wheelchair, and I'll take you to ask her yourself."

Desperately needing to see that her mentor was all right, Sadie got into the chair and let Blair push her down the hall.

When they got to Morgan's room on the next floor up, Blair stepped in before pulling Sadie in. "Morgan, Jonathan, I have a surprise for you."

"What?"

Blair backed out and pushed Sadie in.

"Sadie!" Morgan reached for her, and Sadie rolled to the side of her bed—then she saw what Morgan had in her arms. The little bundle, wrapped in a blue blanket . . .

"Is it—?"

"It's a boy!" Morgan cried. "Oh, Sadie, he's a beautiful, healthy little boy."

"Healthy?" she asked. "Are you sure?"

Jonathan chuckled. "That's exactly what Blair asked. Yes, we're sure. It was a night for miracles."

"Oh, Morgan . . ." Sadie started to cry again. "He's so precious."

"Here. He wants his aunt Sadie to hold him."

Sadie took the tiny thing, feeling his limp weight settling with such trust into her arms. He slept deeply, completely relaxed, oblivious to the dangers that lurked in the world he'd just been thrust into. But he had worthy protectors. Just like she did.

Protectors sent by a sovereign, loving God, who gave them miracles just when they needed them most.

C H A P T E R

53

Sadie stayed in the hospital overnight, sleeping next to Blair in the ICU waiting room. It was the closest she could get to her mother. Morning dawned with harsh insistence, lighting the room through the curtains. Sadie finally gave in and got up, wincing at the pain in her side. At 7:00 a.m. she was allowed to go in to the ICU. She stole a look at Nate when she went past. He looked like a corpse, lying on that gurney, wires and tubes tangling over him. A woman with long, frizzy gray hair stood over him, crying.

Was that his mother? The thought did something to Sadie's stomach. She wanted to run in there and tell the woman she shouldn't weep over him, that he was an evil monster and deserved his time in hell.

The woman turned and met Sadie's eyes, and she saw the despair, the brokenness, the regrets . . . the sheer humanity of another soul who'd been crushed by loss.

And then it hit her: Nate was human. He had a mother who loved him, a grandfather who doted on him.

Had drugs turned him into a killer? Had his past somehow perverted his potential?

She closed her eyes, holding back her tears, and said a silent prayer for her enemy. And she prayed for his grieving mother.

She turned away and rolled her chair to her mother. Sheila looked worse than she had last night. Her face was swollen to twice its size, and her bruises faded from black to blue to brown to yellow. Her arm and leg were in casts, and she had shaved spots of hair where she'd needed stitches. If she woke up and saw herself, she'd be horrified.

But to Sadie, she looked like a hero.

When visiting time was over, Sadie got Blair to push her to the cafeteria for breakfast. Then, on the way back up, they stopped by Amelia's room. The Savannah police had posted a guard outside her door, as Cade had promised.

Since Sadie was on Amelia's visitors list, the guard let her in, but Blair had to wait outside. Sadie rolled herself in. Amelia was awake, and several people were there with her.

Amelia looked much better than she had the last time Sadie'd seen her. She'd showered and eaten, and the IV in her arm had hydrated her.

"How are you feeling?" Sadie asked.

"Great. Glad to be alive." She leaned over and hugged Sadie. "They're letting me go home today. How about you?"

"I'm fine. I just have to stay off this foot for a while."

Amelia slipped out of the bed, her nightgown sweeping the floor over her bare feet. "Everybody, I want you to meet Sadie, my half sister. Sadie, you know my mom and dad. This is my aunt Millie, and Uncle Herbert, my cousin Jimmy, and our next-door neighbors Larry and Myra."

Amelia had a whole family, a community, separate from Sadie's life. People who loved her. And yet, in all the tangle, Sadie felt a bond with her that even she couldn't understand. They were sisters, in every sense of the word.

"Amelia, Sadie's not your half sister," her mother said. "She's a full sister."

Amelia frowned. "What do you mean?"

Sadie smiled up at her. "We have the same mother *and* father."

Amelia's smile faded, and she looked from Sadie to her own parents. "Really? Are you sure?"

"Sheila would know," her father said.

Amelia turned back to Sadie, looking at her with new eyes. "Well, what do you know about that? A real sister."

The two girls hugged again, and Sadie knew that whatever happened in either of their lives or either of their families, they had something special here that couldn't be taken from them.

When they broke the hug, Lana took Sadie's hands and tearfully smiled down into her face. "We owe you so much, Sadie. If it weren't for you searching for Amelia, figuring things out, she might still be there."

"Mom's the real hero."

"Yes, she is. She's been our hero twice now."

Sadie hoped they would say that again to Sheila. She needed to hear it. "You were a hero too, Amelia. You're the one who shot him."

"I wanted to talk to you about that, Sadie. About when I shot him. I don't want you to think I would have taken the chance of hitting you. For most people it was just too close. But not for me. In ROTC, I was the top marksman in my class. I knew I could hit him without hitting you."

She was glad to know that. "I guess that's another instance of God preparing you for something you were going to have to do."

"He sure did," Bob said.

"So are you afraid to go home?" she asked Amelia.

"Kind of." Amelia looked at her parents, and her father took her hand. "The bureau has arranged a place for us to go for a while, so we'll be safe. I guess it's important for them to keep me safe since I'm the only witness who saw the other guy."

"It'll be like a vacation," Lana said. "Just until they catch him."

"I wanted to go to Jamie's funeral—" sudden tears choked Amelia's words—"but they won't let me."

Sadie was glad. "They shouldn't," she whispered. "Amelia, he might look for you there. I think it's a great idea that you're leaving. They'll find him soon. Already, they're probably finding out who all of Nate's friends were. It's not rocket science to boil it down to someone that close to him."

"I hope so."

Sadie said her temporary good-bye, and made Amelia promise to come back and spend time with her this summer, so they could get to know each other under better circumstances. Then she left the room, and Blair rolled her back to the elevators. "Sadie!"

She turned and saw Matt Frazier, coming up the hall behind her. "Hey, Matt."

He caught up to her, hands in his pockets, and looked down at her with soft eyes. "You're okay. I'm so glad." He leaned over and hugged her.

It was the first time he'd had his arms around her, and she liked the way it felt.

"I was so scared for you," he said, holding on. "I prayed and prayed . . ."

"Thank you. It worked."

He followed them down to the ICU waiting room, and Blair left them alone to go check on Morgan and the baby. Sadie told Matt everything that had happened, and how her mother had saved the day.

He took it all in, his eyes misty, and she realized how much she mattered to him. "So how is that Nate person?"

"He's in a coma, just barely hanging on. They didn't even know if he'd make it through the night. But he did."

He sighed. "Well, I sure hope they find the other guy soon. I guess no one's completely safe until they do."

When he started to leave, Sadie rolled herself into the hallway with him. He stalled for a moment before leaving, as if he wanted to say something, but couldn't find the words. "I was thinking that . . . maybe when all this has settled down . . . maybe I could take you to a movie or something, if you still want to go."

She smiled. "I'd like that."

"And I'd love to meet your sister. See if she's as pretty as you."

Warmth burst through her. He'd never told her she was pretty before. "She's getting out today. But I plan to spend a lot of time with her this summer. You can get to know her then."

"I'll look forward to it." He took her hand, looked down at it, then leaned over and pressed a kiss on her lips.

She hadn't expected that, and she felt the blood rush to her cheeks, a warm blush of surprise.

"See you soon." His whisper brushed her ear, then he started back to the elevators.

Sadie just sat there watching him go, feeling as if God had just ordained another new beginning.

Itold him he was gonna come to no good."

Cade and Joe stood in Nate's father's house, listening to the man's angry rantings about his son. It hadn't disturbed him to learn that his son was dying in the hospital. Instead, he'd launched on a tirade about how he'd predicted this. He reeked of alcohol and cigarette smoke, and his house was filthy, with piles of old newspapers and magazines everywhere. Three smelly bulldogs sniffed Cade's and Joe's legs, their paws slipping on the dusty hardwood floor. Two big cats lay on top of stacks of newspapers and magazines that were piled on the couch and in several chairs.

"Ever since he was a little kid, he's been gettin' into trouble. Never could control him. He ran wild, that boy."

"How long since he's lived here with you?" McCormick asked him.

"Years. He done dropped outta school in the ninth grade, wound up movin' in with some drug dealin' friends of his."

"Could you give us their names?"

"I don't know their names. You think he brought 'em home for supper? He didn't show his face around here much. And it was good riddance."

"Where's his mother?"

"She's at the hospital with him. She don't feel the same as me. She always thought there was hope for him. Guess she knows better now."

As Cade and McCormick drove back to Cape Refuge, Joe shook his head. "Well, it doesn't take a genius to see why Nate turned out like he did."

"No, it doesn't." He tried to think where they needed to go next. Even though the state police were still handling the case and trying to find Nate's accomplice, Cade had decided he couldn't leave this to them. If there was anything he could do to help, he would do it.

"Why don't we go to the Flagstaff and talk to that Tina girl Sadie met? She saw Amelia and Jamie getting into the car with them. Maybe she saw more than she's telling."

"Good point. Maybe, now that Nate's out of the picture, she'll feel freer to talk."

Though it was eleven o'clock in the morning, they had to wake Tina up. She came to the door looking as if she'd just crashed after a three-day high. "What do you want?" She squinted out into the light.

"We want to talk to you about Nate Morris."

"What about him?"

"Can we come in?"

"There are people sleeping." She stepped back so they could see in, and Cade saw another girl and a man asleep on the bed.

"How about you get dressed and talk to us outside?" Cade asked.

She sighed and shoved her hand through her hair. "All right, I'll be out in a minute."

They waited just outside the door, and finally, Tina came out. She had pulled on a pair of shorts, but still wore the long baggy shirt she'd apparently slept in. Her hair looked wild and unbrushed, but she'd washed her face of the smeared makeup that had circled her eyes before.

She took a long drag from her cigarette and faced them. "So what do you want to know?"

"We want to talk to you about what you saw the night Amelia Roarke and Jamie Maddox were abducted."

"I've already told you what I saw."

"That's right, you did. But we thought since Nate was off the street, that maybe something else might have occurred to you. Like who the second guy was."

She leaned over the rail, looking down into the parking lot. Her hands trembled, and Cade knew she needed a fix. "I didn't lie to you before."

"We don't think you lied." McCormick leaned next to her. "We just thought you might not have told us everything."

"Nate's not coming back, you know," Cade said. "If he lives, which he may not, he's going to prison."

Tina wet her lips and squinted into the breeze. "I told those girls not to stay here. I warned them it was dangerous."

"You were right."

"The other guy, I didn't know him. He was clean-cut. Didn't look like he belonged with Nate."

"Then you knew it was Nate?"

She straightened and looked from Cade to Joe. "I knew, but I also knew he'd put a knife to my throat without a second thought if I told."

"You could have helped us find them sooner." Joe's tone was hard. "Obstructing justice is a crime."

"So you want to bring charges against me? Get in line."

Threatening her wasn't going to get them anywhere. Cade leaned on the railing. "Tina, we're not here to accuse you of anything. We just want to find the other killer. What can you tell us about him?"

"It was dark, and I only saw him from behind. But I'm pretty sure he had short brown hair. He was wearing jeans and some kind of polo shirt. It was green, I think."

"How tall was he?"

"Taller than Nate. Six feet, maybe."

"Did you hear him talking?"

"No, they were too far away."

"What age would you say he was?"

"Young. Nineteen, twenty maybe. I can tell you for sure it wasn't that crazy writer guy. You couldn't miss him."

She wasn't much help. The description she'd given matched the one Amelia gave, and seemed just as vague. Amelia had even tried to talk them through a composite sketch of the man, but he'd been wearing sunglasses, so she hadn't seen his eyes. That made it even more difficult.

"Look, I do want to help," Tina said, and Cade thought she looked sincere. "That girl Amelia was nice to me. I don't get that a lot. And the other one, her sister . . ."

"Sadie."

"Yeah, her. She was nice too. Gave me her phone number, told me I could come and live with her or something, if you can believe that."

"I do believe it," Cade said. "She lives at Hanover House. They take in people who want to clean up their lives. If you ever want a better life, you should call that number."

The mist in Tina's eyes spoke volumes. "Maybe I will someday."

CHAPTER

55

Cade had just gotten back to the station when Yeager called him.

"I wanted to let you know that we checked out that file on Gibson's computer. The one with the scene describing the murder?"

"Yeah. Did his theory pan out?"

"It sure did. Turns out he's right. Our analysts believe that scene was inserted by someone else. And the initials on the hacker's computer were *SC*."

Cade's mind raced to match those initials. Jotting it down, he said, "So you weren't able to get the whole name?"

"No, that would be too much to hope for. And our cybercrimes guy cautioned us that he could have been using someone else's computer. Or, if he was aware that the Track Changes feature was on and knew what it was, he could have faked the initials. That's doubtful, though."

"Why?"

"He assures me that not that many people know what Track Changes is. It seems like the hacker didn't.

If he had, he would have inserted the scene into one of the other files on the computer. There were other versions of the document that didn't have Track Changes on, and wouldn't have identified him. It looks like he just picked the file Gibson worked on last."

Cade thought about the shoe in his truck, the blood . . . The killer was shrewd, good at setting others up. If it wasn't Gibson, then he'd been set up too. What if the killer was playing with them all? "What if he knew the computer well enough to use the Track Changes feature to throw us off yet again?"

"I guess that's possible. He's not stupid, after all."

Cade ran his pen over the initials again. "It just seems too obvious to think he'd allow his initials to pop up in Gibson's program. I can't see that happening."

"Cade, you've been in law enforcement long enough to know that killers often leave stupid clues behind. All it takes is one mistake. If he was in a hurry, he might have forgotten about the initials."

Cade stared at the wall. His gut told him something wasn't right, but he couldn't figure out what. "Are you sure this isn't Gibson sending us on a wild-goose chase? It was his gun, his work, and he didn't have an alibi for the first two girls. Maybe he has a partner who did all this. Maybe Gibson directed it from his home while he was under surveillance."

"But the girl at the Flagstaff says it was two young men. She was clear that it wasn't Gibson."

Cade sighed. "Yeah, you're right."

"My hope is that this is a real clue, Cade. Do me a favor and mull it over for a while. If you come up with any names, let me know ASAP."

"You got it."

"By the way, you'll be happy to know that we've ruled you out as a suspect, after interviewing Amelia."

Cade breathed a laugh. "Well, that's good news."

"Sorry we ever doubted you, man."

"That's all right. The evidence didn't look good."

As Cade hung up the phone, he stared down at the initials. *SC*. It was someone who knew him, knew he'd been planning to propose to Blair, knew where he was doing it. Someone who held a grudge, wanted to get even.

His mind raced through names . . .

"Hey, Chief."

He looked up and saw Scott standing in his doorway. His heart jolted.

Scott Crown.

"I got that list you wanted of all the tenants at the Flagstaff for the past three weeks." He tossed it on Cade's desk. Cade took it and scanned down it for the initials *SC*. There was only one—Sarah Colvert.

"Thanks." He looked up at the young man who was Joe McCormick's nephew. Was it possible? Could he be a killer? Okay, so he held a grudge against Cade for reaming him in front of his peers, and he knew Gibson's work, knew computers, had found the first girl . . .

Cade swallowed hard. "Tell me something, Scott. You've gone to Cape Refuge schools all your life, right?"

"Right."

"Nate Morris was your age. Did you ever know him when he was still in school?"

Scott hesitated. "No, I don't think I did. Why?"

Cade made a note to check the yearbooks for the years prior to Nate's dropping out. If he could make any connection at all . . .

"Just wondered. We're trying to find out every little thing we can about the guy."

He stared at Scott for a long moment, his mind racing. Scott had overheard him talking to McCormick about his proposal plans. He could have taken Jamie's body out to the cavern, left her there for him to find. He was one of the last ones to see Sadie.

"I've been asking around about him," Scott said. "If anybody tells me anything, I'll let you know."

"Do that."

Scott left the room, and Cade stared at the doorway. He rubbed his face, trying to decide how to proceed. He would have to talk to McCormick, but it wouldn't be easy. Scott was his nephew, his sister's son.

But if he was a murderer . . .

He got up and went to the doorway. McCormick sat at his desk, checking something on the database. "Joe, can I talk to you?"

McCormick got up and came into his office. "Yeah, Cade. Whatcha got?"

Cade sat back down and ran his hand over his jaw. "Close the door, Joe."

McCormick closed it and sat down. "Must be good."

Cade crossed his hands on the desk and looked hard into his friend's eyes. "Joe, I just talked to Yeager. He says that Gibson's theory about his computer file was right. The initials of the hacker were *SC*."

"Good. That's something to start with. Have you looked on the list Scott just gave you?"

"There's only one person at the Flagstaff with those initials, and she's a woman."

"Okay. We need to match it to all of Nate's acquaintances. I'll get right on it."

He started to get up, but Cade stopped him. "Joe, sit down."

McCormick sat back down. "What is it?"

"There's one person that came to my mind. Someone who has those initials, who knew about my proposal, had access to my truck, knows computers, has a grudge against me . . . and even fits Amelia's description."

Joe's forehead creased. "Who?"

"Scott."

Joe just sat there for a moment, staring at him. "No way! Cade, you're way out of line here. You can't seriously think—"

"He found Emily's body, Joe. He wasn't even supposed to be over there. His reason was lame from the get-go. Maybe he put her there."

The skin of Joe's face began to redden, and his lips tightened. "My nephew is not a killer, any more than you are."

"How do you know?"

"Because I *know* him. Cade, he's my sister's kid! I've known him since he was born, and he doesn't have this in him."

"Maybe he didn't do the killing. Maybe he just covered up."

"No! " Joe said. "It's not possible."

"Then help me prove it."

Joe's lips were tight across his teeth. "That's not what you want to prove. You want him to be guilty. You haven't liked him from day one."

Cade clamped down his anger. "You think I'd try to pin a murder rap on him, just because he rubbed me the wrong way? Do you honestly think *I'm* capable of *that*?"

Joe rubbed his face roughly and brought his angry gaze back to Cade. "He didn't do it, Cade. It's somebody else."

"We'll find out. I want to put him in a lineup, and let Amelia decide. Then we'll see."

"Good idea," Joe said. "Then you'll see, all right."

CHAPTER

56

Cade reached Amelia on her father's cell phone and convinced him to bring Amelia back for the lineup. Bob told him they would take the next flight out and have Amelia there by that afternoon.

Since Cade's station didn't have a lineup room with the two-way mirror, he used the one at the Tybee station. He rounded up all of the brown-haired officers under twenty-five, from both the Cape Refuge and Tybee departments, who hadn't been on the scene during the rescue. Only four guys qualified. He filled in the rest with young seamen he'd rounded up at Crickets.

"So Uncle Joe, what is this lineup for?" Scott asked as they started to file in.

"A robbery that took place on Tybee last month."

Scott lowered his voice. "Which one of the guys do they think did it?"

"I don't know."

As the men lined up, Joe shot Cade a withering look.

Cade couldn't worry about Joe's feelings now. If Scott was the killer, they'd know momentarily. He went around to the room where Amelia and her parents waited. Joe followed him in.

Amelia looked small as she sat between her parents, fidgeting with a button on her shirt.

Cade saw fear in the fragile expression on her face.

"Amelia, our suspect is in this lineup that you're about to see. We want you to pick him out. Do you think you can do that?"

"I know I can. He was wearing sunglasses, but I'll know him when I see him. His face is clear in my mind."

"Good. Then let's get started."

Amelia stopped him. "Chief Cade, will he be able to see me?"

"No. They're looking into a mirror."

She nodded, and swallowed hard. "I'm ready then."

Cade spoke into the microphone in the room. "Send them in."

The men filed in, and Amelia held her parents' hands as she looked from one man to another.

Cade held his breath and watched her.

Amelia's frightened eyes scanned across the faces, but there was no sign of recognition. She looked back at the first one, clearly studying his features. Scott was third in line, and her eyes skirted past him.

"Do you see the man who abducted you that night?"

Tears came to her eyes, and he saw the struggle on her face. Was she afraid to name him, or was she just unsure?

"I . . . I don't think he's here . . ."

Cade glanced at McCormick, saw the relief on his face. "Just take your time. Look at each one."

"He seemed thinner, taller. He's just not here." She started to cry. "I wanted it to be him. I was so hoping I could identify him, and you could lock him right up. But I don't want to make a mistake, because if I do, he'll still be out there."

"That's okay, Amelia. But you said he wore sunglasses."

He'd asked each of the men to bring his own pair. He leaned over to the microphone. "Gentlemen, put your sunglasses on, please."

They took their glasses out and put them on. Cade looked at Amelia. "That change anything?"

She looked at them again, one by one, then shook her head. "I'm sorry."

"Don't be sorry. You did good." He must have been wrong. If Scott were the guy, she would have identified him.

They held the lineup until Amelia and her family had left the station, and then they let them all go.

"I hope you're satisfied with that," Joe said. "My nephew didn't do it."

"I have to agree with you. I don't think he did either." But Cade knew he couldn't rule Scott out entirely. Not until they had someone else behind bars.

"Hey, Cade." Chief Grant leaned into the doorway. "Sorry the lineup was a bust. But I have some news you might be interested in."

"Yeah?"

"Nate Morris just died."

CHAPTER
57

One month later

Blair and Cade's wedding day dawned as beautiful as anyone could have hoped. Sadie sat on the window seat in her mother's room, gazing out her window at the activity going on below. Men from the church were setting up chairs that spanned from the front porch, all the way across the lawn, into the street—which Jonathan had flexed his mayoral muscles to barricade off—and across the sand to the new gazebo built on the beach for the occasion.

Everyone in town would be here in a couple of hours. So why did she feel such uneasiness?

Ever since she'd been rescued from the pit, Sadie struggled with the feeling that someone dangerous was watching her, charting her movements, waiting to grab her again. Crowds made her nervous, and she constantly found herself assessing every male face she saw, wondering if Nate Morris's accomplice was near.

Her mother sat wheelchair-bound behind her, Caleb in her lap.

"You have to be a good boy for Mommy, okay? When they put you in your little police car, you're going to ride down the aisle without crying."

"Me big boy."

"That's right. You're a very big boy, and you're gonna smile and wave at everybody."

"Not cry."

"No, not cry."

Sadie smiled. Blair insisted on having Caleb in the wedding, but she knew with her little brother, anything could happen. He could get cold feet and refuse to participate, or he could cry or knock the flowers over, disrupting the whole ceremony as they read their vows.

Blair insisted it was worth it.

"Now I want you to lay down on Mommy's bed and try to take a little nap. I don't want you to be grumpy at the wedding."

Caleb slid off her lap and climbed onto her bed. Letting out a wicked giggle, he began to jump on the mattress.

Sadie got up and caught him. "You rascal. That's not how you take a nap! I guess I'll have to take you to your room."

"No!" He dropped down, lying with his thumb in his mouth.

That wouldn't last long. Sadie turned back to her mom. "You need any help getting ready?"

"*Do* I? As hard as I've tried, I can't put my makeup on with my left hand."

Sheila's face had been reconstructed in surgery, and while the bruising had faded, it was still swollen on one side and bore surgical scars along her hairline that hadn't yet healed. Even with her left arm and leg in casts, Sadie thought she looked beautiful. Like a hero.

"Here, I'll do it for you."

Sadie rolled Sheila's wheelchair to her vanity table and sat down in front of her. She brushed the eye shadow on Sheila's eyelids, then got an eyeliner pencil and lightly outlined her eyes. "I wish Amelia could be here. She'd get such a kick out of seeing Caleb riding down the aisle."

"She really wanted to."

"Yeah, but she's right. It probably isn't safe yet."

She heard the telephone ringing in the hallway, and someone downstairs answered it. At the same time, Blair came running up the stairs.

"What an idiot! How could I do something so stupid?"

Sadie stood up and looked out into the hall. "What is it?"

Blair looked like she might cry as she came to Sheila's doorway. "I just had my hair done, and I wore this stupid T-shirt. How will I get it over my head without ruining my hair?"

Sadie pulled on the neckline, hoping it would stretch. But it didn't. "I see your problem."

"Just cut it off, hon," Sheila said. "Sadie, I have some scissors in my dresser."

"Great idea." Sadie got the scissors and handed them to Blair.

"Thanks." She let out a huge breath. "You saved the day, Sheila." She started out of the room, then turned back. "Sadie, when did Matt say he and his mother were bringing the flowers?"

"Two. They should be here soon."

"I hope so. They're late, and it's going to take awhile to decorate the gazebo."

"It'll all be done. Just go relax. Try to enjoy this. It's your wedding day!"

Morgan came up the stairs, carrying her baby, who slept blissfully in her arms. "Sadie, you have a call. A girl named Tina."

Sadie frowned. The only Tina she knew was the girl from the motel. She took the cordless phone. "Hello?"

"Yeah, uh, Sadie? This is Tina. We met at the Flagstaff?"

She caught her breath. "Tina . . . how are you?" She went out of her mother's room and stepped into her own so she could hear.

"Uh, not so good." She could tell that the girl was crying, trying to control her voice.

"What's wrong?"

"I've just . . . got to get out of this place. I've been trying to stop doing dope, and I've been sober for two weeks. But it's getting really hard. And I remembered you saying that I could come there. That maybe there was help for me."

"Yes, there is. You need to come and talk to Morgan and Jonathan Cleary. They run the house and the program."

"I don't have any money. I don't even have a job. I couldn't pay anything."

"You don't need money. Please, just come. Do you know where Hanover House is?"

"Yeah, I know. It's that beautiful house on the Sound. I could walk over right now . . ."

Sadie looked out the window, saw that Matt's florist truck was pulling in. She started to tell Tina that it wasn't a good time, then stopped. If she put her off, she might change her mind, or someone else might coerce her into staying. A delay of even a few hours could send her back to drugs. "Yes, come now . . . When you get here, you'll see a lot of activity out in the yard. We're having a wedding today, but it's not until four. If anyone stops you, tell them you're looking for me."

The girl sniffed. "Are you sure? Maybe I should wait."

"No, don't wait. Come now, okay? I'll be watching for you."

There was a long pause. "Okay, I'm coming."

CHAPTER

58

Blair stood in her parents' bedroom, feeling almost giddy as she looked out the window. So far the weather was beautiful. No artist's brush could have painted such an azure sky, and the ocean was calm, rolling against the shore in whispered approval of what was soon to take place.

She hoped Jonathan had been right to block off the street and line so many chairs across to the beach. If they didn't fill them up, it would be embarrassing. But she felt sure they would. Everyone wanted to see the town's favorite bachelor tie the knot, and they were trying to accommodate them all.

Blair fluffed her veil again and laid it back on the bed. She'd just had her hair and makeup done, and she stood in her wedding gown, afraid to sit down for fear she would wrinkle it. Maybe she'd put it on too soon.

Morgan sat in the rocker across the room, nursing little Wayne as she smiled up at her sister. "You look gorgeous."

Blair looked into the mirror. "That makeup artist was good. She almost covered the scars." Almost. It would have to do. The veil would cover them on the way down the aisle, but after it was pulled back, there would be no hiding them.

But it would be okay. Cade thought she was beautiful no matter what. And so she was.

What would her mother and father have thought of her marrying Cade? Were they watching from heaven, tears of joy streaming down their cheeks? Even if they weren't, she hoped they'd gotten word.

"I miss Mama and Pop," she whispered. "It won't be the same without Mama fussing over me, telling me some story about her wedding day. Pop kissing me on the cheek and making me cry before I walked down the aisle. They were supposed to be here, Morgan."

Her sister's eyes filled with tears, and she looked down at the precious little baby sleeping in her arms. "They were supposed to be here for him too. But we got through it okay, didn't we?"

Blair picked up one of the pillows off of their bed, brought it to her face. It used to smell of salt air and sea breeze, her father's aftershave, her mother's shampoo. But she couldn't find that scent any longer. It was long gone. The memories this room represented were etched more on her heart than they were on the items her parents had left behind. "I think it's time to clean the room out. It's crazy leaving it like this."

Morgan looked around at all the things her parents had left. She walked through it, stopping at her mother's closet. Her mother's shoes were still lined up on the shelf unit her father had built. On one side of the closet, her mother's dresses and pantsuits still hung. On the shelves above them were things they had collected over the years. A porcelain Christmas tree with Lite-Brite lights that fit into the holes. A couple of suitcases. Extra pillows. An old iron that didn't work. A box of pictures and papers.

Blair followed her and looked in. On the other side was her father's closet, much the same. His shoes, lined up on the floor, said so much about his habits. His gardening shoes with dirt still on the bottoms, his deck shoes for boating, his church shoes for preaching, his tennis shoes for walking. As long as they'd left them here, just as her parents had, it had seemed like they were coming back, picking up where they'd left off.

But Blair knew better than that. "Someone can use all these shoes, and the clothes. They're in good shape. Mama had good taste."

"I don't know if I can do it." Morgan's words came out tight, strained. "It's too hard."

"I'll help you. When Cade and I get back from Maui, we can do it together."

Morgan swallowed. "I'll think about it. But not today." She blinked back the tears rimming her eyes and laid the sleeping child on the center of the bed. "Today you're getting married. And I know Mama and Pop wouldn't want one minute of sadness for you. They prayed about this day since you were born, and if they'd searched the whole world, they couldn't have found a better husband for you."

"It's too good to be true. Mama would never have believed it."

"Yes, she would. I think in their hearts, she and Pop always had Cade picked out for you. Pop was so close to Cade. Remember how he took him under his wing and discipled him? It's almost like he knew he was training him to be a godly husband."

Blair blinked back her tears. "So they truly are a part of this."

"Of course they are."

Blair went to the window and gazed out again. She saw Sadie, already dressed in her bridesmaid dress, walking toward the house, her arm around the girl who'd called earlier. She was small, skinny, and wore a pair of cutoff shorts and high heels. Her hair strung into her face, and she looked scared as they walked toward the porch.

"That girl's here."

Morgan came to look out over her shoulder. "She actually came."

"She's just a kid. Probably a runaway."

"We'll deal with that. Right now, I think she just needs a safe place, away from the world she was in."

"So you'll take her without an application?"

Morgan just looked at her. "Sadie promised to help her. What do you think Mama would have done?"

"Morgan!" She heard Sadie's voice coming up the stairs.

Morgan opened the door. "We're in here, honey."

Sadie stepped into the doorway. At the sight of Blair, she threw her hands over her face and giggled. "Oh, Blair! I'm breathless."

The reaction gave Blair confidence. She hoped Cade would feel the same way.

"There's somebody I want you to meet." She brought the girl into the room. "This is my friend, Tina."

Tina looked like she wanted to turn and run. "I'm so sorry. I didn't mean to barge in on you while you're getting ready."

"It's okay," Blair said. "I have more than an hour before the wedding. I'm just trying to kill time until the photographer gets here. Come on in."

Morgan took Tina's hands. "Welcome to Hanover House. I'm so glad you came. I know what a big step that was for you."

Tina burst into tears, and Morgan pulled her into a hug. "Oh, honey, don't cry. This is your new beginning. We don't have a room ready right now, but I'm sure Sadie won't mind sharing hers until we can get another room cleared out."

Tina looked at her through her tears. "Really? You'd let me stay here?"

"Didn't Sadie tell you that we're here to restore people? Jesus said he came to bind up the brokenhearted and set the captives free. We're just continuing that work. God considers you His treasure, and we're going to help you find your luster."

Sadie laughed and put her arm around Tina's shoulders. "See? I told you they'd take you. And it'll be fun sharing a room. But, Morgan, which room are you going to clear out? Since you fixed up the nursery for little Wayne, there isn't a vacant room upstairs. Are you putting her in Mrs. Hern's room downstairs?"

"No, I'll put her upstairs." Blair met Morgan's eyes, and she saw the peace in them. "It's time Jonathan and I moved into this one. That would free up our room."

Sadie's smile faded. "Are you sure?"

"Yes, I'm sure." Morgan swallowed hard and turned back to her baby, picked him up, as if she needed to cling to the new beginning that made such a good-bye possible. "Now, Sadie, why don't you go find something of yours that Tina can wear to the wedding?"

Tina shook her head. "Oh, no, I can't. It's okay. I can stay inside . . ."

"No way," Sadie said. "You're coming with me."

As the two girls left them alone again, Morgan turned her tear-filled eyes to Blair.

"There you go. Mama *is* still here. She's in you, Morgan."

With her free arm, Morgan hugged her the way her mother would have done, and the sadness for her parents' absence seemed to fade away.

CHAPTER

59

An hour later, Melba Jefferson knocked on the bedroom door and stepped inside. Her mother's best friend looked on the verge of tears. "Oh, honey, you look like a princess. I just know your mama and daddy are giggling in heaven, tickled to death that things have turned out the way they have. But it's time for the wedding to start, hon. Are you ready?"

Blair drew in a deep breath. "I think so."

Morgan picked up the veil. "Then let's get this on you. Turn around."

Blair turned back to the window and looked down. The lawn was full of guests, hundreds of friends taking their seats. The string orchestra that Cade had hired from South University had already begun to play.

Excitement bubbled up inside her. It was really going to happen. Today she would become Cade's wife.

Cade took his place on the raised altar that Horace Jenkins had built for the occasion, and tugged at his collar. The tux was unbearably hot for such a warm day, but it was worth it. *Thank You, God, for giving us such a glorious day*. Blair deserved it. The guests all smiled at him, and he began to feel self-conscious. He glanced over at Joe McCormick, his best man.

"Kind of makes you wish you could tap-dance, huh?" Joe muttered.

Cade laughed and turned back to the crowd. Some of the guests were still being seated, and the City Council members who were up for reelection were making the rounds, shaking hands and politicking, as if they thought the event was for them. Sarah Williford's hat was so huge she looked as if she might become airborne if a strong wind blew. He felt sorry for anyone sitting behind her.

The music began, and he watched, amused, as everyone hurried to their seats.

The police officers on his force lined the aisle in full dress uniform. The child-sized police car was brought to the end of the aisle, and Sadie put Caleb into it. With her small bouquet in one hand, she took the floral rope in the other and pulled the little car slowly up the aisle. The crowd laughed softly as the toddler bucked and laughed, clutching the pillow that had their mock rings sewn on, and waving like royalty.

Caleb was the hit of the show, Cade thought. At least until the bride came out.

When they got to the front, Sadie took Caleb out and, holding his hand, went to stand next to the gazebo. Caleb was compliant for now, but if he started to get disruptive, Melba Jefferson would swoop him away.

Sadie's dress was the color of sunshine, beautiful against the backdrop of the ocean, and she had flowers in her hair. She looked radiant. No one would have ever imagined that she'd been held prisoner in a pit just a month ago. Cade thought of how he'd found her, two years ago, beaten up and sleeping on the beach. She'd come such a long way.

And then came Morgan, walking slowly and smiling, in her own yellow dress. He'd always thought his best friend's wife was beautiful, but he had to admit that she'd never been more lovely than she was since having the baby. Her skin glowed with contentment and joy, and she wore her hair up, with some of her stray curls cascading down to her shoulder.

Finally, the music changed, and the strings launched into the famous wedding processional.

And there she was. He saw her all the way across the street, floating like an angel out of Hanover House, on Jonathan's arm. She was beautiful, more radiant than he'd ever expected, and he fought the urge to break and run for her, scoop her up in his arms and carry her, laughing, down the aisle. But he knew the walk was important. It was the walk that every little girl dreamed of.

And boy, did she walk it. The guests came to their feet, and he heard their collective gasp as they caught sight of her. Tears stung his eyes as she started up that long aisle. He'd wanted her for so long, and now she was going to be his. *Thank You, God.*

Their gazes met as she came closer, and he could see that she had tears shimmering in her eyes under that veil. She could have come barefoot down the aisle, in a terry cloth robe, and he would have thought she was beautiful. But forever he would remember the sight of her in flowing white, that pure white veil covering her shoulders, framing her in light . . .

As Jonathan brought her to him, he took her hand. Jonathan pulled her veil back over her head and kissed her on the cheek.

Then he stepped into the preacher's spot and turned to face the audience.

The crowd chuckled at his double role.

"We are gathered together to join Matthew Cade and Blair Owens in holy matrimony . . ."

CHAPTER
60

Amelia and her parents got to the wedding late. She had changed her mind about coming at the very last minute, even though Nate's accomplice hadn't been caught. She'd hidden out for a month now, but she longed to be at the wedding. So many of the residents of Cape Refuge had prayed for her while she was missing, and she'd been barraged with cards and letters from them expressing their joy that she was all right. She wanted to meet them and to see her sister and little half-brother dressed up in wedding clothes. It had suddenly become important to her.

She decided she would feel safe enough, with so many police officers there. Surely no one would hurt her at the police chief's wedding! Her parents agreed to come with her, so they'd all hurried here.

Blair had already gone down the aisle when they arrived, so they went to join the standing crowd at the back. Caleb stood up at the front, next to Sadie, squirming and trying to break his hand free of hers. He looked

like a little doll, dressed in a miniature tuxedo that looked comi-
cally uncomfortable.

She watched him tug at his tie, trying to get it off. Sadie
whispered something to him, but her words seemed to fall on deaf
ears. Finally, Sadie looked out into the guests, and a sweet-looking
woman came forward, picked Caleb up, and whisked him away.

Amelia was glad she'd come. She smiled at the picture before
them, struck by the purity of this ceremony and the newness it
represented. The sky was so blue, and the ocean so quiet. Sadie
looked beautiful, and the police officers lining the aisle looked
sharp in their dress uniforms. Blair's dress looked like something
from the cover of a bridal magazine, and Cade looked as if he'd
never been happier.

Jonathan came to the question that stopped every wedding.
"If anyone here has reason that these two should not be joined
together, let him speak now or forever hold his peace."

There was a moment of tense quiet, and then the crowd
erupted into laughter.

"Guess we can go on with this," Jonathan said with a grin.
The crowd began to cheer.

Amelia listened, warmth in her heart, as they exchanged
their vows.

"I, Cade, take you, Blair, to be my lawfully wedded wife, to
have and to hold from this day forward . . ."

Hope bloomed inside her. For the past few weeks, since
Jamie's death and her captivity, Amelia had felt a lingering sense
of hopelessness and defeat, as though she lived on borrowed time.
For the first time in a month, she found herself looking past today,
to a future in which she was the bride, standing at an altar with the
man God had chosen for her. Would that day come, or would her
time in that pit, at Nate's mercy, keep her from ever trusting a man
again? *No*, she thought. She wouldn't let him steal that from her.

"I, Blair, take you, Cade, to be my lawfully wedded husband, to have and to hold from this day forward . . ."

She hardly knew these two, but she felt somehow a part of
this union, as if she had a stake in its success, just because she'd
witnessed it.

Jonathan pronounced Cade and Blair man and wife, and told Cade to kiss his bride. Amelia held her breath as he took Blair's face in both his hands and kissed her so sweetly that an "Awwww" went out over the crowd.

Then they turned to face their friends and family.

"Ladies and Gentlemen, may I introduce Mr. and Mrs. Matthew Cade."

The crowd erupted in cheers, and Amelia applauded with the rest, caught up in the joy around her. She laughed as Blair and Cade walked back up the aisle they'd come down, their faces beaming with joy.

She waited as Morgan and Sadie made their way up the aisle, then the uniformed police officers made their way out. Finally, Jonathan invited them all to the reception in the backyard.

As the crowd broke up and began to move out of their rows, Amelia sought out Sheila. She saw her in her wheelchair, and a girl walked beside her. She squinted in the sunlight, trying to remember where she'd seen her before.

The girl turned and met her eyes . . . and then she knew.

It was that girl Tina from the Flagstaff.

Her heart constricted, and a sense of apprehension fell over her again.

"Sweetheart, are you all right?" Her father touched her arm. "You look a little pale."

She nodded. "I'm fine. I just . . . saw the girl I told you about from the Flagstaff."

Her parents followed her gaze to the girl walking next to Sheila. "Are you afraid of her?" her mother asked.

"I have no reason to be. She wasn't involved. It's just that . . . well, she was there that day."

She watched Sheila as she rolled across the street, toward the reception in the backyard. She hadn't yet seen her, and Amelia thought that might be for the best, at least while Tina was with her. She didn't think she was up to talking to the girl right now.

"Let's go find Sadie."

Her father took her clammy hand and led her through the people. She looked for Sadie, knowing she'd feel better when she found her sister.

Sadie reached the backyard and watched Cade spin Blair around. "She actually *married* me!" he shouted to the wedding party.

They all laughed as the photographer snapped pictures.

Scott came to stand beside Sadie. "You look good, Sadie. The bride was pretty and all, but it was you I couldn't take my eyes off of."

She smiled. "You don't look so bad yourself." She hugged him, but as she did, she saw Matt over his shoulder. He was brooding, clearly not happy to see her in Scott's arms. She pulled back.

"Hey, Matt! You and your folks did a great job with the flowers. They're gorgeous. I don't know how you do it."

Matt shot Scott an unappreciative look, then bent down to hug Sadie. "I'm glad they turned out all right."

She stepped back to look at him. "You clean up nice. I've never seen you in a suit."

"You look pretty too, but I'm sure I'm not the first one to tell you."

"Thank you." She felt the tension between the two men and wished she knew how to handle it. She bit her lip and looked at the people coming around the house. Her mouth fell open when she spotted Amelia. "My sister came! Amelia!"

Amelia looked in Sadie's direction. She lifted her hand in a wave . . . then froze . . .

Across the lawn, Amelia heard Sadie call her, turned to see her sister, standing between two men. Both turned to look at her.

And then she saw him.

The man who'd been with Nate the night they'd abducted her, the one who'd bound her with duct tape, wrestled her out of the car, watched as her best friend was shot . . .

Dizziness wafted over her, and a scream tore from her throat.

CHAPTER
61

The terrified scream cut through the crowd, and Cade turned from his well-wishers, searching across the heads for its source. Amelia was backing into people, hysterical. "It's him!"

Blair looked at Cade. "The accomplice?"

Cade saw McCormick and yelled, "Seal off the place! Don't let anybody leave."

"Everyone stay where you are!" McCormick yelled out. "Sit down at the nearest table, please!"

But no one listened. Everyone strained to see what had set Amelia off.

Sadie looked all around her. What was happening? One minute Amelia was calling to her, smiling and waving, and the next she was screaming.

"It's him! You *monster*! You killed my best friend!"

As the words registered, Sadie stepped toward her. "Who? Amelia, who is it?"

"*Him!*" But the crowd had filled in, and Sadie couldn't tell whom she was pointing to.

Amelia's screams went up an octave. "Stop him! He's getting away!" She fought her way through the crowd.

Sadie turned and saw Scott running, and her heart jolted. Was he the one? She watched him, horror-stricken, as he ran.

Then, up ahead of him, she saw Matt Frazier, dodging through the crowd flowing around the house. Scott . . . was chasing *him.*

"Matt Frazier!" Sadie screamed. "It must be Matt!"

Matt jumped into his van, parked on the side of the property, and pulled out toward the crowd, spinning up a cloud of dirt.

The crowd split and people screamed as he drove through them.

Sadie turned to find Cade. He was already running.

CHAPTER

62

The moment Cade jumped into his police car and took off after Matt, Blair hiked up her big skirt, grabbed the camera out of the hands of the photographer, and took off running to her own car.

"Blair, you can't follow them!" Morgan shouted. "He may have a gun. You could get shot!"

"I'll be all right," Blair shouted back.

"But your wedding dress! You'll ruin it!"

"No, I won't." She flicked the tulle from her veil back over her shoulder and got into her car.

Morgan stepped in front of it to keep her from leaving. "Please, Blair. Get out of the car!"

When Blair started the engine and began backing away from Morgan, Morgan turned to Jonathan, who was running toward them. "Jonathan, stop her!"

"You know better than that. The only thing to do is to go with her."

He grabbed her car door and flung it open. "Hold on, Blair. I'm coming too. Come on, Morgan."

Morgan jumped into the front seat, and they started to pull out. "You're crazy, you know that? Cade's going to be all right. He's a professional. He doesn't need you to follow him when he's in pursuit of a criminal."

"Somebody has to get the story," Blair said as she drove. "It might as well be me."

CHAPTER

63

Matt tried to make the curve to Ocean Boulevard, back toward Hanover House, and saw that he was cornered. Police cars surrounded him on three sides, and on the fourth, there was nothing but ocean.

Instead of stopping his van and surrendering, he turned into the South Beach Pier's parking lot, drove through it and out onto the sand. Then, leaping out of his van, he took off running down the long pier.

Cade jumped out of his car and took off running, as well. He heard other footsteps pounding the planks behind him.

Matt had a gun now and was waving it around, threatening to use it if anyone got too close. He reached the end of the pier and turned around, holding the gun out with both hands.

"Don't come any closer!" he shouted. "Stay back or I'll kill all of you. I have nothing to lose! I'm not going down for two murders I didn't even commit!"

Cade stood several yards from him, arms extended, his own gun pointed at the kid. "We know you were just the accomplice, Matt. We know you didn't pull the trigger. A jury will go easy on you if you surrender now."

"I'm not taking my chances on a jury! They won't understand!" He was crying like a frightened child. "I never meant for it to get like this. I was trying to help my cousin! He killed Emily. He was on crystal meth and he came on to her at the concession stand. When she rejected him, he got violent, like he always did, and he forced her to go with him. After he killed her, he came to me all panicked, begging me to help him dispose of the body. The boat was the easiest thing, and I had just read about doing that in one of Marcus Gibson's books. But I shouldn't have helped him!"

"The jury will listen to that, Matt. Just don't make it any worse. Now drop the gun."

Matt shook his head. "And then I went to see him at the Flagstaff, to warn him that he had to go to treatment, because things had gone too far. We argued, and I told him that because of his stupid addictions he had dragged me into this. I threatened to turn him in. And then he warned me that if he went down, I was going down too, because I helped him. But those girls . . . they were listening to everything, and we couldn't take the chance of their reporting us."

"So you abducted them to shut them up?"

"It all happened so fast. I panicked, then Nate said we had to make sure they didn't talk. I didn't think far enough ahead to realize what that meant. I just knew I couldn't go to prison. But after we got them into the car and took them out to his grandfather's land, one of the girls tried to run for it, and he shot her. After that, I didn't want any part of it anymore. But I was in too deep."

"Then you didn't kill anybody yourself? If that's true, Matt, then Amelia and Sadie will tell the jury. It may not even be a murder charge."

"Don't lie to me! I know what happens in court! You're not going to let me get away with this!" He kept his gun trained on

Cade and backed up to the railing at the end of the pier. He pulled himself up on it, put his leg over.

He was going to jump.

Cade heard McCormick behind him, talking into his radio, calling for the Coast Guard.

And then Matt put the gun to his head.

"Don't do it," Cade shouted. "Matt, suicide is not the way out. Put the gun down."

"What do *you* care? It'll save the taxpayers money. I'll get what's coming to me, and I won't have to suffer through a trial."

Cade suddenly felt sorry for the kid. "I care, Matt. You got caught up in something bigger than you. You're not beyond redemption."

"Aren't I? *I'm* the one who set you up! When you came by the florist that Saturday to buy the flowers for your proposal, I heard you telling my dad your plans."

Cade moved closer, trying to keep him talking. "So you took Jamie out to Breaker's Reef?"

"No! I didn't. But I told Nate, and he did it. He thought it would throw everybody off, and he got all excited about implicating the chief of police. All I did was hack into Gibson's computer to make him look guilty too. I figured the more suspects there were, the less likely they were to trace any of it to me."

As he spoke, Matt moved the gun's barrel to his throat. Cade moved two steps closer.

"You did a good job. We never traced it back to you. The initials *SC* threw us off."

"Scott Crown." Matt's smile was bitter. "He deserved it. Going after Sadie when she was vulnerable . . ."

So that was it. Matt wasn't the innocent victim he imagined himself to be. He'd used the deadly situation to his advantage.

"You've made things hard for yourself, Matt, but you can overcome it. Drop the gun. Just drop the gun."

As Cade came closer, Matt lowered the gun . . .

. . . then tossed it to the floor.

Cade went for it, as Matt dove into the water.

Cade ran to the railing, looked over into the surf. Matt was swimming out toward the deep . . . straight toward the Coast Guard boats speeding toward them. Within minutes, they had surrounded him, and divers went in and apprehended him, pulling him out of the water and into the boat where he was restrained.

Cade breathed a sigh of relief. It was over.

He wiped the sweat on his forehead and turned to shake McCormick's hand. "Good going, guys," he said to the other officers.

He looked through the crowd of police officers, and at the entrance to the pier, saw his bride in her wedding dress and veil, snapping pictures with a big, clunky camera he'd never seen before. She was working, he thought with a grin. Recording the story for her paper, intent on getting the scoop. Did she plan on spending their wedding night getting out a special edition?

Oh, no. Not if *he* could help it.

He straightened his tie, raked back his hair, and cut through the people. "Excuse me, everybody. Mrs. Cade and I have some business to attend to."

Before Blair could protest, he swept her off her feet. She laughed and put one arm around his neck, thrusting the camera at Jonathan. "Get this, Jonathan. It'll make a great front-page shot."

Cade laughed and kept walking until he reached the police car where Scott Crown stood. "Give us a ride back to our wedding?"

Crown laughed. "Sure thing, Chief. I'd be honored."

McCormick rushed ahead, opened the back door, and Cade set Blair down, got in, and pulled her onto his lap. "We'll take it from here, Cade." McCormick's grin almost split his face. "Don't you worry about a thing."

Scott turned on his siren and lights and made his way the mile or so back down Ocean Boulevard, followed by Blair's car with Jonathan and Morgan, until he got to Hanover House where the guests waited.

"So . . ." Blair looked down into Cade's eyes. "Tell me every little thing Matt said. I couldn't get close enough to hear."

Cade grinned. "When I'm ready to call a press conference, you'll be the first to know."

The guests cheered as Scott pulled his car around the barricade and up onto the Hanover House lawn.

Cade got out of the car, pulling Blair with him. "Everything's under control now. The perpetrator has been arrested and is in custody. Now, I intend to celebrate my vows."

Applause rippled over the crowd as the string quartet began to play again. Cade pulled Blair into a kiss. "I love you, Mrs. Cade."

Her smile burst with joy. "I love you too. I think I've always loved you."

"Dance with me?"

She took his hand and let him pull her close, and they began to dance their first dance as husband and wife. Everyone around them seemed to fade out of mind. It was just the two of them.

"What a perfect day." Blair sighed. "A wedding and a crime solved in the space of an hour. And pictures, to boot."

"Stick with me, baby, and your life will never be dull."

Their laughter rose on the breeze, making their witnesses smile.

And Cade felt the pleasure of the greatest Witness of all, smiling down on the union He had created.

AFTERWORD

I wish I were the kind of person who had lived life according to God's best plan for me, but my free will got in the way so many times, leaving me with a series of regrets that rear their ugly heads with hair-trigger consistency. I read the words that Paul wrote in Philippians 3:13–14—"But one thing I do: Forgetting what is behind and straining toward what is ahead, I press on toward the goal to win the prize for which God has called me heavenward in Christ Jesus." And yet, I find myself constantly looking in my rearview mirror, working through the things I should have done, wondering how different things would be if I had.

I judge the paths I took and the decisions I made with the critical eye of a prosecutor determined to win the case, indicting myself, convicting, and executing all at once. I run through my parenting mistakes with the skill of a DA. I was too lenient, too strict; spoiled them too much, deprived them of what they needed; I was naive, I was suspicious, I let them have too much freedom, I didn't give them enough. And then there's my divorce, and my writing, and the people I've offended or hurt, or those I failed to validate or acknowledge . . .

I wake up nights and file through these things in my mind, asking God how He could ever forgive me for any of them, when compared to so many good people I know, I'm such a wretch. How can God use a loser like me? How can He count on my lazy, slow-learning spirit?

My friend Nell has the same thoughts late at night when she lies awake on the six-inch mattress provided by the county's Department of Corrections. She's been in jail on drug charges for fourteen years, since her children were small. They've grown up without their mother. If anyone has a right to regrets, she does.

She looks thirteen months ahead, to the date of her release, and knows that she won't be able to step right back into her family and her life. She can't get back the years her drug abuse cost her. But during the time that she's been imprisoned, she's learned of Christ's forgiveness and has been discipled and mentored by people who love her because Christ loves her. Her faith has had time to grow deep roots, and she's become something of a missionary among her cell mates.

She looks back on the last fourteen years and thanks God for all the suffering and the lessons she's learned, for it's given her a new life and transformed her into a new person. Instead of throwing up her hands as her children have grown up without her, she prays earnestly for them and shares Scripture with them on the phone. During occasional visits, she talks to them of the things the Lord is doing in her life. She looks forward to the day when her sons will marry and have children of their own. "I didn't get to raise my boys," she says, "but I'll be the best grandmother you've ever seen!"

Nell has learned the lessons of pressing on and not looking back. She's a poignant example for me.

The apostle Peter learned this lesson too. After the Passover meal that we often call Christ's Last Supper, Jesus looked at Peter. "Simon, Simon," he said, "behold, Satan has demanded permission to sift you like wheat; but I have prayed for you, that your faith may not fail; and you, when once you have turned again, strengthen your brothers" (Luke 22:31 – 32 NASB).

Peter didn't know that in just a few hours, he would betray Christ three times. But Jesus knew. And don't you know that Jesus' words played through his mind over and over for the rest of his life? Jesus had told him—before the betrayal—that he would mess up, but when he repented, it would be time to move on and fulfill his calling. Jesus didn't say, "Peter, you are going to really blow it a few hours from now. You're going to turn tail and run, and then you're going to lie through your teeth about even knowing me. And it's a shame, because you had a lot of potential, but you'll be of no use to me then." Instead, He anticipated Peter's sincere repentance and reminded him that his calling would still be there when he came back. And for two thousand years, Peter has strengthened his brothers through his writings in the New Testament, and reminded us that you can't move forward if you're always looking back.

I realize that God is in control of the universe, that the mistakes in my past, while dramatic to me, did not ruin God's plan beyond repair. God is sovereign, and His plans cannot be thwarted by someone like me. He can fill in the blanks of my mistakes, teaching my children what I failed to teach, restoring what I destroyed, rebuilding what I tore down, redeeming what I sold away.

And He tells me to stop looking back, to press on toward the prize . . . He knew my mistakes before I ever made them, yet He still planned to use me anyway. He didn't see me as The Great Loser, but as someone uniquely gifted with something to be used in His kingdom work. Where I see myself as a disappointment, He sees me as an asset. He already knows the fruit I will bear for Him, and my future is on His mind so much more than my past.

If He can see me that way, why wouldn't I want to press on toward that goal, and wave good-bye to my fragmented, imperfect past? The future is so much brighter in Christ, and I have so many sisters and brothers who need strengthening.

Thank You, Lord, for seeing my potential instead of my past.

ABOUT THE AUTHOR

Terri Blackstock is an award-winning, *New York Times* bestselling author who has written for several major publishers including HarperCollins, Dell, Harlequin, and Silhouette. Her books have sold over six million copies worldwide.

With her success in secular publishing at its peak, Blackstock had what she calls "a spiritual awakening." A Christian since the age of fourteen, she realized she had not been using her gift as God intended. It was at that point that she recommitted her life to Christ, gave up her secular career, and made the decision to write only books that would point her readers to him.

"I wanted to be able to tell the truth in my stories," she said, "and not just be politically correct. It doesn't matter how many readers I have if I can't tell them what I know about the roots of their problems and the solutions that have literally saved my own life."

Her books are about flawed Christians in crisis and God's provisions for their mistakes and wrong choices. She claims to be extremely qualified to write such books, since she's had years of personal experience.

A native of nowhere, since she was raised in the Air Force, Blackstock makes Mississippi her home. She and her husband are parents to three adult children—a blended family that she considers one more of God's provisions.

Blackstock is the author of numerous suspense novels, including *Intervention*, *Vicious Cycle*, and *Downfall* (the Intervention Series), as well as the Moonlighters Series, the Cape Refuge Series, the SunCoast Chronicles, the Newpointe 911 Series, the Restoration Series, and many others.

www.terriblackstock.com

An excerpt from *TWISTED INNOCENCE*, by Terri Blackstock

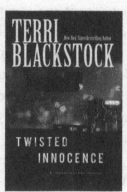

CHAPTER 1

Holly Cramer pulled to the curb of the condemned apartment building, her yellow taxi grinding gears and threatening to die. Though the sun hung bright overhead, the street was colorless, oppressive, with moldy, rotting houses and garbage festering in yards. Men loitered on the road up ahead in front of another boarded house. She shouldn't have accepted this fare, but the customer had called her cell phone personally instead of going through the agency. She must be a repeat customer.

Holly tapped her horn and looked out her passenger window. The house showed no sign of life, but it wasn't the wrong place. The girl had clearly said it was the green house on the corner of Burke and Darby. Holly checked her phone for the caller's number and called her back.

It went straight to voice mail.

Holly sighed. Maybe this was a prank, some kid trying to yank her chain just to see if she'd come. She had done that enough herself as a kid. Back when she was still Panama City's party girl, she'd done things under the influence that had been even more childish, like calling a guy fourteen times when she knew he was with his girlfriend, just to create trouble in paradise. She and her friends would giggle hysterically at the fight they imagined ensued, but the next day, as she nursed the punishment of a hangover, she would hate herself for it.

Not ready to give up on this fare just yet, Holly honked the horn again. The men up the street turned to look at her. Getting nervous, she reached into the pocket of her door, but of course her pistol wasn't there. It was against the law for a cabbie to carry a firearm inside the car while they were on duty. It was locked safely in her trunk.

She thought of bucking the law and getting it out, but that would call more attention to her. This was stupid. She was a mother now, and the last place she should have been was in the slums, waiting for someone to blow her head off just for target practice.

But what if the woman who'd called wasn't a kid at all, but someone stranded here who desperately needed a ride?

"Two minutes, then I'm leaving," Holly whispered.

The loiterers up ahead were showing too much interest in her, and two swaggered toward her. *That's it. I'm outa here.* She shifted into drive.

"Wait!"

Holly pressed a foot on the brake and looked back, saw a man and woman coming out from behind the abandoned house. They were both skin and bones, and as they hurried closer, she noted their rotting teeth and the sores on their faces. Meth addicts, no doubt. She hoped they had cash.

"I almost left you," she said as the wispy girl slid into the back.

"We came when we heard you." The girl had an irritating smoke-scarred voice.

The guy opened the front door and thunked into her passenger seat. "I'd rather you sat in back," Holly said, moving her money bag and purse to the center console.

"I like it up here," the man said.

"Stevie has a phobia," the girl added, as though that explained it. Holly decided it wasn't worth fighting.

Body odor filled the cab, along with the acrid smell of their habits. Breathing through her mouth, Holly set her meter. "Where to?"

"How much to take us downtown?" Stevie asked as Holly pulled away from the curb, past the dealers.

"Where downtown?"

"Just anywhere."

Holly sighed. She hated nonspecific destinations. "Probably about ten bucks, give or take. Depends on traffic and whether I have to take detours, and where I drop you off."

"Okay, whatever. Just get us out of here."

That didn't sound promising. The man jittered as she turned off the street. "Have I driven you before?" she asked, glancing at the girl in her rearview mirror. "You didn't call through the agency."

"Yeah, you drove me once. Few months ago, you picked me up when my boyfriend ditched me. I still had your card in my purse. Not too many chicks driving cabs."

Yes, she recognized the girl who had run out in front of her cab when Holly was following a subject. She'd had no choice but to give her a ride. The girl had deteriorated since then. Her habit was slowly eating away at her.

Holly didn't try to figure out why they'd wanted a woman

driver. Tweekers were always paranoid, so maybe they considered a woman to be safer. Relieved to be out of that neighborhood, she breathed easier and pulled onto a road where businesses had long ago closed. She would be glad when she got back onto more populated streets.

Just as Holly's sense of security returned, Stevie slid up his dirty T-shirt and took hold of something in his waistband. She gasped as he pulled out a .38 revolver, cocked it, and pointed it at her.

"Are you kidding me?" She swerved and almost ran off the road. "What are you doing?"

"Keep both hands on the steering wheel and pull over!" He jabbed at her temple. "Do it!"

That would make as much sense as driving off a bridge. Pulling over would ensure that they stole her car and killed her, leaving Lily to grow up without her mother. Holly slowed and pretended to pull over, then stomped the accelerator, swerving hard to make the man lose his balance as she tried to knock the gun from his hand. Shrieking, the girl leaned forward and threw a belt over Holly's throat, threatening to choke her. "He said pull over!"

Holly groped at the belt but kept her foot on the accelerator. "Are you brain dead?" she choked out. "I'm driving!" The car picked up speed . . . sixty . . . seventy . . . "You kill me and you're both dead too!"

The girl loosened the belt, leaving it around Holly's neck, and the man steadied his aim. Holly deliberately ran off the road, then swerved sharply back onto the asphalt. This time she knocked the gun from his hand. He groped for it on the floorboard, found it, then swung it up into her face, its metal splitting her lip.

Tasting blood, Holly swerved again and stabbed her fingers into the soft tissue of Stevie's eyes. He cried out in pain, and she knocked the gun free again.

The girl jerked the belt, forcing Holly's head back against the headrest. Holly clawed at it and slammed on the brakes, throwing her passengers forward. The girl lost her leverage, and Holly got her fingers between the belt and her throat and ripped it away, then slammed the accelerator again.

The crazed man grabbed the wheel and pulled, forcing her to turn into a parking lot. She stomped to a screeching halt just before ramming into a building.

Holly dove for the gun on the floorboard, but the guy kneed her in the face, then thrust a knuckle punch to her eye. Recoiling, she tried to grab the gun, but he came up with his finger on the trigger. "Give me your cash! All of it!" he shouted.

"I don't have any," she lied.

The girl bent over the seat, snatched the money bag and Holly's purse, and bolted out the back door. Holly watched, astonished, as the girl left Stevie behind and ran behind the building.

Cursing, he flung the door open, lunged out, and ran after the woman. Holly stumbled out, wiping the blood from the bloody gash over her eye. She opened her trunk, grabbed her gun, and aimed at him over the hood. "Stop or I'll shoot!" He disappeared around the building.

"I have to pay my mortgage!" she cried, knowing it was useless.

She couldn't run after them. She'd only given birth four weeks ago. She dropped back into the car and pulled around the building, looking for them. The girl had scaled a fence and dropped to the other side. Now she was running into the woods. The man was almost over the fence.

Holly slammed her fist against the steering wheel and tried to calculate how much money they'd gotten. She would have to start all over . . . be away from Lily twice as long.

She pulled her phone out of her jeans pocket and called the

police, then looked at herself in the rearview mirror. Her lip was already swelling and blood was smeared across her cheek. The gash over her eye dripped blood and her lid was puffing shut.

She looked like someone who belonged here. Someone like them.

CHAPTER 2

Holly stopped at a convenience store on the way home and washed her face in the dirty bathroom, splashing away her tears. She looked like she'd been in a drunken fight with a no-good boyfriend. Her sister Juliet would come unglued.

In fact, Holly didn't want to let anyone see her, but the police had encouraged her to go by the bank to cancel her credit cards. She hoped it didn't take long—she needed to see her baby. Maybe then she'd stop shaking. Breathing in strength and trying to look strong, she took care of business, then headed home.

Juliet sat on the floor in Holly's small living room, holding Lily against one shoulder as little Robbie slept in her lap. Only Juliet could pull that off.

"Hey." Holly dropped her keys on the counter, keeping her face down and hidden.

"Just in time. I think Lily's going to want to be fed soon."

"Yeah, sorry I'm late." Holly couldn't keep her face away from Juliet forever. She needed to hold her child. She crossed the room and took Lily from Juliet.

Juliet gasped. "Holly! What happened?"

Lily nuzzled against Holly's neck, and Holly held her for a moment, breathing in the calming scent of her.

"Are you all right?" Juliet said. "Do I need to take you to the hospital?"

"No, I'll be okay. I got mugged."

Juliet came to her feet and laid Robbie on the couch. "Mugged? Holly!"

Holly burst into tears again. "They cleaned me out. Two dopeheads that I should have realized were bad news when I picked them up."

"Oh, honey." Juliet rushed into the kitchen and searched through the cabinets. "We have to clean that. Come here. Did you call the police?"

"Yeah, I called them. They came, but it was too late. The dopeheads had gotten away. I had to go by the bank to cancel my debit card. Real classy, going in with a bloody lip and eye."

Juliet found hydrogen peroxide and poured some over a paper towel. Wadding it, she dabbed at Holly's lip and eyebrow.

"I feel so stupid."

"Holly, I've worried about this very thing happening."

"Well, it finally did. Are you happy? You can say I told you so. But I have to make a living, Juliet." The baby started to cry, and Holly pulled away from Juliet and went to the couch to feed her.

"How many were there? Can you identify them?"

"I'll recognize them if I ever see them again, but the chances of us finding them are pretty slim. They were meth heads. Skinny as toothpicks and pocked with sores. One of them was named Steve or Stevie, but who knows if that was his real name. I doubt the other one would have called him by his real name, knowing they were going to rob me. The money's gone. I'll just have to earn it back."

"Thank God you're okay. That's the important thing. Oh, Holly. I wish I could help you."

Juliet had financial problems of her own. Holly's oldest sibling had once been rich, the wife of an orthopedic surgeon. Now she was a widow with three children and had to live on a budget. She couldn't bail Holly out of her messes anymore.

But that didn't mean she wouldn't try. "Maybe it's time for you to work full-time for Michael. Business is getting to be more than we can handle working part-time."

"You'd think the fact that he's in prison would've put a damper on business, wouldn't you?"

"For any normal guy. But Michael's not a normal guy."

Holly smiled. Everyone in the area knew Michael's whole felony conviction was a farce.

"Anyway, what if you gave up driving the cab and just did that?"

Holly couldn't believe Juliet would suggest such a thing after loaning her the cash to buy the cab. It had been a way for Holly to hold down a job she couldn't be fired from—unlike all the other jobs she'd had. Juliet had a friend from church who owned a taxi service, and they'd agreed to add Holly's cab to their fleet in exchange for a commission when she was on the clock. By the time she paid them, bought gas, maintained her vehicle, paid taxes, and made her loan payment to Juliet, she could barely pay her personal bills.

Welcome to the adult world—a world she had studiously avoided until her pregnancy.

"How would I pay you back?"

"You could sell the cab to the agency and buy a normal car."

Holly sighed. "I can't live on ten bucks an hour."

"Maybe we can raise your pay." Juliet poured more hydrogen peroxide on the paper towel and dabbed at Holly's eyebrow again. "Are you sure you don't need stitches?"

"I don't know. Maybe I'll go to the doctor after I feed Lily. I just don't know how I'll pay for it. I have a huge deductible." How was she going to pay her mortgage, utilities, diapers, babysitters . . . ?

While Holly nursed, Juliet sat on the coffee table across from her. "Holly, what if I can get Michael to raise your pay to fifteen dollars an hour? Could you give up cab driving then?"

"What am I going to do with Lily if we're both working the same hours?"

"We can go in together and get a babysitter. Somebody who can keep Robbie and Lily at one of our houses. And sometimes we can have the babies there at work with us. Robbie has a little separation anxiety, so maybe at first the babysitter can just hang out with us at the office, until the babies are used to her."

"I don't know. That place is moldy."

"It's not moldy. I already had it checked. It's just old."

Holly looked down at the peaceful face of her nursing child. She wanted to cry again, but it would just upset Juliet more. If only she could stay home with her baby and focus on her all the time. But when you had a baby without involving the father . . . well, staying at home was a luxury you couldn't afford.

At least it would be years before Lily knew that her mother was an idiot who always did things in the wrong order.

"It'll be hard for me too, Holly," Juliet said, leaning toward her. "I stayed home with Zach and Abe. It feels all wrong to leave Robbie, but most mothers have to work, and the kids turn out fine."

Holly shot a look at her. "Please don't give me that quality over quantity stuff. I don't want to hear it."

AN EXCERPT FROM *TWISTED INNOCENCE* 329

"We can interview babysitters together. Bottom line, I don't want you driving a taxi anymore."

Holly thought about the investment she'd made in the car. She would be way happier working as a PI full-time than as a cabbie, but she had responsibilities, and it didn't really matter what would make her happier. She had to support Lily. "Like it or not," she said, "I make more driving a cab. If Michael will raise my hourly pay, I'll drive less and work for him more, but I can't afford to give up the cab driving altogether."

Juliet clearly didn't like it. She touched Holly's pink-tipped hair. "I guess you're making a mature decision, even though I hate it. You're growing up."

"Twenty-eight years old, it's about time, right?"

Lily looked up at her, her round eyes unfazed by the bruising, bloody wounds. Holly would never get used to that unconditional adoration. That gaze had the feel of God in it, and it calmed her spirit more than anything ever had.

Whatever motherhood cost her, it was worth it

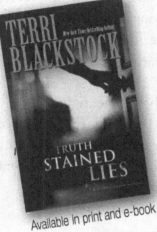

THE RESTORATION SERIES

In the face of a crisis that sweeps an entire high-tech planet back to the age before electricity, the Brannings face a choice. Will they hoard their possessions to survive—or trust God to provide as they offer their resources to others? Terri Blackstock weaves a masterful what-if series in which global catastrophe reveals the darkness in human hearts—and lights the way to restoration for a self-centered world.

Bestselling books with Beverly LaHaye

Softcover: 978-0-310-23519-4

Softcover: 978-0-310-24296-3

Softcover: 978-0-310-24297-0

Softcover: 978-0-310-24298-7

Pick up a copy today at your favorite bookstore!

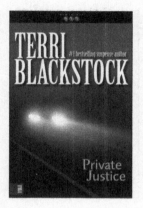

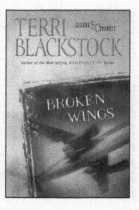

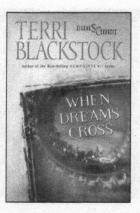

More great books from Terri Blackstock

Sun Coast Chronicles

Softcover: 978-0-310-20015-4

Softcover: 978-0-310-20016-1

Softcover: 978-0-310-20017-8

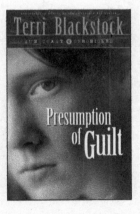

Softcover: 978-0-310-20018-5

Pick up a copy today at your favorite bookstore!

7/16